LIBBY'S STORY

Libby's STORY

JUDY BAER
BEST-SELLING AUTHOR

TYNDALE HOUSE PUBLISHERS, INC., WHEATON, ILLINOIS

12916805

Visit Tyndale's exciting Web site at www.tyndale.com

Scripture quotations are taken from the Holy Bible® New Living Translation, copyright © 1996. Used by permission of Tyndale House Publishers, Inc., Wheaton, Illinois 60189. All rights reserved.

You may wish to contact the NARHA after reading this book. Here's how: North American Riding for the Handicapped Association (800) 360-RIDE; P.O. Box 33150, Denver, CO 80233

Edited by Curtis H. C. Lundgren

Designed by Jenny Destree

Library of Congress Cataloging-in-Publication Data

Baer, Judy.
    Libby's story / Judy Baer.
        p. cm.
    ISBN 0-8423-1923-9 (sc)
    1. Adult children of aging parents—Fiction. 2. Alzheimer's disease—Patients—Fiction.
3. Congregate housing—Fiction. 4. Aging parents—Fiction.   I. Title.
PS3553.A33 L5 2001
813′.54—dc21

00-47969

Printed in the United States of America

04   03   02   01
5   4   3   2   1

For my late-night coffee buddies—Loren, Katy, and Babe—with love and gratitude. You were there when I needed you.

For my Saturday morning Bible-study group and proxy brides-maids—you are one of the dearest groups of Christian women I have ever met. Sharon, Sherida, Laurie, Cheryl, Arnella, Ginny, Becky, and Cindy—it was a joy and a blessing to study, pray, and grow with you.

And for my Tuesday evening Bible-study friends—I admire you all so much. You are an amazing group of people who have triumphed over adversity and healed emotionally when the prognosis looked grim. And we learned to laugh together—a true miracle!

For Kathy F.—thanks for sharing your home and your wonder-ful children with me. You are an extraordinary person, and I'm proud to call you my friend.

And last but never least, to my agent, Karen Solem, who knows exactly when to give me pep talks. You are the best.

All of you should be of one mind, full of sympathy toward each other,
loving one another with tender hearts and humble minds.

1 Peter 3:8

PROLOGUE
. . . .

"Shhh. It's my mom!" Libby Morrison leaned over the edge of the Best Friends Forever tree house platform and thrust her denim-covered rump in the air. Her pigtails dangled over the rough wooden edge. "Up here, Mommy."

Tia Warden lay on her back gazing at the speckling of light that drifted through the leaves and at the glimpses of cerulean sky beyond. "I don't always answer when my mom calls," she admitted with a tinge of defiance.

Libby scowled at her friend. Tia rarely did what she was supposed to from Libby's point of view.

"She's saying something." Jenny Owens put a chubby finger to her lips. Her blonde ringlets quivered in the sunlight.

"Supper will be a few minutes late tonight, Libby. Dad is still working." Mrs. Morrison's cheerful voice sang through the branches. The girls could hear her humming as she returned to the house.

"OK, Mommy."

Libby sat down and crossed her legs. A faint crease marred the perfectly clear expanse of her round, childish forehead. "You're supposed to listen to your mom, Tia. You're only nine, you know."

"So?" Tia, resident insurgent, responded. "Big deal."

"But your parents love you and worry about you!" Libby persisted. "Don't you care about them?"

"Sure, but I'm just a kid. They are *supposed* to worry about me." Tia, as callous and coldhearted as a boot camp sergeant with a fresh group of recruits, wiggled into a sitting position. "Did you eat all the licorice?"

Before supersensitive and compassionate Libby could respond, Jenny produced the licorice from the interior of their battered clubhouse cooler. "Want some before she eats it all, Libby?"

Libby halfheartedly tugged two twisted red cords out of the bag. "You'd hurt my feelings if I were your mom."

"What's the difference? I hurt your feelings when I'm your friend!" Tia pointed out. "That's 'cause you're too sympa . . . sympath . . . sympathetic. My mom says you're 'tenderhearted.' Who wants a mushy heart, anyway?"

"Not you," Jenny muttered as she stuffed an entire rope of licorice into her mouth and chomped down hard.

A look of sudden comprehension crossed Libby's features. "Did you get a bad grade on your geography test today, Tia?" she asked.

"No." Tia jiggled one foot over the edge of the platform.

"Then did you get in trouble at recess?" Libby moved her dog-eared copy of *Black Beauty* aside to scoot closer to Tia.

"Of course not."

"Tia has to stay after school tomorrow night 'cause the teacher found a whole bunch of spitballs in her desk," Jenny said. "She was just juicing up the first one to throw at Mike Adams when Teacher caught her. You were still in the library when it happened, Libby."

Tia sprang to her knees like a little jungle cat in the treetops. "He threw one first!"

"You were ready for him," Jenny said.

"He always throws them just before the bell 'cause that's when he never gets caught."

"But you did get caught and now you're grumpy."

Tia crumpled like a pricked balloon. Tears threatened in her dark eyes. "And I have to tell my mom. She's going to be mad!"

"Then you *do* care what your parents think!" Libby crowed righteously.

"Only if they think like I think," Tia said honestly.

"They know what's best for you," Libby intoned piously.

"That's what you think because you're an only child!" Tia protested. "You'd know better if you had a sister like I do. They're always sticking up for her!"

"Do you want to stay at my house on Saturday?" Jenny asked, changing the subject. "I can have a sleep over."

"Sure." Tia's dark eyes sparkled with anticipation. "Can we have that popcorn-and-peanut-butter stuff your mom makes? And dip pretzels in melted chocolate to eat in the tree house, and . . ."

"You could come to my house," Libby offered timidly. "I don't think I could come to Jenny's, but . . ."

"Why? 'Cause sometimes you get homesick and one of your parents has to come and get you?" Tia asked bluntly.

A glaze of tears shadowed Libby's green eyes and her lower lip trembled.

"Tia!" Jenny hissed through her teeth.

Even Tia, scowling little imp that she was today, had the grace to look repentant. "I'm sorry, Libby. I didn't mean to say you were a baby or anything. . . ."

"Tia!"

"We'll come to your house," Tia sighed.

"It's OK, Libby. We like sleeping over at your house," Jenny assured her friend.

She glared at Tia. It was unspoken knowledge among the Best Friends Forever that Libby occasionally got homesick and was exceedingly embarrassed by it. Tia had crossed the line by mentioning it today.

Libby brightened. "We can study our Sunday school lesson together."

"I already did mine," Jenny said. "I had to because Tia asked to borrow my book."

"I can't help it that I lost mine. Maybe someone stole it."

"A Sunday school book? Who would do that?" Libby wrinkled her nose.

"Maybe our lesson is on the wrong commandment," Jenny said with a giggle. "It should have been on 'Thou shalt not steal' instead of 'Honor your father and your mother.'"

"What do you think God meant by that, anyway?" Tia mused. "Anything like the honor roll at school?"

"It means *respect,*" Jenny retorted. "I looked it up."

"And that means listening," Libby added. "And answering when your mom calls you."

"How long do you have to listen to them?" Tia asked. "My baby-sitter says she's going to quit listening to her parents when she's eighteen."

"I thought it meant forever." Jenny frowned. "That's a long time."

"Not for me," Libby said. "I'm going to listen to my mom and dad my whole life."

"What happens when they get too old to love you?" Tia asked.

Libby smiled serenely. "Love doesn't get old. It only gets bigger and better. My mom said so."

Tia rolled her dark expressive eyes. "Oh, Libby, you just say that 'cause you're used to doing everything they say. Someday you'll change your mind."

Libby's sweet features grew pensive. "No, I won't. My mom says I'm their 'special blessing' because I was born when they didn't think they'd ever have any kids. She said they were so excited that when I was a baby they wouldn't go anywhere without me. I never even had a baby-sitter!"

"Boring." Tia yawned so hugely that her pink mouth and white, evenly spaced teeth were on display for Libby and Jenny. A piece of red licorice was stuck in one tooth. "Isn't there anything else to talk about?"

Tia picked up Libby's book and studied the cover flap. An awesome black horse reared and pawed from the page. "Is this good?"

"You haven't read *Black Beauty*?" Libby grabbed the book away as if to protect it from an invader. "It's so cool. . . ."

"Are horses smelly?" Tia persisted. "I wouldn't want a horse if it stunk."

"I'm going to have a horse someday," Libby announced. "And I don't care if it's smelly. I'll love it anyway."

"Where are you going to put it?" Tia challenged. "You don't live on a farm, and you can't keep a horse in your garage. Especially not if they stink."

"They do not!"

Fortunately, at that moment, Mrs. Morrison's voice drifted up through the branches. "Libby, come wash your hands. Tia and Jenny, your mothers both called, and you girls are supposed to go home for supper right away."

Tia sighed and wrinkled her nose. Jenny gathered her small bag of jacks and checked for the ball in the pocket of her pants. Libby scrambled down the ladder and into her mother's arms.

Life was good. The future shone brightly ahead of them, and Best Friends Forever had adjourned for another day.

CHAPTER ONE

*Victorian crazy quilts were so called because they were wild
and haphazard, broken into splinters of color and shape.
While appearing unplanned, much time was spent cutting
and arranging the random pieces of fabric into beautiful, practical art.*

A tiny red toboggan careened out of control down a snow-and-pinecone-frosted cardboard hill, skidded sideways across a mirror-glass pond, and scattered miniature china figurines on ice skates before embedding itself in a toy pine tree near the front steps of a ceramic Victorian house.

Libby Morrison watched dispassionately as the holiday display self-destructed as the wayward sled wreaked havoc with her work. She felt no sense of frustration or anger at having to rebuild the scale model Christmas scene for Tia Warden's store window or that one of the tiny figurines now had a missing arm and that another had snapped in half.

She'd become accustomed to chaos. Libby sat back on her heels, her jean-clad legs balancing athletically, her long spine straight. She studied the mess and murmured, "One step forward, two steps back." The display for Tia's Attic was a microcosm of her own reality right now, a tedious upward climb punctuated by far too many backward slides. If Libby had ever liked toboggan rides, she didn't anymore.

"Did I hear a crash?" Tia materialized over the top of the display cabinet. Like a life-size Christmas elf, she was dressed in a holiday-red, figure-fitting wool dress with oversized green buttons. She wore a pointed felt hat and gigantic globe earrings that resembled Christmas tree ornaments.

"I'm having trouble setting up the miniature village display the way you want it. Fake snow is slippery."

"Don't worry about it. I'll sell every item out of this cabinet by December 24 anyway. Leave the toboggan on a flat surface if it keeps sliding down the hill. I don't want to risk breaking anything more if it falls again."

"Good idea." Libby moved the little sled to a safer resting place and stared at the village she was creating. If only her own problems could be solved so easily. She sighed and inquired wistfully, "Isn't it about time for tea?"

Jenny Adams, the third portion of the trio that had been friends since childhood, joined them at the table in the storeroom. While Tia brewed the tea, Jenny and Libby moved wrapping paper, packing peanuts, and bubble wrap to make a space for themselves and two plates of Christmas goodies.

"Who baked the *Krumkaka*?" Jenny picked up a pale flaky roll of the gossamer-thin cookie, stuck her tongue in one open end, and bit down. "Melts in your mouth."

Blonde and blue-eyed, Jenny was as Scandinavian as the cookie she was eating. "Mike would love this," she said, referring to her second husband, a mutual childhood classmate. She sighed blissfully with sugar-induced pleasure on her face.

"Who else?" Tia put a chipped sugar and creamer set from her damaged goods inventory on the table and poured tea into three colorful mismatched mugs. "Libby, Princess of the Kitchen, of course."

"I thought Jenny was Kitchen Princess now that she has her

own bakery and catering business." Libby took an elaborately decorated Christmas cookie from the tray Jenny had brought for them when delivering baked goods for Tia's upcoming Christmas open house.

"Sanbakkles, fattigman, lefse, and rosettes." Jenny itemized the delicacies on the plate. "How do you find the time, Libby?"

"It's therapy. Nothing like immersing oneself in a mixing bowl full of sugar, butter, and flour. That's about all Norwegians use except for a little flavoring to make this stuff." *And work keeps me from thinking too much about what's going on at home.*

Tia groaned and fell into the chair like she weighed three times her one hundred and fifteen pounds. "Oh! It feels good to take a load off." She chewed on a Santa cookie's head and inquired, "Jenny, do you think we'll have enough food for the open house?"

"I added 20 percent to your estimate, and I'm baking every day until Christmas. If you run low, I'll refill your order. No problem."

"You're a gem. I can't tell you how much it means to me to have your help. This is the first year I haven't had to agonize over goodies for the sale. And, Lib, you've put in more nights here this month than a cat burglar. Thank you."

A crease marred Tia's flawless ivory forehead. "Tell me again why I do this every year?"

"Because you have the prettiest, most innovative gift shop for miles around, silly." Libby poured herself more tea.

"Then why do I suffer from a guilt complex every December?"

"Are we going to have the commercialism-versus-the-true-meaning-of-Christmas debate again?"

Tia put her head in her hands. "Every year I try harder to put Christ back into Christmas in my personal life, yet at the store I order more cutesy knickknacks and gewgaws for people to lust after. Do I have a double standard?"

"Not everyone is as passionate about what Christmas really means as you are, Tia," Jenny said. "Without your store and your seasonal parties, some people would never be reminded what the holidays really represent."

"You think?"

"You are the only store owner I know who serves birthday cake on December 24 with 'Happy Birthday, Jesus' written on it. And, despite those gewgaws you sell, anyone who comes by your front window knows they're shopping with a Christian."

"The manger scene gets more beautiful every year," Libby agreed. "Love that new camel."

"Its fur is real—llama fur or something. Little kids love it." Tia brightened. "During the school holidays, I've hired high school girls to read the Christmas story to them while they eat the camel cookies Jenny supplies. Mothers love that."

"Creative marketing at its best—both secular and Christian," Libby murmured. "Tia, sometimes you amaze me."

"After all this time? You should be accustomed to me by now."

"There's no getting accustomed to a kaleidoscope, Tia."

Tia was about to respond when the phone rang. She picked up the extension hidden under a pile of bubble wrap on the table. "Tia's Attic, Tia speaking." Then she extended the receiver to Libby. "For you."

Libby frowned as she reached for the phone. "I wonder who's calling me here. Mom and Dad are at the Senior Citizens' Center for the Christmas dinner and pageant."

The frown turned into an expression of concern as she listened to the voice on the other end of the line. When Libby hung up, she was as white as the artificial snow that had seeped throughout the entire shop during the holidays.

"That was the Senior Center. Mom wandered away during the pageant."

Tia stood up. "I'll get my coat. . . ."

"They've already found her. Daddy alerted the staff, who went right out to look for her. She'd fallen in the snow near the sidewalk." Tears flooded Libby's eyes. "She was trying to get to the

Nativity scene." She brushed away the moisture with the back of her hand, leaving a trail of mascara across her cheek. "She told the man who found her that she wanted to touch the baby Jesus."

Tia and Jenny were on their feet embracing their friend almost before the words were out of Libby's mouth.

Without a word, they spun into action. Jenny threw a sheet of butcher's paper over the boxes of baked goods and scooped her jacket off a stack of undecorated Christmas wreaths. She bundled Libby into her fleecy coat and hat while Tia informed her clerks that they would be leaving for the day. Tia had the keys for the car out of her purse and the door open when Jenny led Libby into the garage and to Tia's car.

Snow fell like the fleecy white puffs in the snow globes in Tia's gift cases, and night closed in on them as quickly and suddenly as a clamped hand.

"Are they still at the Senior Center?"

"No. The staff insisted she be checked out at the hospital. They're at Oakview Community."

"Gotcha." Tia expertly navigated rush hour traffic, intensifying snow, and the onslaught of night. They were at the emergency room in record time.

"I'll park. You find Mr. Morrison," Tia directed as she pulled up to the entry.

....

Jenny led the shaken Libby into the harshly antiseptic light of the ER waiting room and steered her toward the reception desk to avoid an emergency triage occurring in the hallway. Libby moved like a block of wood in her hands.

Jenny's stomach lurched at the unwelcome glimpse of a man lying on a gurney, mouth open, skin pale and waxy, his eyes fixed. A trickle of blood meandered from the corner of his mouth.

Lee. Her first husband's memory loomed in her mind. His face during the last moments of his life had not been unlike that of the man on the stretcher. *Get a grip. This is Libby's time, not mine.*

She hadn't been in a hospital since Lee's death other than a time or two for her stepson Luke's appendicitis. Tonight brought back deep, gut-wrenching memories.

"You both look like death warmed over." Tia's brisk, business-like voice was a welcome splash of cold water on their psyches. "Mr. Morrison is over here. I'll check on Libby's mother."

They found the old man shriveled into an uncomfortable-looking plastic chair with chrome legs and arms. Jenny was shocked at the sight of him. What had happened to him, the man she'd always considered a second father? When had he gotten so old? How had she missed the deterioration of this man so dear to her?

Libby sank to her knees in front of her father, and it occurred to Jenny that Libby had aged, too. She was the athlete in their trio, leggy and strong. Libby had won the races, gathered the trophies in competition, played a bruising game of tennis, and displayed a wickedly accurate golf swing, yet tonight her shoulders were stooped and her agile frame carried far too little weight.

"What happened, Daddy?"

"I looked away for just a minute!" Mr. Morrison bleated. "She was there and then suddenly she wasn't! A lady in a Mrs. Santa Claus suit was handing out candy. I know how much your mother loves those hard Christmas candies, so I . . ."

"And she wandered away?"

"I don't know how she had time to get so far," the old man said, puzzled. "She isn't as steady as she used to be, and . . ." His face collapsed and tears leaked from the corners of his eyes. "They found her outside in the snow flailing like a big fish, trying to get to Jesus."

"Oh, Daddy . . ." Libby felt something breaking inside.

Libby was grateful when Tia distracted her. "Your dad can see your mom now. While he's with her, the doctor wants to speak with you."

"Pray for her, Libby," her father whispered as a nurse led him away.

....

Libby and Jenny followed Tia to a cubicle behind the registration desk.

Waiting inside was a brisk, no-nonsense-looking woman with graying hair knotted carelessly into a bun. She wore her unused glasses just above the furrow line on her brow as though she had eyes in her forehead. Her jaw was square and abrupt, but her eyes were pools of soft, compassionate blue.

"Hello, Libby." The blue eyes shifted to Jenny and Tia.

"These are my friends Tia Warden and Jenny Adams. I'd like them to hear what you have to say about Mom."

"Very well. Please sit down. There are extra stools along the wall."

They perched like three large sparrows on a high line wire as they waited for the doctor to speak.

The physician studied the chart a long time before looking up. "I'm Dr. Hazard, by the way." A twinkle in the doctor's eyes stopped Tia from opening her mouth. "And I've heard all the jokes about my name and my profession, thank you. Besides, I'm not nearly such a hazard as is avoiding medical attention when one needs it." Now that Dr. Hazard had everyone's full attention, she turned to Libby.

"Your mother was very confused when she came in. She hadn't been outside long, but at her age it doesn't take very long in these temperatures to show signs of hypothermia. I'd like to keep her here for observation overnight, if you don't mind."

"Of course," Libby said, "but is she . . ."

"Going to be all right?" Dr. Hazard poked the glasses with her index finger and they slid to her nose. "Mentally or physically?"

Libby sagged weakly against the wall. Did the doctor already suspect the family matters she had been so deliberately trying to hide?

"So you *are* aware of your mother's mental state?"

A pang of anxiety shot through Libby. *Exposed.*

"She's confused sometimes, but usually not at home. I thought she'd be fine at the Senior Center. She and Daddy go there often. I can't imagine what she was thinking. . . ."

"About Jesus, apparently." The doctor smiled. "All in all, a very good thing to think about—just not when you feel the need to get across a snowy yard and crawl into a Nativity scene. She behaved as a child might, wanting the prize without considering the cost."

"It's just been the past few months that she's done odd things like this," Libby said.

"She's acted like this before?" Tia was shocked.

"It wasn't anything, really. Just getting turned around in a store or not being able to find her way back from the bathroom. Once Daddy searched the entire mall before finding her in a sporting goods store holding a volleyball, asking anyone if they'd like to play."

"No way! Your mom?"

"They both laughed it off. Acted like it was the funniest thing either of them had ever seen or done. I thought if Mom and Dad weren't upset, then I shouldn't be. Besides, one incident wouldn't have scared me so much, but . . ."

"There have been others?" the doctor prodded.

"Mom hasn't been sleeping at night. She prowls the house like a cat getting into mischief."

"What kind of mischief?"

"One night last week she turned on the oven. She thought she was baking and filled it with Tupperware and cereal boxes. The smoke alarm went off, and I had to call the fire department."

"Oh, Lib, and you didn't tell us?" Jenny cried.

"Is there anything else?" Dr. Hazard persisted.

Libby steeled herself. "Mama wandered away from us at the Mall of America while I had her trying on shoes."

"Are you kidding? That place is *huge!*" Tia blurted, horrified.

"I called security right away. Daddy was so frantic he was no help at all." Libby tugged agitatedly at her hair. "What was I thinking to bring a confused woman and her elderly husband into a space so filled with lights, color, and sound that it would overstimulate a stone?"

Tia moved forward on her perch. "So what happened? Obviously, you found her again."

"I combed the store in which we'd been shopping. People poured past me. It was dizzying. I nearly frightened myself to death imagining what Mother must be thinking. Have you ever thought about how many hiding places there are in a department store? Racks of clothing are angled together in rows long enough to hold an entire battalion of snipers. There are mirrored walls hiding changing rooms and enough storage cubbies to confuse a SWAT team. I was going in circles around a maze of racks and half walls designed to direct traffic in circuitous directions around every bit of merchandise. I couldn't walk a straight line. After a while, the mannequins began to look like predators. And poor Mama had left her shoes behind. . . .

"I couldn't imagine what she must be feeling. Everything took on the speed and color of a carousel ride—spinning, whirling, splashes of light. Voices turned into a cacophony of noise."

Libby had a rapt audience.

"I ran around like a chicken with my head cut off until I decided I had to calm down and start thinking outside the box, like my mother instead of myself."

Like a confused mind rather than a logical one.

"I knew Mother wouldn't go near the escalators. I was scared of them as a child, afraid that if I didn't jump off in time, I'd be sucked into the basement or wherever all those stairs were disappearing. Mom made it a habit never to use them and it's held over until now. I knew she'd be reluctant to use an elevator either because she was trapped in one once during a malfunction. Logically, she probably hadn't left the store, but she'd been gone nearly an hour by then. . . ."

Wiping away a tear, Libby murmured, "Then security found me and took me to the lingerie department. She'd crawled under a bottom rack full of pajamas to hide. The clerk had spied her soiled bare feet and the hem of her dress."

"How did you get her home?"

"They took her to the clinic at the mall and had her checked out." Libby's voice broke. "All she would say was, 'Somebody stole my shoes.'"

When Libby had composed herself, Dr. Hazard gently continued. "Does your father spend a lot of time with your mother?"

"Almost exclusively. They are each other's best friend. They've always shared similar hobbies and interests, and the older they get, the more they depend on one another."

"Is it possible that he's been covering for her? Perhaps your mother has been confused for a longer period of time than you realize."

Libby wanted to put her hands over her ears and pretend this wasn't happening. Unfortunately, she couldn't deny what she'd seen and experienced in the past few weeks.

"It's very threatening when a spouse changes," the doctor continued. "It's easier to do whatever it takes to make things appear normal than to admit something is going wrong."

"What do you mean?" Tia demanded when Libby remained silent.

"I'd like to run some tests before answering that. We have excellent neurologists and geriatricians on staff. We'll do a comprehensive medical history and a complete physical workup."

"What exactly would be involved?" Libby couldn't prevent the tremor in her voice. She felt terrified inside, as though her organs were turning soft and shivery.

"You and your father can help with the medical history. We'll need to know if any family members have suffered dementia or related problems. We'll want to access her medical records. It is also routine to check her thyroid and to do a mental status test."

"What's that?"

"We'll start by asking her things such as who our current president is, the date, et cetera. She'll be asked to remember lists of things we give to her as well as answer questions that will give us an idea of the clarity of her thinking."

"How long will it take?"

"It could last a few hours." The doctor's expression softened. "It sounds difficult, I know, but it's necessary. It will give us an objective view of your mother's impairment."

As though she could read Libby's mind, Dr. Hazard added, "I'm afraid the family's subjective impressions of the patient just aren't enough. It will also provide us with a baseline. Then, when your mother returns to us, we will be able to measure whether or not her condition has progressed or if medication we might give her is working."

"I see."

Libby's thoughts whirled with strange behaviors her mother had exhibited recently and the angry emotions she'd experienced as a result.

It was like being angry at a baby for crying or messing her diaper when she was doing the only thing she knew how to do—be a baby. How could she be upset with her mother for the regression Mom surely must hate as much as Libby did?

Libby felt tears forming in her eyes. "I try to understand her, Doctor. Sometimes I think I try too hard."

"What do you mean?"

"I'm so afraid. Everything I see or hear, I've begun filtering through what my mother must experience. One day I opened my closet and was so bombarded with all the color and texture that it was impossible to decide what to wear. Standing there feeling overwhelmed made me realize what Mom is going through.

"It has to be ghastly—not remembering the flavors of her

favorite foods, opening familiar cupboards and being surprised by what's inside, looking at photos of people she used to love and not recognizing them anymore. It breaks my heart to think of her suffering that way."

"Libby, you're running on emotion, not logic, right now," Dr. Hazard interjected. "With some rest you'll be able to put things in perspective. You may feel better once we have a better handle on your mother's condition. We'll do the usual blood work, an MRI—that's magnetic resonance imaging—and whatever else we need to do to rule out things such as a tumor."

Libby was not consoled.

"She won't be in here much longer than I'd keep her anyway," the doctor soothed, "but as long as we're in the business, we might as well see what we can see."

"And what do you think you might find?" Jenny inquired. Libby appeared too shell-shocked to ask more.

"Dementia. Senility. Beginning Alzheimer's. Her thyroid could be over- or underactive. She might have a vitamin deficiency. This could stem from something as simple as too little nourishment to—"

"I feed my parents!" Libby's shoulders trembled indignantly beneath her woolen sweater.

"I simply mean that some older people—not necessarily your parents—do not get proper nourishment and as a result have problems with confusion. Your mother's problem could be very simple or very complex—like Parkinson's or a series of small strokes."

Libby's silence spoke volumes.

....

"What can we do for you?"

Libby shivered. "Get Daddy settled first." The house was cold and silent without Mother.

"He's already lying down," Jenny said. "I told him we'd have soup later."

"I've got an idea." Tia disappeared into the kitchen where the others could hear loud clanking and the rush of running water. She returned with a wash bucket filled with warm water and a hint of suds.

"Soak your feet in this. Famous old Warden wives' method of getting the chill out of your bones. I grew up seeing my grandmother's feet in a bucket of water. If it wasn't for the chills, it was for corns and bunions, pedicures, or who knows what—soup for supper for all I know."

"Yuck!" Libby yelped.

"Speaking of soup," Jenny said tactfully, "maybe I'll make my grandmother's famous Friendship Stew."

"What's that?" Libby asked suspiciously.

"Dump together whatever kinds of canned soups are in the cupboard and make dumplings out of store-bought biscuit mix. According to my grandmother, it's good enough for anyone's best friend."

After dinner, Libby's bones felt considerably warmer. She donned a pair of wool socks and a jogging suit while she was upstairs to check on her father.

Mr. Morrison was lying on the bed reading a Bible—her mother's Bible.

"Whatchadoin', Dad?" She sat on the side of the bed, her hip tucked into the curve of his body.

"Just looking at your mom's Bible." He chuckled softly. "Look at these pages, will you! Have you ever seen so many notes and underlined passages in a book before? I can't see how she was able to read this anymore."

"She probably didn't have to. She had most of it memorized."

"That's true. All the years she taught the Bible classes at church, the Sunday school lessons . . . She gave a lot of years and energy to the church or, more correctly, to the Lord."

"You gave a few yourself," Libby reminded him.

"But most of what I had to give involved my back, not my brain—building projects at the Bible camp, shoveling snow, fixing the plumbing at every ladies' meeting because they never seemed able to find a plumber. . . ."

"And you don't think that's important? Who could even listen to Mom teach if the toilets were overflowing? You two are a good team."

"Were. *Were* a good team. We're faltering now." His voice cracked.

"No, Dad, that isn't true. You've been everything Mom needed you to be. When you were down, she helped you up. Now you are helping her. That's what you taught me about good relationships."

She stroked his forehead and saw how weary he was. Gently, she pulled the comforter over his body.

"Daddy says he doesn't want any more stew and that he thinks he'll just doze off for the night," Libby announced when she returned. A smile quirked the corner of her lip. "And he wants me to get the recipe for your stew, Jenny."

"Ha, ha!" Jenny chortled. "Friendship Stew never fails." She took the recliner across from Libby and Tia.

"I made a fire. If you are still chilled, I don't know how to help you. My bag of tricks is now empty," Tia said.

"I'm fine." Libby looked at a small stack of literature on the coffee table. "Physically, at least."

"The doctor said you didn't have to read the material she gave you right now, Lib. Do it when you can absorb it. Besides, just because she gave it to you doesn't mean . . ."

"That Mom might have Alzheimer's?" Libby inclined her head. "I'm not an ostrich, Tia. It's entirely possible. But it will have to slap me in the face before I accept it."

"Can they be sure if it really is Alzheimer's?" Jenny asked.

"They announced it to the world when President Reagan got

it," Tia pointed out. "I heard a commentator talk about the early symptoms. Memory loss—short term first, then longer term."

"You mean like calling someone on the phone and forgetting what you wanted to tell them or that you've *already* called them?" Libby received dozens of calls from her mother in a workday.

Tia ignored the question to skim the material the doctor had given them. "Another sign is change in behavior. Sweet, quiet individuals may become grouchy, short-tempered, or quick to argue. Irritability is a common symptom, as is having trouble performing normal, familiar tasks."

"Like cooking dinner and paying bills?" Libby often found her mother agonizing over the checkbook. It wasn't as though she didn't remember to pay the bills. It was more like she couldn't remember *how* to do it. The checkbook had become such a source of trouble in the house over the past year that Libby and her father had taken over the task that Mrs. Morrison had been in charge of since before Libby was born.

"Or being unable to express oneself, to find the right words for what you mean. I do that now," Tia said.

"You're never at a loss for words," Jenny pointed out.

Libby shivered in her warm outfit. "Let's change the subject, OK?"

"Cold again?"

"Mostly around my heart." Libby stared out the window at the swiftly falling snow and was reminded of the little sled in Tia's shop display. What would become of this toboggan ride with her parents? Would they make it safely through or would they crash somewhere along the way?

"I'm making tea," Jenny announced abruptly.

The tea-with-cream-and-sugar ritual had helped them think through many a crisis since childhood. Foggily, Libby hoped it would help tonight.

Then the doorbell rang and Mike, Luke, and Spot Adams burst into the entry on a gust of wind.

Mike and his son had blended seamlessly into the trio that had, as children, vowed to be best friends forever, adding a masculine point of view to the mix. Luke added the energy of youth; and Spot, total affection and a dash of comic relief. It was a recipe that was turning out just right.

Jenny struggled to shut the door against the bitter gale before turning to kiss her husband in greeting. "Brrr. Your nose is like a Popsicle! Yours, too, Luke." Then she eyed the eager dog at her feet. "And yours has its own built-in refrigeration system!"

The dog gave an unrepentant whine and dropped onto the discarded snowmobile suit his master had shed. He gave Jenny one long, loving stare; closed his eyes; and fell asleep.

"If I could learn to relax like that dog does," Tia commented, "I'd be limp as a wet noodle at work."

"Whoooeeee!" Mike squatted in front of the fire and poked at it with a tool from the basket by the fireplace. "It's turning nasty out there. We're in for some bad weather." Jenny moved to stand next to him, her hand on his shoulder. He tipped his head to one side and rubbed his cheek on the back of her hand. Love radiated between them. "Luke and I brought our sleeping bags just in case you ladies decided to get stranded. We didn't want to miss a party."

That, Jenny translated, meant "We want to be here for Libby, too."

Meanwhile, Luke scooted on his belly under the Christmas tree to rattle the gifts.

"I can understand why you do that at home," Jenny observed, "but why are you doing it here when you know none of the gifts are yours?"

"For practice. Dad calls it 'fine-tuning my craft.'" He held one to the light. "This is socks. Six pair. Probably Gold-Toe brand 'cause I've seen Libby's dad wear them before."

"You're good!" Libby said with a touch of amazement.

Luke grinned modestly. "I know. So far I'm getting a model car, books, two pairs of jeans, and a tape player."

"Ha!" his father said. "It's a set of measuring spoons, a used toilet seat, bib overalls, and a karaoke machine."

"Aw, Dad!" Luke grinned at his father.

"You'd better watch out, Luke. Someday he might decide you actually deserve bib overalls and a used toilet seat."

Nonplussed, Luke asked, "Do we have food for this storm?"

"Too bad you're so shy and retiring, young man. You'll never get anything you want that way." Jenny rumpled her stepson's hair. "Come. Help me take in the tea things. Libby has enough Christmas baking in the kitchen to carry us through Easter."

The Morrison kitchen looked like Jenny's own shop. Sometime in the last twenty-four hours, Libby had baked enough dough to make sidewalls and roofs for half a dozen gingerbread houses. There were bags of gumdrops, licorice sticks, pretzels, and other various and sundry sweets to use for housing materials and decorations.

"Wow! Did we ever pick a great place to get snowed in!" Luke's eyes gleamed, the proverbial kid in the candy shop.

"Hold on, buster. First of all, you can't eat Libby's housing development. Second, who says we're snowed in?"

"Dad. He told me Libby needed moral support. Besides, I know how Dad gets when you aren't around."

"How's that?"

"Lonesome," Luke said, as if she'd asked the world's dumbest question.

Jenny's heart felt as though it might swell right through her chest wall and float away. After Lee died, Jenny had never expected to find a love so sweet and so right as the one she had now with her childhood classmate Mike Adams. Mike and Luke were gifts to her from a God who knew all she needed in her life and had given it to her tenfold.

God did answer prayer. Even those so deep and wordless that the heart didn't know for what it was asking.

"Can we have these tonight?" Luke held out a plate of assorted goodies that Libby had put together for the break room at Tia's shop. At the rate the weather was deteriorating, there'd be no shop to open or employees to feed.

"Probably. Let's ask Libby." Jenny left the cozy clutter of the kitchen carrying the teapot and mugs. Luke followed with the food.

Mike and Tia were hooting with laughter over an old Burns and Allen routine on television in the other room. Libby was smiling wanly at Spot who, ever sensitive to underdogs like himself, was licking Libby's hand.

Two hours later Luke unfurled his sleeping bag near the fireplace. He slept on his back, his arms thrown wide, in a trusting, childlike pose. Spot, who sometimes seemed more human than canine, slept next to him. He, too, was on his back, doggy legs splayed wide, tender underbelly exposed.

"Utter trust and contentment," Mike observed. "Look at those two. Can you see what they're saying?"

Tia looked at Mike as if he'd lost his mind. "They're saying they're exhausted, of course."

"More than that. See those exposed bellies? If Spot were still out fending for himself, he'd never let that soft, vulnerable part of him show, in case something wanted to take a hunk out of him. Here, he trusts us to not hurt him. Luke, too, by the look of it."

"You do say the most amazing things sometimes, Mikey." Tia reverted to his childhood name. "I never dreamed that you'd grow up and turn out so well."

"You never dreamed I'd grow up at all. Remember the time you got a detention because I was throwing spitballs at you?"

Tia's cheeks reddened. "That was one of the *few* times *I* was in trouble at school."

Mike covered his head with his hands. "OK, OK, sorry about the spitballs."

"Just for that, you can mulch my lawn in the spring—free of charge." Mike was the owner of a successful landscaping firm called How Does Your Garden Grow?

"You drive a hard bargain, lady."

Tia reached for Libby's hand. "Looks like you have plenty of company tonight. Has anyone looked out to see if the storm is still raging?"

"Can't see in front of your nose," Mike said. "Guess we really are snowed in. It must be true—be careful what you wish for, you might get it."

"Or pray for," Jenny added.

As if on cue, they shifted themselves until they were in a circle, holding hands, silent but for the wind shaking the eaves and the crackle of dry wood burning.

"Dear heavenly Father," Jenny began, "thank you for this safe haven in the storm and for friends to share it with. Even the storms—especially the storms—are yours, Lord. We can't change them; we can only rest in your protection until they pass. Help Libby to remember this as her parents weather their own personal storm. Bless the doctors and nurses who are caring for Mrs. Morrison. Give Libby and her father wisdom and courage and insight for whatever is to come. Help us all, Lord, for you are the only true help we have. Amen."

A chorus of amens reverberated through the room and into the night.

CHAPTER TWO

*Through simplicity comes great beauty. Amish quilts
are usually made of conservative patterns and solid colors,
including black. The combination of intricate quilting stitches and the
dramatic play of black against other deep hues
makes a beautiful and distinctive quilt.*

Libby felt more free than she had in a long time as she ran the pedestrian path around the lake near her home. She'd had to look hard for her running shoes and thermal-lined black pants. It had been months since she'd taken time to run, and she'd nearly forgotten the euphoric high of endorphins pumping into her system and the lightness of body she felt when gulping deep breaths of fresh, crisp air. The wind against her cheeks was turning them ruddy. For a few moments nothing mattered but the lithe strength of her body and the pounding of her feet against the snowy ground.

But she was out of shape. The heady run was brief and soon Libby dropped onto a park bench next to old Mr. Sorenson, her parents' lifelong neighbor. He made this trek to the lake for exercise every day—summer and winter.

"Still the fastest kid on the block," he said with a smile as he moved aside to make room.

She unwound her muffler to speak. "Not anymore. I'm in terrible shape."

Mr. Sorenson had always followed Libby's athletic accomplishments with interest. His own children were grown and gone when Libby was in high school, and he'd taken a special interest in the little neighborhood girl who showed such promise.

"Not compared to me." He chuckled. "People with canes don't run races."

"You haven't changed a bit," Libby responded. "You're just as I remember you when I was a child."

"Sweet words, my dear." The old man looked pleased. "I did enjoy watching you back then. You were always running. I wasn't sure you *could* walk. *I* had no proof of it."

"I was a little monkey, wasn't I?" Libby scraped the hair out of her eyes and shook out her legs.

"Marathon monkey."

"I don't run marathons anymore. I'd last about twenty yards now." Libby hadn't had time or inclination to think about the races she'd run or the ribbons she'd won in the past. She just knew that now, after having a taste of running again, she'd missed it.

"How are your parents, my dear?"

"Not great. Just getting by."

"That's how it is for me too these days. Golden years, ha! Whoever coined that phrase hadn't been there yet. I should stop by and say hello one day soon."

"Do that. Dad would love it."

"Your parents are good people, Libby. In all the years I've known them, they've never been anything but cheerful, good-hearted, kind, and honest."

"That is a beautiful thing for you to say."

"But true. In the early years I wondered why they were always able to stay so cheerful. We were all struggling with bills, young children, troubles. I finally decided it had something to do with their being Christians."

He tapped the toe of his shoe with the tip of his cane. "That realization certainly made a difference in my life."

"How?" Libby loved hearing stories about her parents.

"I came to know Christ through their example. They didn't talk much about their faith, but they always lived it. It made a big impact on me and my family."

"I'm so glad you told me!" Libby took his hand. "Thank you."

Mr. Sorenson nodded. "I thought you'd like to know."

They visited a few moments longer, and when she was rested, Libby jogged along beside the old man as he made his way home. Then, with a spurt of new energy, she bolted home. Tia wouldn't let her in the store without a shower.

....

"Jenny, you are a lifesaver!" Tia met her at the door of the shop and took a stack of boxes out of her arms. "I'm convinced that no one is doing their own Christmas baking this year. They're just coming to the store to eat mine!"

Libby, close behind Tia, helped Jenny with a cooler. "She grumbles, but this is the best sales season she's ever had. And," she added with a whisper, "she's sneaking all the chocolate for herself when she thinks the staff isn't looking."

"I heard that!" Tia sniffed haughtily and forged back into the store.

Jenny pulled off her coat and stomped the snow from her boots. "How's everything going?"

"Good. We ordered more gift boxes yesterday. And another three giant rolls of gift wrap. Tia's been so cheerful that the Salvation Army guy outside our store is bursting his buttons. She stuffs a wad of money in his kettle every time she goes by."

"I mean, how is everything going for you?"

Libby sighed and scraped a stray lock of hair from her eye. She was wearing rusty red denim bibs, a green flannel shirt, and a

Santa button whose nose lit up when she pulled his beard. Her expression was far less cheery than her outfit.

"Do you want to know or do you *really* want to know?"

"Skip 'fine, thanks' and go right for the meat."

"OK." Libby pushed aside a stack of catalogs to make room for Jenny's delivery. "I'm totally bummed. Zonked. Brain fried. Every time I pick up the stuff on Alzheimer's that the doctor sent home, my eyeballs roll back in my head.

"I can't think. I can't make a lucid decision, and yet I'm supposed to bring Mom home from the hospital after work today."

"Need help?"

"No. Daddy will come with me. He's so anxious to have Mom home that he's been sitting with his overshoes on, waiting to leave, since before breakfast. We'll be fine."

"If this gets to be too much for you, Mike will help. Your parents both love him. They won't mind if he's along. Call him on his cell phone and he'll be at the hospital before you get there."

"I know and I'm very grateful. But this is something I have to do. Mom will feel more comfortable if it's just Daddy and me."

"She's lucky to have you, Lib."

Libby's chin lifted and her jaw tightened. "I'll be here for her for as long as she needs me. I've never taken that 'Honor your mother and father' stuff any more seriously than I do now that the shoe is on the other foot."

"What do you mean?"

"Have you ever considered the amount of responsibility God gives parents?"

"For example?"

"Proverbs 22:6, for one: 'Teach your children to choose the right path, and when they are older, they will remain upon it.' Or Deuteronomy 4:9: 'But watch out! Be very careful never to forget what you have seen the Lord do for you. Do not let these things escape from your mind as long as you live! And be sure to pass them on to your children and grandchildren. . . .'

"Parents are examples of his hands and voice here on earth. My parents brought me up to love the Lord. Now it's my turn to show God's love to them."

"You do know, Libby," Jenny said cautiously, aware of the fire her words might ignite in her friend, "that if your mom ever does get to be too much for you, there are places that are available for nursing care, and . . ."

"No." Libby's tone was flat. "That's not for us. Nursing home. More like nursing warehouse. What I have with my parents right now is a *home*."

"Libby, that's your first reaction, but you can't generalize. . . ."

"Jenny, I grew up hearing my parents talk about their fears of the nursing home. You know how active and involved my parents were—church, bowling, their gourmet club, volunteering for any good cause . . . and now a home? Mom always said she'd rather die first. Knowing that, how could I send her to one now?"

"You don't have to. Certainly not for the time being. But if you need help . . ."

"I won't." The determination in Libby's voice was cold and steely, her will ironclad in this area. Of course, even iron, under the right conditions, has been known to snap.

. . . .

"Delivery!" Jenny called as she opened the Morrisons' back door and wrestled a huge basket of sweet breads and rolls onto the kitchen table. "Thought you might enjoy my miscalculation in the amount of bread I needed for a catering job."

"Looks great." Libby's voice was flat and lifeless. "Want some coffee?"

"Sure." Jenny peeled off her hat and jacket. "And I'll take a piece of banana nut bread. I've been too busy to taste my own wares." Then Jenny became aware of someone else in the kitchen. "Oh, hello there."

Mrs. Morrison was seated on a chair pulled up to a window overlooking the backyard. The elaborate birdhouse outside was a bustling arena of finches and downy woodpeckers. "Libby's mean," the older woman complained without preamble.

"She is?"

"Birdies," Mrs. Morrison muttered condemningly.

"She's been asking for bread to feed the birds all morning," Libby explained.

"Then why don't you give her some? I certainly brought enough for both you and the birds."

"We've already gone through an entire loaf. She just doesn't remember that we've done it. The Humane Society will be over here to tell me I'm killing birds with kindness if I don't quit feeding them. I saw a downy woodpecker that could barely fly after making a pig of himself out there."

"I see." Jenny looked sadly at the older woman, who was pouting like a small child at the perceived indignity of Libby's refusal. "Mrs. Morrison, would you like to have coffee with me? I brought treats."

"Libby's mean." Mrs. Morrison's eyes narrowed.

"Now what has Libby done?" Mr. Morrison arrived in the kitchen with a frown on his face, a ratty sweater across his shoulders, and scuffed slippers on his feet.

"I won't give the birds more bread, Dad."

"Good. I think we should get rid of the bird feeder entirely. I'm tired of crawling out there to fill the thing. I don't know why you put the messy contraption there anyway. Too much bother."

"Daddy," Libby said tightly, "you put the feeder there two years ago."

"Whatever. You should have it moved. I'm not as young as I

used to be. Can't do the work and you don't ever seem to get it done."

Startled by the uncharacteristic crabbiness of Libby's parents, Jenny jumped in to divert the conversation. "Banana nut bread? Cranberry? Or would you like a blueberry muffin? I'll fix a plate for you."

"One of each," Mr. Morrison decided. "I'll take it to the living room. *Let's Make a Deal* is on in a few minutes."

"What's behind door number two?" Mrs. Morrison asked, some small part of her memory triggered by mention of the game show.

"Come with me and we'll find out, Mama," Mr. Morrison said to his wife.

"Door number three is behind door number two."

"Jenny, butter a little more of that nut bread, would you?"

"A lovely car!"

"And fill my coffee cup?"

"Am I a winner? I pick door number two."

The Morrisons were still engaged in the strange exchange as Jenny helped the pair into the other room and settled them in front of the television set before escaping into the kitchen.

Libby still stood at the counter working silently, forming ground meat into tiny balls.

"Libby? Libby? Lib!"

"What is it?" Libby turned and scraped a hand through her bangs, leaving a smear of hamburger on her forehead.

"Come here and sit down."

"I've got work to do."

"So do I. Give it a break for a minute."

Libby moved stiffly across the room and sank into a chair.

"What's the deal?"

"Probably behind door number two."

"Quit being sarcastic, Libby. You know what I mean. I've never seen your parents so cross and unreasonable!"

"Tell me about it. Every week it gets worse. The more confused

Mother gets, the more difficult Daddy becomes. They're a pair sometimes." Anger roiled inside her. "Sometimes I could just strangle them both!"

Guiltily, Libby recanted. "Oh, I don't mean that, Jen. Not at all. It's just that . . . ."

"You don't have to explain to me. I understand. It's obvious they aren't themselves. I've known your parents most of my life. Other than my own parents, they are the ones who taught me most about Jesus! What's happening now isn't really them. They are both victims of your mother's disease."

Jenny studied Libby for a moment, compassion glistening in her eyes. "And you are the third victim."

"Now I feel like a mother with two very large, naughty, hard-to-handle children. I love them but I can hardly stand them at times!" Tears stained Libby's face. "And I can't believe I just said that about my own parents!"

"You're just being honest about how you feel, sweetie. You've got to vent sometimes."

"And you're the lucky recipient." A weak smile trembled through Libby's tears. "You must have been standing behind door number two."

When Jenny smiled, Libby continued. "My Bible's pages are so thin they're practically see-through. And God's ear must be worn out. I mutter and fuss to him all day long. With his help, I manage to hold my tongue. I know my parents can't help what's going on. They're suffering far more than I am. I have to keep reminding myself of that."

Libby pointed to a set of old wooden duck decoys she'd placed on the table. "I found those in the basement. They're from Daddy's hunting days. I brought them up to remind me to be a duck in water, to be impervious to the pain and hurt by letting it roll off my back just like a duck's oily feathers allow water to roll away. Even though he's in water, a duck never really gets wet."

A smile quirked her lips. "There are a few more decoys downstairs. I'm considering bringing them up and setting them everywhere in the house. Maybe it would help if I turned the whole house into a quasi flyway for decoys."

"It's that bad, huh?"

"Jenny, I've come closer to losing my temper with my own parents more this week than in the entire first twenty years of my life! They are behaving like crotchety, cranky children."

Jenny picked up a knife and calmly began spreading butter on a slice of bread. "You'd be horrible if you weren't upset, Libby. At least this way we know you are human."

"All too human."

"Good. That's just how I like my friends." Jenny smiled beatifically. "Mike and I were talking about Simon Peter just yesterday. Mike says he so strongly identifies with Peter because he messed up so many times and he could still be loved and used by God. It's a comfort, isn't it? Sometimes I think that God especially enjoys proving that there are no hopeless cases where he is concerned. He views our frail humanity as opportunity. Maybe we should, too."

"Opportunity for what? Witnessing from a padded cell?" Jenny could always make her feel better, Libby thought gratefully.

Jenny handed Libby the slice of bread. "I wouldn't get myself measured for a straightjacket just yet. I think he has far better things planned for you."

Jenny sat down. "What God wants of us is our trust in and dependence upon him. He has plans for us far greater than any we can imagine for ourselves. But we have to lean fully on his grace in order to—pardon the crass expression—cash in on those plans."

"And I'm not leaning fully on him?"

"Only you know that, Lib."

Libby felt a stirring of guilt. She had been trying to do it all herself—honoring her parents, caring for them, loving them. She was the one fighting the idea of professional care. And when she wondered why she was feeling so angry, she'd justified it by reminding herself that she was doing it all out of obedience.

But if the obedience was grudging and resentful, was it really obedience at all? Was she becoming Little Libby Martyr in the process?

"An only child has a very unique relationship with his or her parents." Libby spoke more to herself than to Jenny. "They were my advocates, my champions, my daylight. They were my security. My rudder."

Tears leaked from her eyes. "Mom and Dad were my daylight," she whispered, "and now my daylight is fading into night."

Jenny rose from her chair and embraced her friend. Libby put her forehead against Jenny's temple and they stood together weeping.

When Libby caught her breath she added, "Jenny, what is worst of all is that this nighttime has no stars."

. . . .

Four hours with nothing to do! Libby felt as light and directionless as a loosed helium balloon. One of her mother's friends had come bearing a casserole and shooed her out of the house for a few hours.

She'd called three different friends hoping to pick up a game of tennis at the indoor courts at the club but had gotten three separate answering machines. Then she'd gone to the YMCA for a swim, only to discover that they were cleaning the pool and it wouldn't be refilled until tomorrow.

Talk about being out of the loop!

There'd been a time, Libby mused, when she'd have had tennis partners lined up two weeks in advance and the Y's pool schedule memorized. Now she didn't even recognize the receptionist behind the desk. Her plans thwarted, she felt directionless and disoriented.

That was how she ended up at an old standby, the shopping mall just a mile from her home. Without making a conscious decision, Libby found herself in the fabric store and drew a breath of relief. At least this felt familiar.

"Hello, Libby," the clerk greeted her. "Ready to sew a new quilt?"

Libby brightened at the sight of her old friend. "Hi, Patty. My legs brought me here of their own accord. But now that I'm here, what's new?"

"I'm just setting up a spring display. Come visit with me while I'm unpacking and you can see the bolts of fabric just as I see them for the first time."

"I'm not going to be in the way, am I?" Libby and Patty had golfed together in high school, had grown up in adjoining neighborhoods, and kept in touch through Patty's fabric store and a Bible study they both attended.

"You? Never."

"So," Patty continued as Libby helped her arrange bolts of fabric, "how are you? I thought you'd dropped off the face of the planet."

"That's how I've felt, too. Mom hasn't been well, and I don't get out much."

"Ummm," Patty clucked sympathetically. "I know all about that. My dad lived with us for a year before he entered assisted living."

Libby's antenna went up.

"I felt so isolated, so responsible for him, and in the end he was still miserable." Patty complacently studied a fabric bolt, oblivious to Libby's intense interest.

"What?"

"I scrambled between work and home. I never went out because I didn't want to leave him alone. Worse yet, I was dreadful company for him and didn't even realize it." Patty calmly pulled another bolt of fabric out of the shipping box. "Remember how much time we spent on the golf course when we were on the school team? I finally realized that I didn't even know where I'd put my clubs. No wonder he was miserable!"

"I had no idea! You never said a thing. But how . . ."

"I was playing martyr. Poor me. See how much I'm sacrificing for my dad? Don't you admire me?" Patty mimicked. "Though I felt responsible for Dad, I didn't really consider his needs."

"But staying at home with you . . . surely that's what he wanted!"

"At first maybe, but it got boring fast. He didn't get out because I was at work. And when my husband and I came home, I was so tired and cranky, and he had to listen to me slap pots and pans together while fixing supper. It took me a while to see how lonesome he was for peers, for friends of his own generation, but I finally got it through my thick head." Patty expertly arranged the fabrics by color family, having no idea what this conversation was doing to Libby.

"So, he isn't still at home with you?"

Patty laughed. "No way! He ditched me for a more interesting group of people. He lives in an assisted-living facility, plays cards and games with a group there, eats in the dining room, and has his eye on a sweet lady down the hall. He gets out every week to movies or shopping and is happier than he's been since Mom died.

"It's been great for him—and me, too. Once I got over the fact that I wasn't the only one who could care for him properly, that is. I thought I was being noble, but it was really my pride at stake." Patty shook her head. "Oh, the lessons God teaches us!"

Then, with a quick change of subject, as Patty had always been wont to do, she inquired, "What have *you* been doing for fun lately?"

. . . .

"If Christ is planning to come any time soon, I hope he does it today so that I don't have to keep the appointments I made for this afternoon!"

Jenny and Tia looked up as Libby erupted into the shop like frosting from a pastry tube. Whenever she could, Jenny made a point of slipping over to Tia's store for a morning check-in before opening time. Sometimes, if the bakery had already been going full tilt for hours, she provided "castoffs"—the misshapen éclair or broken cookie—for morning coffee. Today the castoffs were delicate Scandinavian butter cookies, which were not, to Jenny's experienced eye, in a perfectly satisfying pretzel shape.

"Now that we have your end-times opinion, do you mind telling us what motivated that outburst?" Tia, accustomed to Libby arriving late and flustered, poured another cup of coffee for her friend and then topped off her own cup and Jenny's.

"I have to ask for more time off to take Mom in for tests. She has been poked and prodded beyond reason, and they still aren't done with her! The doctor assures me that they are being so thorough because research into Alzheimer's is growing explosively and there may be good options for Mom. But the poor thing can't understand why she has to be inspected from stem to stern. Last time we went to her appointment we had a little episode just outside the hospital. Mom was confused and frightened. She couldn't remember where she was and didn't want to get into the car. Daddy finally calmed her down."

"We're sorry, Lib."

"Poor darlings, they were both so scared. I wanted to weep but didn't even have the time for that."

"How is she today?"

"Daddy has her propped up in bed like a queen. He's waiting on her hand and foot, hovering over her like a bodyguard."

Libby inhaled a whiff of her coffee before taking a draught. "As I was getting her settled, he kept trying to help me. All he did was get in the way and he knew it. He swung his cane like a conductor's baton to give me directions. When he hit me on the hip as I was rummaging under the bed for her slippers, we both realized that only one person can take care of Mother at a time."

"And that's why you are here today?"

"I ran away from home. About time, huh? Especially since I never took Tia up on any of her offers over the years."

"I remember the time she wanted to go with the circus. You were going to be a trapeze artist, weren't you?"

"Hey! I was a kid. What did I know?" Tia protested.

"Can your dad handle it?" Jenny asked.

"I left a meal in the refrigerator. They're watching television and holding hands like geriatric lovebirds." Libby dropped her head into her hands and her braided hair draped over one side of her slender neck.

Tia reached out and rubbed the pale, vulnerable spot near Libby's hairline. "Deep breaths, kiddo. It will be all right."

Libby's green eyes were grieved. "I'm sorry I've been such a lousy employee lately, Tia. I haven't contributed to the store like I should have, and I've asked for way too much time off because of things cropping up at home. Fire me if you like. I wouldn't blame you."

"Don't be an idiot. That would be like me trying to tell my right arm to stay home from work. Besides, you as a part-time employee is like hiring two normal full-time employees. I'm no fool. I know a good deal when I've got one."

"You're just being kind."

"Right. Kind. That's me all over—especially when it comes to business. Isn't that right, Jenny?"

Jenny smiled at Tia's implication. Tia was a generous employer but also a consummate professional. She might not be able to squeeze blood from a turnip, but she could press work from an employee with the best of them.

"You don't have to feel sorry for Tia. Wasn't she the one who talked you into hanging garland from the vaulted ceiling in the front of the store? And putting thirty-five zillion lights on that monster of a tree? And sewing miniature stockings for all the fireplaces in her dollhouse display? And . . ."

"Enough!" Tia yelped. "You really will make her quit!"

Libby finally laughed. "OK, OK. I get your point. Nothing has changed between us since we were little kids. We need each other. We're good for each other. I'm the best employee Tia has and the only one who tolerates her nutty ideas. She, on the other hand, gives me total freedom because she knows I'll always get my work done."

"There you have it." Jenny pushed her cup away and stood up. "My job here is done. Calm reigns once again."

"Don't go quite yet." Tia reached for Jenny's hand. "Let's pray for Libby and her parents. Seems to me that's about all we can do right now."

With a grace born of much practice, the threesome slipped into the familiar pattern of praise and prayer that had carried them through so many dark times over the years. Once again they gave to God what had been his all along and asked for strength for themselves and for Libby and the trial through which only she could walk.

....

Mr. Sorenson was as good as his word. He turned up at Libby's back door with a smile and a small box of chocolates. "Is your dad home?"

"They're both watching television. They will be so happy to see you. I'll bring you some coffee."

Nodding, the old man disappeared through the kitchen door.

Libby put the coffee on to brew and then opened the dishwasher to retrieve some mugs. Her heart leaped into her throat at what she found. Groceries. A vacuum-packed pound of raisins, a bag of marshmallows, assorted cans of vegetables, and the soggy remnants of a loaf of bread.

"Oh, Mom . . ."

Then, biting her tongue, Libby cleaned out the mess. Yesterday it had been cooking utensils in the refrigerator. Her mother so wanted to help around the kitchen that Libby couldn't deny her the pleasure. Still, it was getting to be a real challenge to remain patient.

When Mr. Sorenson returned to the kitchen, he wore a troubled expression.

"Did you have a nice visit?" Libby inquired.

"Yes . . . and no." He scratched his chin. "It's been some time since I saw your parents. I hadn't realized how much they'd declined."

"I know. And I'm here to see it every day."

"Your mother . . ."

"Has moments of clarity and can be very lucid, but most of the time she's like you saw her today."

"How sad. And your father?"

"He's been under a great deal of pressure watching Mother disappear before our eyes. He never complains, but I know he has dizzy spells—stress, I suppose. It's a wonder we're not all dizzy all of the time!"

The old man put his hand on Libby's wrist. "If you'd like to get away, I'll come and visit with your parents. Your dad and I restored an old car when you were a baby. I'll bet he'd enjoy visiting about that. And I'm sure you don't like leaving them alone."

Gratitude welled in Libby. Though she probably wouldn't ever call on him, just knowing he was there for the asking lifted a load from her heart.

. . . .

"Who's cooking Christmas dinner this year?" Tia mumbled from her nest on Jenny's down-filled couch.

"I thought you volunteered," Jenny mumbled back.

"If I did, I plead innocent by reason of insanity. Are there any pillows left? I need one under my left knee."

"Get your own," Libby yawned. "Ours are in use."

"Are you guys gonna lay around all night?" Luke asked.

"Yup," Tia answered. "We're exhausted, Luke. Jenny has baked her last Christmas goodie, and Libby and I have wrapped our final last-minute gift. This is the gift we give ourselves—rest."

"I could have stayed at Benjamin's tonight if I'd known how boring it was going to be here," Luke complained.

"Play with Spot," Jenny suggested.

"He's sleeping, too."

"Smart dog," Tia muttered.

"Tia, are you really cooking dinner? I mean, can you even cook?" Luke's question brought open one glaring dark eye.

"Like Julia Child, my boy."

"Who's that?"

Tia rolled over and scowled at Jenny. "The mother of this child should entertain him so the rest of us can recuperate."

Jenny groaned. The bakery had put out more product in the past week than in the entire month of August. "Where's your dad, Luke?"

Luke shrugged. "He said he had a surprise to arrange and that I wasn't supposed to let you guys fall asleep till he gets back."

"The plot thickens." Libby sat up. "Then how about a rousing game of Monopoly?"

"OK!" Luke jumped to fetch the board.

"I'll just pass go and collect two hundred dollars," Tia suggested.

"Get up, lazybones. I worked as hard as you did today."

Tia grumbled but sat up. By the time Mike returned, they'd divvied out the play money and were debating who deserved which playing piece. Tia insisted on the hat because she was more fashion conscious than the others.

Mike filled the doorway with his snowsuit-clad frame. "OK, everyone, get dressed. Your surprise is going to be here in fifteen minutes."

"What are you up to?" Libby asked.

"I'm not interested unless it involves Tom Cruise or large, extravagant gifts of diamonds and roses," Tia growled.

"It's a beautiful night. Snow is falling and there's no wind. You can't lay around like slugs on a night like this."

Mike took Jenny by the hand and pulled her up from her seat. Then he took a ski cap out of his pocket and tugged it over her ears. "Dress warmly. You'll be outside for a while."

Grumbling and complaining filled the air as they ransacked the closets for warm clothing. Luke and Spot darted from person to person, making sure that no one hung back.

When they were dressed in a strange combination of ski clothes, old winter jackets, snow pants, and woolen hats, Jenny stood back and giggled. "We look like we're going *Julebukking!*"

"What's that?" Luke asked.

"Christmas fools. It's a Norwegian custom. Between Christmas and New Year's, people dressed up in strange costumes and traveled from neighbor to neighbor. When they arrived, the person they were visiting had to identify his guests and offer them a treat."

"Cool. Can we do that?" Luke was interrupted by his father's shout from the driveway.

"He's here!"

"He had better be Santa Claus or the president," Tia grumbled. "There's no one else I'd go outside for tonight. Especially dressed like this."

They all trudged to the driveway and gasped in unison.

On the street before them stood a huge red sleigh with gleaming runners and filled with bales of hay and thick quilts. The body of the runnered vehicle was adorned with fresh green garland and red bows. Pulling the sleigh were the most massive cream-colored Belgian horses any of them had ever seen.

The butterscotch-colored horses with manes like pale tea with cream stood patiently in their darkly oiled harnesses. As they shifted, sleigh bells shivered a tuneless melody on the chilly air.

"How beautiful!" Libby gasped. She moved toward the animal nearest her.

"Be careful," Tia warned. "They have feet like serving platters. Don't let one step on you."

Libby glided toward the magnificent animal and instinctively put her uncovered hand out with the palm down to let him catch a whiff of her scent. While the others oohed and aahed, she stood quietly stroking the massive neck.

"Ready?" The man who'd been driving the rig touched Libby on the shoulder. "Everyone else is in."

"I could stand here all evening and just look at this beautiful creature."

"You can still look at them. Now you'll just have a different angle." He led Libby to the sleigh and helped her up.

As she snuggled in next to Luke, she burst out laughing. From this vantage point she could see the horses' massive rumps— each tail sporting a festive red ribbon.

With a click of his tongue, the man moved the sleigh onto the street.

"Mike, this is wonderful!" Jenny gasped. There were hot bricks covered with canvas along the bottom of the sleigh for their feet and fuzzy robes that felt as if they'd just come from the oven. "Whatever gave you this idea?"

"You three have been working hard this season," he said as he poured hot chocolate from a thermos into disposable cups and passed them around. "I thought you might like a reward for jobs well done. Soda crackers, anyone?"

"As if you haven't been working hard yourself."

Mike's company, How Does Your Garden Grow?, was a large landscaping firm in the city of Minneapolis. In the winter months, especially before the holidays, the company did a great deal of seasonal decorating, sold Christmas trees and garland, and had an entire staff of decorators designing whatever holiday fantasyland a customer could imagine. He'd built the business from nothing into a very prosperous enterprise. Not bad for a preacher's kid with a knack for mischief.

"This is a perk of my job. Bill Reynolds, the fellow who owns the sleigh and these beauties, offered to do this if I'd do some work on his horse farm in Medina. Seemed like a fair trade to me."

"Bliss," Libby murmured, rocking with the tug-and-pull motion of the sleigh, savoring the smells of steaming chocolate and sweet hay. "Pure bliss."

Jenny, Tia, and Luke couldn't stop chattering. Libby, however, chose to tilt her head skyward and stare at the stars. The cheerful jingling of the bells, the crunch of the snow beneath the runners, and the sounds of her friends' voices talking, laughing, and occasionally breaking into song lulled her into a relaxation so deep and unfamiliar to her these days that she felt as though she were floating.

It was some time before Libby realized that she was not alone in her corner of the sleigh. A man, burrowed deeply in a hooded parka, rode next to her.

"Oh! I'm sorry. Was I leaning on you?" Libby felt herself blush in the moonlight. "I didn't even realize Luke had moved."

"Forget it." Though she couldn't see the face, the voice was low, musical, and masculine.

"Are you a friend of Mike's?" The others were singing now, loudly and out of tune, but with genuine zest.

"No. My brother coerced me into coming along for the ride."

Was that irritation in his voice? Libby strained for a better look at the man but they'd taken a dark path along a lake and she could see nothing.

"I'd go with him on every outing if I were you. This is wonderful."

"Whatever."

Sensing that her riding companion didn't want to talk, Libby relaxed against the sled. She closed her eyes and sagged into the hay, unaware that her arm was wedged against a warm and solid body. Mike couldn't have given her a better gift than this, she thought dreamily as her mind drifted off. They'd been riding quite some time when a jolt of the sleigh woke her.

"Wha . . ." She sat up with a sputter.

"You had a good nap," the musical male voice commented.

Embarrassed into wakefulness, Libby realized she'd nodded off with her head on his shoulder. "I'm so sorry. I didn't mean to doze off, especially not right on top of you!" She felt herself blush in the darkness. "I don't even know your name. . . ."

"Reese Reynolds. And I didn't mind a bit. It made me feel useful. I don't get much of that these days."

"I'm Libby Morrison."

She struggled to escape the nest of hay into which she'd burrowed but kept falling back against the man's broad chest until he said, "Stay where you are. It's too crowded in here anyway. You aren't a problem to me."

Libby eyed the bodies ahead of her in the sleigh and realized he was right. "I've had a hectic few weeks," she admitted. "The motion of the sleigh and the warmth of the hay . . . I just couldn't keep my eyes open."

"Bad time?" came the faceless voice from the dark.

"I work two jobs. One for Jenny at her bakery and another for Tia at her gift shop. They're both very busy this time of year." It was strangely comforting to confess into the darkness. "And I've been having some trouble at home. . . ."

"Married? Kids?"

"No. Parents. My mother hasn't been well." She drew a ragged breath. "Not well at all."

"Want to discuss it?"

It was, Libby thought later, so easy to talk to him. Was it the darkness? Or the underlying current of genuine concern in his voice?

"She's losing her memory. Alzheimer's."

"Tough for all of you."

Libby nodded in the darkness. She appreciated the fact that he didn't offer any platitudes or useless advice. The sympathy in his voice was surprisingly heartfelt, as if he knew suffering personally.

Without invitation, Libby began to tell him about the incident at the Senior Center and the events of the past few days. He listened with what Libby could only call later "active" silence. He drew out her pain and frustration with hardly a word.

". . . but I'm sure I'm boring you," she murmured when she realized how much of herself she'd spilled to this stranger. But it had felt so good to think out loud, to summarize the chaos her family had been experiencing.

She turned to him in the darkness and could make out only a rugged profile with high cheekbones and short-cropped hair peeking out from beneath his ski cap. As they passed beneath a streetlight near the lake path they were taking, Libby noted a somber expression and a face that seemed familiar with pain. Then he was blotted out again by darkness.

Before she could say more, Spot came scrambling into her lap and put his icy nose on the bare spot at her throat. Luke soon scrambled to the back of the sleigh and Tia after that to haul Libby closer to the front to help them remember all the words to an old Christmas carol. Libby's new acquaintance didn't move.

They rode until Jenny complained that even with Mike's love to keep her warm, her toes were freezing. As they unloaded at the house Libby heard Mike give the driver an invitation to come in for coffee.

"Well, I don't know. . . ." Bill sounded doubtful. "I don't think my brother . . ."

Libby held her breath. She didn't know if she wanted to see her confessor's face or not.

"Whadayathink, Reese?"

"Do what you want." Libby was surprised by the gruffness in his voice. What had made him so testy?

"We'll be in after I load the horses," Bill said.

Libby followed Jenny and Tia inside.

"That was just too fun!" Tia babbled. "Wasn't it great?"

"We didn't hear much from you, Libby," Jenny commented as she put trays of Christmas baking and mugs on the table. "You were tucked so far back, I could barely see your outline. Did you have fun?"

"Probably more than I've had in a long time." *Thanks to a complete stranger who let me bend his ear.*

A door opening, a thunk of rubber against wood, and a muttered expletive drew Libby's attention to the door. Her eyes widened at what came through.

Bill Reynolds backed up and steered his brother's wheelchair through the door this time.

"That's yours?" Libby blurted. She hated herself the moment it was out of her mouth. Tia and Jenny both stared at her uncharacteristic lack of tact.

"All mine." His face was bland but she could sense strong emotion behind his words.

"I didn't mean . . . I didn't know . . . ."

"That I'm a cripple? Then you're the first to miss it." Anger flared in his voice like sparklers on the Fourth of July. Bill deftly faded into the other room.

"Excuse us," Tia muttered and grabbed Jenny by the elbow and towed her into the living room where the others were gathering, leaving Libby to untangle the faux pas.

"But you were in the sleigh!" Libby burst out, immediately making her gaffe worse.

"Tucked in by Bill and Annie, to give the pitiful relative a night out. I get to go on a lot of hayrides. They think it's good for me." His resentment was palpable. "They used to think of themselves as my brother and sister-in-law. Now they view their job as my keeper."

"I-I'm so sorry," Libby stammered. "I don't know what's wrong with me lately. I feel terrible. . . ."

Reese relented. "I'm sorry, too. You didn't know. Bill says I'm

too touchy about—" he looked at his legs with near hatred—
"you know."

Luke broke the tension by skidding into the kitchen with Spot
at his heels. "Are we going to eat or what?"

With relief, Libby grabbed a carafe and fled to the others. It
only occurred to her later that she'd left Reese alone in the
kitchen to fend for himself.

"I loved your horses," Libby murmured to Bill. She'd decided it
was prudent to steer clear of Reese, who seemed content to talk
to Luke and play with Spot in the far corner of the room.

"They're good old girls, no doubt about that. You should see
the colts those two have thrown." He whistled through his teeth.

"So you have a lot of horses?"

"I have a broodmare operation and do some training and
farrier work as well." Bill grinned. "And I run a nursing home for
old horses that no one else wants. Let them live out their last
days in comfort is my motto. Besides, kids love my old horses.
Those are the ones with all the smarts and patience. An old
riding horse has seen just about everything, I figure—including
every kind of idiot who thinks that just anyone can crawl on a
horse's back and ride."

"What's a *farrier*?"

"Let's just say I give pedicures to horses, put shoes on them,
and keep their feet in order."

Libby liked the man. He was solid, down-to-earth, and obviously in love with his work. "And your brother? Does he work
with you?"

"Reese? No. Not anymore. He was a wonderful horseman at
one time but in the past couple years getting him to come near a
horse has been as easy as getting a camel to do back flips. But I
keep trying. He owns half the broodmare operation, and he
could still train and work young horses in the round pen. I know
if he'd break down and try it, he'd enjoy it."

Libby identified with the sadness that came over Bill at the mention of his brother. They had both lost something precious when their loved ones changed.

Later, after the guests had gone and Jenny and Libby were clearing away the dishes, Tia broached the subject.

"What was that little scene in the kitchen all about?"

"The gorgeous guy in the wheelchair, of course," Jenny drawled.

"Did you know he was in a wheelchair?" Libby inquired.

"Not until he came in. Why?"

"I put my foot in my mouth—big time."

"You didn't know," Jenny soothed. "Your tongue just got a bit ahead of your brain, that's all."

"He acted as if I were throwing his disability in his face!"

"The man obviously has issues with his handicap," Jenny said, still unconcerned.

"How can you be calm when I'm all flustered?" Libby muttered. "The wheelchair must be recent. He said that Bill and Annie hadn't always seen themselves as his keeper."

"Deep issues," Jenny concluded.

"I feel so stupid," Libby moaned. "I hurt his feelings."

"You can apologize later if you think he's still angry."

Libby wasn't sure she wanted to see Reese again. Even to apologize.

Libby was still dwelling on the fiasco when Tia announced that the hour was close to midnight and, since she had volunteered to cook this Christmas, it was time for her to go home and start thawing a turkey.

"How big is it, Tia?" Libby asked.

"Twenty-five pounds."

"You should have had that in the refrigerator by now."

"Don't worry. It won't be a meatless Christmas." Tia waved a hand cavalierly. "But I *must* go. I need to plan my menu."

Luke's head spun to Libby, his expression dismayed. "Aren't you going to cook at all, Aunt Libby?" He sounded so worried they all burst out laughing.

"Don't worry," Luke's father assured him. "Mom and Libby are cooking Christmas Eve. You can pack enough food away that if Tia's meal doesn't turn out all right, you won't starve."

"Very funny," Tia harrumphed. "I can cook Libby and Jenny under the table any day I want."

"There's no stove under the table," Luke pointed out.

Laughing, they dispersed to their own houses to prepare for Christmas.

....

Dismantling a Christmas tree is like a backward walk down memory lane, Libby thought as she lifted a ballerina ornament from the pine branches of the tree. She'd been nine years old the year she received the slender pink dancer and aspired to the stage. *A prima ballerina.* Libby smiled ruefully. What else had she dreamed of doing before the reality of life had intruded and taken her on a more mundane path?

One by one the ornaments told her. A tiny basketball commemorated the year her team had played in the state tournament. Miniature track shoes representing the miles she'd run. A smiley face she'd received from the owner of the hamburger joint in which she'd flipped burgers and gorged on French fries. A white dove with a slender pink ribbon around its neck and an olive branch in its mouth, given to her by the boy she'd thought she'd marry one day.

Libby sat back on her heels and stared at the tiny dove. What had ever happened to . . . what was his name again?

I really must have loved him. I can't even think of his name!

Libby picked up the clay thimble she'd made at school so many years before. She'd poked a hole through the clay while it was soft with the lead of her pencil. Then she'd strung a bit of ribbon through the hole so it could be hung on the tree. It was her mother's favorite Christmas present that year.

Her mother loved quilting, more even than Libby. Over the years, her designs became more and more fanciful. They were truly works of art stitched with fabric and sometimes even sewn with glittery silver or gold thread.

Then Libby discovered her dad's clay fish. She'd made that the same year—third grade, perhaps—to represent the hours her father loved to spend on one of the many lakes nearby. He'd caught hundreds of fish—and turned every one back into the water saying he fished for the fun of it, not to eat.

One by one she wrapped and put away the memories for another year. She was almost done when she ran across her favorite ornament of all, a tiny sewing machine given to her by her textiles instructor at the university. What had she been planning then? To be a famous clothing designer. To make her mark on New York City. The irony of it all nearly made her weep.

What will next year's ornament be? Did they make miniature wheelchairs and hospital beds? Maybe they don't design remembrances for the kind of life I'm living now. Maybe it's the kind of life no one wants to remember.

Libby sighed and closed the lid on the storage container. She couldn't think about next year when she was having difficulty thinking about tomorrow.

"Jenny? Jenny?" The whispering voice on the other end of the line was barely recognizable.

"Lib? What's wrong?" Jenny sleepily kicked at the edge of her comforter and fought the sleep that still embraced her. It was 4 A.M.

An exhausted sob quivered on the line. "Mom must have been overstimulated by the excitement of Christmas. When she lays down she always wakes up with horrible nightmares, screaming and clawing at the air. She's been prowling the house, and I'm terrified she'll fall and break a hip. She won't let me comfort her. I need help, Jenny."

"I'll be right there." Jenny swung her legs over the edge of the bed as she hung up the phone.

Mike grabbed the back of her nightgown. "Where are you going in such a hurry?"

"Libby is having trouble with her mother."

"I'll come with you." He gave a catlike stretch and started to get up. His dark hair was ruffled and boyish, his eyes heavy lidded.

"You don't have to . . . ."

"From what I've observed of Mrs. Morrison, she's a strong woman. If she wants to do something, I doubt either you or Libby could physically stop her. If there's any lifting or carrying to do, I'll be the one to do it."

"Thanks." Jenny hadn't really wanted to go alone. It was cold and dark, and she knew that they would find very agitated people at their destination. It was so like Mike to have such concern and consideration—and one of the reasons she loved him so much.

Jenny was even more grateful for Mike's support when she saw her friend.

Hair mussed, flannel nightgown torn, feet bare, and eyes sleep deprived, Libby met them at the door. In the background, Jenny could hear Mrs. Morrison sobbing.

"She thinks I'm lost," Libby explained, voice trembling, "and that I'm five years old. I can't convince her that I'm me!"

Jenny dropped her coat on the foyer floor and walked into the living room where Mrs. Morrison rocked back and forth on the couch, braying forlornly that she couldn't find her daughter.

"Hi, Mrs. Morrison. It's me, Jenny."

Mrs. Morrison quieted for a moment, and before she could start to cry again, Jenny added quickly, "Libby's at my house. We're playing with dolls."

The woman blinked and scrubbed away the tears on her cheeks. "She is?"

"Uh-huh. My mom wants to know if she can stay for supper. Can she?"

Mrs. Morrison frowned. "Be sure she washes her hands."

"OK." Then Jenny touched the older woman's hand. "You look tired. It must be nap time. Should I help you lay down?"

Mrs. Morrison nodded like a child and allowed Jenny to lead her to the bedroom where Mr. Morrison was snoring, relaxed as a baby, his hearing aid resting on the bedside stand.

When his wife had been tucked in next to him, Jenny tiptoed from the room and closed the door.

"Boy, do I feel dumb," Libby muttered. "I had to wake you up in the night to do that? Even the night after she'd been to the hospital wasn't this bad. Now any sort of disruption of her schedule sends her into a night fit."

"Is it getting worse?"

Radically. Libby averted her eyes. "Yes."

Mike put a cup of decaffeinated coffee and a meatball sandwich he'd made from Christmas Eve leftovers in front of Libby. "Eat this. We're tucking you in next."

"I don't know if I dare go to sleep now. I might not hear her if she wakes up again. I'll lay down when Daddy gets up for breakfast and puts his hearing aid in."

"Don't be silly," Jenny said. "I'll sleep on the couch if that's what you're worried about."

"I can't let you do that. You have a husband and family at home."

Mike sat down across from her. "It appears to me that the husband is already here. And the family—Luke and Spot—won't be up for five hours yet. I left Luke a note on the refrigerator. He'll find it on his way to the leftovers."

"This is ridiculous. I should be able to manage. I'm just tired from the busy season at the store."

"Maybe we could swap favors, then," Mike said.

"What do you mean?" Libby stirred sugar into her coffee, wishing Mike had made the leaded variety.

"I'm leaving for Arizona on Wednesday to get my parents settled into a new retirement community. Luke is going on a ski trip with his best friend's family. That means Jenny will be alone for a week. If you let one of us watch your mother for the rest of the night, then I'll let you watch Jenny and Spot this week."

"Very funny . . ."

"It's a great idea, Libby," Jenny chimed in. "I'll sleep here at night. That way, you'll have help for your mom if you need it and I won't have to be alone."

"You don't mind staying alone and you know it."

"Please? It will be nicer for me," Jenny pleaded.

"And I'd feel better—about both of you," Mike added.

"No. You'll never rest here. Don't you have a lot of catering to do this week?"

"This is the post-Christmas season. Everyone is gearing up for a diet. Fruit and cheese plates, shrimp cocktail, crudités, one dessert instead of seven. Easy as pie, if you don't mind my saying so. All my New Year's accounts are under control. And I wouldn't cook at night anyway."

Libby sighed. "Oh, all right. But only because Mike and Luke are going to be gone." Then tears flooded her eyes. "And because I'm so tired I can't hear myself think."

Jenny gently guided her friend back to her room and tucked her into her bed, much as she had the older Morrison woman. Libby was asleep in moments. Then Jenny found a down comforter and made a bed for herself on the couch. She waited for Mike to close the door behind himself before shutting her eyes.

"Oh, Lord," she prayed, "help Libby and her parents through

this mess. Show me how to be the friend I need to be and support Libby through her mother's illness."

There were no more sounds from the bedroom and slowly Jenny drifted off to sleep.

CHAPTER THREE

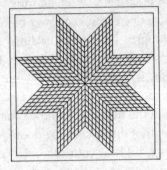

As the Civil War dragged on, blankets were needed
for the troops. Southern women sewed what they called "secession"
quilts, while Northerners made "union" quilts. It was a way to help
their loved ones, to make patriotic statements by the symbols they
stitched into their creations, and to aid the soldiers fighting
and dying for the causes they held dear.

"When you said you'd move in for the week, you really meant it, didn't you?" Libby watched Jenny lug a bag of dog food up the front step. She took it from Jenny's hands and put it with the suitcase, pillow, garment bag, and sack of groceries Jenny had already toted in from the car. Spot, who knew something big was afoot, stuck close to Jenny's suitcase, in hopes that wherever it went, he was going, too.

"It's too quiet at my house. Besides, I don't want to waste time running back and forth. You don't mind Spot coming along, do you?" Jenny wiped a blonde curl out of her eyes. "Love me, love my dog and all that?"

"Actually, by the look of it, you could have stayed home and just sent Spot." Libby pointed into the living room.

Spot had abandoned his vigil by the suitcase to take up residence beside Mrs. Morrison's chair. She'd put down her crocheting—a tangled wad of yarn due to a plethora of dropped stitches—and started petting Spot on the top of his silky head. They stared at each other with sweet, adoring eyes.

"They say petting a dog or cat can lower blood pressure," Jenny observed. "Animals have many healing properties."

"Then Spot sleeps with me tonight, not you. I need some of what he's got." Libby started up the stairs with Jenny's suitcase. "I'll put you in the room next to Mom and Dad. I don't trust myself to hear her in the night. Right now I think I could sleep through an explosion of the house next door."

"I'm a light sleeper. If I hear your mom, I'll get up. There'll be no need to call you."

"Don't try to do this alone, Jenny."

"You are."

"That's different." Libby's expression tightened. She dropped the suitcase and walked down the hall to her room.

Jenny followed close behind. "How?"

"She's my mother."

"And the mother of my best friend. Let me do this."

Libby dropped onto the bed and fell back in a sprawl. "Let's just hope you don't hear anything. Changes have been occurring so quickly with her lately that I can only hope and pray that they will slow down soon."

Jenny didn't comment as she walked around the room, allowing a lifetime of memories to flood over her.

Libby's room reflected her personality—homey, warm, cozy. There were a dozen brightly colored pillows in florals, stripes, and prints overflowing the bed. Two homemade quilts and a big pillow-type backrest with arms—a creature Libby jokingly called her "husband"—made the bed look like a downy sea. The rocking chair that had been in the room since Libby was an infant sat in an incandescent pool of light from an antique floor lamp.

Oh, the slumber parties they'd had in this room—the spooky stories, popcorn, butter crackers, and cheese spread from a can! And the adventures—like the night Tia attempted to crawl out the window and down the trellis to meet a boy and ended up with a broken arm when the trellis unhooked from the house and sent her flying into the yard. . . .

Spot's bark brought them both to their feet.

Downstairs, Mrs. Morrison stood at the front door ineffectually trying to release the dead bolt. Her age-spotted hands fluttered with frustration over the latch she'd opened so many times before. Spot, sensing that this was unacceptable behavior, barked and nudged at the woman with his nose as if to dissuade her from the notion of going outside.

"Mom?"

Mrs. Morrison turned to look at her daughter with surprise in her expression. "Libby? My goodness, what am I doing?" She looked genuinely confused.

"You shouldn't be trying to go out. It's cold."

"I know that!" Mrs. Morrison snapped. "My goodness, Libby, don't treat me like a child!" With that, the older woman shuffled off, indignation bristling from every pore.

"What was that about?" Jenny whispered after Libby's mother was settled in her rocking chair with Spot, self-appointed guard dog, again at her side.

"She does it to me all the time." Libby ran her fingers through her hair as if she were going to pull it out by the roots. "She's usually so quiet and tentative that I'm not sure she grasps what's going on. Then she has these moments of perfect clarity. Suddenly I'm the child and she's the mother again, and she accuses me of talking down to her. I never know which person I'll be talking to!"

"It's the nature of the disease. The doctor told you that when she confirmed the diagnosis of Alzheimer's," Jenny said gently. "It has nothing to do with you."

They moved into the kitchen, out of earshot of the living room. Libby slumped onto a tall stool. "The harder I try, the more upset I seem to make her."

"If you think like that you'll drive yourself crazy. If you couldn't remember what had gone on earlier in the day or found yourself in places you didn't mean to be, doing things you didn't plan to do when your clarity finally snapped into focus, wouldn't you be alarmed, too? Or defensive? Or angry?"

"I never thought about it that way," Libby admitted. "I've been too tired to think at all, I guess."

"And that, my friend, is why I'm here." Jenny made shooing motions with her hands. "Go to bed. Sleep like a baby. I'm going to watch television with your parents and help your dad get your mom to bed. Don't show your face down here again."

"What if I can't sleep?"

"Then read. Do your nails. Write letters. I don't care. You can put lipstick kisses on your mirror for that matter. Just get out of here. You aren't needed for the next twelve hours."

"Music to my ears." Libby gave Jenny a bone-crunching hug and disappeared through the door, humming.

Libby slipped her favorite CD into its player, turned on the lamps, and lit every candle. Then she put on her oldest, fuzziest pajamas and stood in the middle of the floor wondering what to do next. Her eyes fell on the dog-eared Bible on her nightstand.

"OK, God, let's see what you have to say to me," Libby murmured. She picked up the book and allowed it to fall open. She'd learned from experience that she could read a passage time and time again and then, when she was ready, read it again and gain utterly new and profound insight. Tonight she'd read the Bible but allow God to pick the passage.

The first passage was clearly a puzzle. Her eyes fell on "Husbands must love your wives with the same love Christ showed the church. He gave up his life for her."

Libby chuckled and closed the Bible. "I'll try again, Lord. Maybe you weren't prepared."

This time it was Ephesians again. "In the same way, husbands ought to love their wives as they love their own bodies. For a man is actually loving himself when he loves his wife."

Twice was rarely a coincidence. This was more like a God-incidence. *But why?*

Marriage was out of the question. One needed a man to have a marriage. And one needed a *date* to have a man! Libby tucked her toes beneath her and wiggled them. She hadn't met a new man in ages. Except for Reese Reynolds.

Her eyes opened wide. "Oh, no, Lord. I'm sure you don't have that thundercloud picked out for me." The absurdity of it made her giggle. It reminded her of the prophecy in Isaiah 65 saying the wolves and lambs would someday eat together in peace. Of course, she believed in prophecy, but surely not . . .

She would stick with the next verse no matter how inapplicable it might seem. And she would keep her mind and heart open. After all, God did work in mysterious ways.

"First Timothy," Libby murmured aloud. "'But those who won't care for their own relatives, especially those living in the same household, have denied what we believe. Such people are worse than unbelievers. . . .'"

Her heart raced as she laid the book on her bed. "What do you mean, God? I don't know *how* to do any more for Mom and Dad. I'm providing all I'm capable of doing."

But what if it's not enough?

Libby swallowed the lump and stared at the passage. How could it not be enough? She was killing herself for them already! Is that what God wanted?

Or was killing herself just what he didn't want?

Libby leaned back on her husband pillow and stared at the wall on the far side of the room. She hadn't been the greatest of daughters lately, she admitted to herself. She'd been a perfect *caretaker* but she'd been too busy feeding, washing, and cleaning to be much real company to either of her parents.

Her father loved practical jokes. He loved both to pull them and to have them pulled on him. Once Libby and her father had a marathon month of short sheeting each other's beds. And he was wicked with a whoopee cushion. But since her mother's problems began, the pranks had stopped. Had the well of his zest for life dried up? Or had his daughter had too little time to encourage the fun?

Libby tried to imagine what it would be like if her only responsibilities were to spend time with them, to have devotions, and to read to them. She and her parents used to play games at night before bedtime. They could still do that if she had the energy. It wouldn't matter if Mother got confused as long as she felt a part of the activity. Had that conversation with Patty been more than an accident?

I've taken care of their physical needs at the expense of our emotional ones.

Though nothing was settled in her mind, Libby felt a growing calm within her. What was God trying to tell her? Was she on the track of an answer for the huge, life-altering question of her parents? Or was God just giving her a break?

It's up to you, Lord. I'm stepping back now. I'm out of this. You handle it.

And Libby's soul said *amen*.

. . . .

Jenny woke to the smell of coffee and frying bacon. She opened one eye to peer blearily at the bedside clock. Eight A.M. How on earth had that happened?

Spot had already disappeared from the bed. Jenny pulled on her robe and padded downstairs. Libby was in the kitchen in her playful footed pajamas, hair scooped into a clip at the back of her head. She was swinging a pair of tongs in time to an old-time gospel hymn on the radio. Spot was hovering near her feet, waiting for food droppings.

"Why'd you let me sleep so late?" Jenny poured a mug of coffee and plucked a fresh biscuit from the counter beside the stove.

"Homemade strawberry jam on the table. Made yesterday," Libby said.

"How'd you manage that? Do you grow strawberries in the basement?"

"Frozen. Bacon with that?"

"Stop pushing food!" Jenny yelped. "Is this what happens when you get enough rest?"

"It was great, Jen. I'd forgotten how it felt to relax. I let my body melt into those sheets. . . ." Libby shivered with pleasure. "Sublime."

"Then why did you jump out of bed this morning and start to cook for an army?"

"Mom. She's been eating like a bird."

"She's not exercising much. Maybe she isn't hungry."

"It's more than that, Jenny." Libby sat down, and bacon grease dribbled off the tongs onto the tablecloth. "I'm trying to nudge her memory with food. She's always talked about her mother's big breakfasts on the farm—biscuits and gravy, eggs and bacon, oatmeal with cream and sugar. I've asked Daddy what her favorite foods are and made every one of them. Once in a while she'll say, 'Mama used to make these' or 'Is this my recipe for trifle?' and then I think it's working. . . ."

"But most of the time, you're just making your friends fat." Tia stood framed in the doorway, her cherry red coat and dark hair making a dramatic picture in the middle of the cluttered, fragrant kitchen.

"How long have you been standing there?" Jenny asked.

"Long enough. I thought something was up with the food. I've gained six pounds since Mrs. Morrison got sick. Libby can't deal with the leftover problem alone. It's a dirty job, but somebody has to do it." Tia poured herself a cup of coffee and sat down.

"It seems to me that you'll have to accept the fact that your mother isn't going to be brought back by the smell of sugar cookies or the sight of your family vacation slides. Offering care and comfort are one thing, killing yourself in the process is quite another." As usual, Tia went right to the heart of the matter. Then, having said what she needed to say, she buttered a biscuit and stacked it high with bacon.

"Then what am I supposed to do?" Libby snapped. "Watch her disappear before my eyes?"

Before anyone could say more, the subject of their conversation meandered into the room, followed by Libby's father. Her uncombed white hair was flattened at the back of her head, showing a childlike-looking swirl and a small bald patch where she had lain. Her cheeks were pink and wrinkly looking, her eyes rheumy.

She was an old baby, Libby thought, not the young, freshly pink kind of infant people loved to cuddle and care for, but rather the elderly variety, the ones easily cast off and hidden away. But that would not happen to her mother. Never. Ever. She would not let it. That couldn't be what God meant to tell her in that verse last night.

In a well-rehearsed family ballet, husband and daughter settled Mrs. Morrison into her chair, tucked a napkin into the collar of her bed jacket, and readied her to eat. Mrs. Morrison allowed them to move around her as a queen bee might permit access to her drones. She hardly seemed to know they were there.

Libby set a plate of food in front of her dad and one before her mother. "Mama, would you like me to cut your food?"

Mrs. Morrison's plate flew across the table so quickly that no one had time to stop it. "No!" Her eyes narrowed to stubborn slits, and her mouth pulled down at the corners. She appeared as irate as Libby was shocked. Hunks of biscuit clung to the cupboard and slid down the front in an ooze of pale gravy.

"We'll get it." Jenny jumped up to clean away the greasy stains. Tia picked the pieces of the glass plate from the floor and disposed of them.

"Mama?" Libby leaned toward her mother. "Would you like another plate? Just some bacon? You've always loved bacon."

Mrs. Morrison's lips curled into a pout and Libby sighed.

"I'll go in the other room, Dad. See if you can get her to eat. For whatever reason, she's not going to eat while I'm around."

Tia and Jenny followed Libby into the dining room where she sat with her head in her hands.

"You can't blame yourself for that little outburst," Jenny soothed.

"Then why do I have the distinct sense that Mother is being intentionally perverse with me?" Libby asked wearily.

"You said it yourself. You and your mom have switched roles. You are becoming the mother and she the child."

"But I don't want . . ."

"It doesn't appear that what you want has any bearing on this matter," Tia said bluntly. "It's happening anyway."

"But she's my mother!" Libby felt her throat constrict. "She can't do this to me!"

"She's not doing it 'to' you. She has no choice in the matter, Lib, any more than you do. It's just what is."

"Well, I don't like it!" Libby paced the floor, feeling as though she might burst. "It's got to stop. We can get a handle on this. I know we can. I just have to think . . . think of something . . ."

"Sit down and take a deep breath," Tia ordered. "Hyperventilating won't solve anything."

"Didn't Doctor Hazard suggest a Living with Alzheimer's class at the hospital?" Jenny asked. "Maybe that would . . ."

Libby turned on her, struggling to quash the thoughts of betrayal that had come to her in the night. "Nothing will help! They don't understand. No one can." Like a balloon deflating, Libby sank to the floor and cried in sharp, jerky sobs that sounded as though they were shredding her insides.

. . . .

"Dad, can you help Mom with her jacket? I'll take her with me to the grocery store."

"Shouldn't we do something about her blouse first?"

Now what? Libby walked toward her parents.

"Oh, Mom . . ."

Mrs. Morrison had pulled her blouse from the confinement of her skirt and tied the ends together in a knot. The skirt was askew on her hips, and the leather belt was missing from its loops.

"Let's just straighten this out a bit."

"She's been messing with her clothes a lot, hasn't she, Lib?" her father ventured.

"Just trying to look prettier, aren't you, Mom?" Libby retucked the blouse and made a mental note to look for the belt later. This, in the scheme of things, was minor. Rearranging clothes was one thing. Rearranging cupboards, as her mother had done yesterday, was far more work to undo.

At the market, Libby gave her mom the job of pushing the cart as she threw items into it. Between the potato chips and the soft drinks, they ran into Tia.

Tia had two pizzas, a grapefruit, and a package of diet cookies in her cart.

"Nutritious," Libby teased.

"Fruit, vegetables—tomato sauce is a vegetable, you know— protein, carbohydrates. Seems perfect to me."

"What's up?" Libby asked.

Tia didn't answer. She was staring at something over Libby's shoulder. "Libby, your mom just opened a can of soda and is drinking it."

Libby spun around in time to see her mother swill down the last of a grape soda. "No! You can't . . ."

"But she did." Tia's voice was unconcerned. "Frankly, I've often wanted to do that very thing. If I'm buying the milk and cookies anyway, why can't I start eating them right away? I'll *pay* for them."

Calmly, Tia took the six-pack minus one can of soda and put it in her cart. Then she freed another can from the plastic web and opened it and took a long deep drink. "Ahhh," she murmured in satisfaction.

Libby stared at Tia for a moment and then back at her mother. Mrs. Morrison was smiling at Tia as if they were cohorts in a great and exceedingly funny crime.

"Leave your mother alone, Lib," Tia said. "She was thirsty and had a drink. Don't embarrass her by making a fuss. Just accept it. I'll pay for the sodas." She threw her own can in the cart with the others.

Libby rubbed her temples for a moment, not sure whether to laugh or cry. Finally, she said to Tia, "My mother has Alzheimer's. That's why she took a drink off a shelf and tasted it. What's your excuse?"

Tia grinned widely. "There's no excuse for me. I'm just made this way. Come on, I'll buy you a piece of cheesecake to wash down the soda."

Tension diffused, the threesome made their way to the coffee shop.

....

She *had* to talk to someone. Libby paced the floor like a caged lion. She'd bent Tia's and Jenny's ears enough for one day. Who could she call? Ellen? Dorothy?

The answer that came into her head was like an unwanted slap in the face. *Reese?*

Libby, alone in her room, blushed. What would he think of that? A woman he'd met only once—and who had been utterly tactless and rude—calling him to pour out her troubles? But he'd had troubles of his own—big ones. Wouldn't he understand? *Maybe. When he quit laughing.* But this wasn't a male-female sort of thing. More of a lost souls sort of thing. Libby's hand reached for the phone as though it weren't attached to the rest of her body.

"Libby?" Patty's voice came on the line. Libby could hear the cash register at the fabric shop ringing in the background. "Are you all right?"

No! her mind screamed. "Yes," she said.

"You don't sound all right."

Libby began to cry. "I'm so sorry to call you but Jenny and Tia are about worn out and my pastor is on a retreat with the junior high kids and I couldn't think of anyone else but you who might understand. . . ." Libby snuffled loudly into the phone. "I think I'm going nuts and don't have anyone to talk to about it."

"So you thought of me? Should I be flattered or insulted?" Like a sluice opening to allow water into a dam, words poured out of Libby's mouth. All about her parents, their current predicament—Libby's fear and exhaustion came rushing out until she felt purged and empty. Then she hit a wall of silence.

"And?" Patty's voice was compassionate.

"That's it. Isn't that enough?"

"That's plenty, it seems to me. Do you feel better now?"

Libby took an inventory of her emotions. "Much."

"Have you asked your parents how they feel? Your father, at least?"

"I can't until I can accept the option in my own mind," she said honestly. "I grew up thinking that families were families forever, and they never let each other down. Until I can convince myself that a nursing home would be better for them than their own home, I don't feel strong enough to ask my dad. I'm afraid he'll say the nursing home only to give me some relief."

"What's so bad about that? He's your father. He wants you to be happy, right?"

"But I am happy!" Libby wailed.

"I can tell," Patty responded so dryly that Libby almost laughed.

"OK. This is enough. Thank you for listening. It's made me feel human again. I promise I'll never do this to you again."

"Until next time. That's what friends are for, Libby."

Libby hung up the phone and stared at herself in the mirror. Though Patty had done nothing but listen, she felt better.

....

"Are you up to it?" Tia inquired as she stuck her head inside the back door of Jenny's house.

Grimly, Jenny nodded. "Maybe we should have our heads examined."

"For walking into the lion's den with only our faith to protect us?" Tia was staying nights at Libby's with Jenny, in a show of moral support.

"Something like that."

"I know it's bad at Libby's right now, but that's when she needs us most." Tia gave a quirky grin. "Besides, I need my number one employee back. The sooner Libby gets her head screwed on right, the sooner life will return to normal."

"Whatever normal is," Jenny pulled on a sky blue ski jacket and matching hat that enhanced her Scandinavian good looks and stunning eyes. "Let's go."

"Remember now," Tia whispered, "no matter how crabby Libby is, we have to be calm."

"The door is open." Tia pushed at the Morrisons' door and it swung wide. Mrs. Morrison wandered off occasionally. Libby had started dead bolting the doors to prevent escapes. To find it unlocked was highly unusual these days.

Mr. Morrison was sitting in the living room staring at the television, his eyes fixed on the center of the screen as he gazed through the tube into its electronic bowels. He didn't hear them come in.

"He gets quieter and sadder by the day," Jenny whispered. "It's as though he's disappearing by degrees." They stared at the man who had been a surrogate father to them both. "Didn't he used to be . . . bigger?"

"They're all disappearing in one way or another. It's horrible to watch."

"Libby says his blood pressure is very high—stress, I suppose. And he complains of feeling dizzy—"

A sudden noise in the kitchen startled them.

"Don't drop the pans on the floor, Mom—you'll disturb Daddy." Libby's tone was one she might use with a small, recalcitrant child.

Jenny and Tia followed the noise. "What's up?" Jenny asked cheerfully as they entered the kitchen.

Libby was stirring something fragrant on the stove. Mrs. Morrison was stirring something imaginary in an empty kettle.

"Rhubarb dumplings. I found the recipe in Mom's grandmother's cookbook. Tell Dad to get Mom set up at the dining-room table and we'll have a taste. She's got a good sweater on, Jenny. Don't forget to use her bib. . . ," Libby faltered.

She sank onto a stool by the stove. "I'm so tired of being a parent to my parents! This is all mixed up. Everything is out of order. I'd give so much if I could be the child again—even for a day."

There was nothing Jenny or Tia could say.

"Where do I find someone to baby-sit an old woman so I can escape from the house for a few hours?"

"We're here," Jenny pointed out.

"I can't bother you all the time. You do too much as it is."

"There are places . . . ," Tia began. "Adult day care . . ."

Libby took Tia's hand and skewered her with a gaze. The intensity of her voice caused it to quiver. "I want to be here for them like they were for me—to comfort them when they are afraid, to let them know that, no matter what, I love them. We're family. If I send Mother away, we will no longer be complete. I don't want any more holes in my heart."

These last words resonated in Libby's skull. *She* hadn't wanted more holes in *her* heart? A pang of guilt pierced her. Was this about selfishness on her part or real and total desire to do what was right? She wasn't sure anymore.

"All right, all right," Tia sighed. "But you have to understand that it's very painful for us to watch you go through this. Promise you'll consider what we're saying."

....

They carried the steaming kettle of rhubarb sauce filled with featherlight dumplings into the dining room. Jenny handed out dishes, while Tia distributed spoons and napkins. When everyone had a serving, Libby sat down next to her mother and picked up a spoon to help feed her.

Instead of opening her mouth, Mrs. Morrison clamped her lips shut and shook her head.

"Take a bite," Libby cajoled. "You'll like it."

The lips grew tighter.

When Libby touched the tip of the spoon to her mother's lips, a whimper escaped.

"It's not too hot, is it?" Libby touched the spoon to her own lips. "It's fine. Just open up. . . ."

When Libby set the spoon on the rim of the bowl, Mrs. Morrison spoke. "I want to go home."

"You are home, Mom. Right here in your dining room. Now if you'd just take a taste . . ."

"I want to go home!" Her tone was more emphatic this time.

"But you are. . . ."

"I don't think that's what she means, Libby." They'd all nearly forgotten Mr. Morrison was present.

"Then what, Daddy?"

"I think she wants to go to her heavenly home."

Libby froze. "Daddy!"

Mr. Morrison shrugged. "It's not such a bad thing, Libby. She'd be happier there."

"Don't think like that! We need her here!"

"*We* need her. But maybe she needs to be somewhere else. Don't be afraid, Libby. It won't be bad when it happens. Perhaps your mother is trying to prepare you in the best—the only—way she has left."

Silently, Libby left the table.

Tia slipped into her spot and, by some sort of perversity, was able to feed Mrs. Morrison an entire bowl of the dumplings.

While Tia remained in the dining room, Jenny followed Libby up the stairs.

"I can't believe he said that!" Libby said furiously when they were out of earshot. "That's his wife and my mother he's talking about!"

"And he didn't say anything bad, Lib. Your mom is a Christian. Maybe he's right. Maybe she knows. . . ."

"Am I wrong, Jenny? Am I being selfish? What if being at home *isn't* the best for her?"

"It's not mine to say. That's between your family and your doctor. But from the outside looking in, things don't appear to be so great. Your mom is ill, your dad is in mourning, and you are terrified because your mom, the heartbeat of your family, is failing. More than that, you've given up practically everything else in your life to care for them."

"What's the right thing, Jenny? What does God want me to do?"

"For now, just listen. He'll get your attention when the time is right."

. . . .

Libby had been asleep for several hours when she heard a scream so loud that it sent her upright in her bed. Dazed, she wiped her hair out of her eyes. Her forehead was damp with perspiration.

Jenny burst into the bedroom at full tilt and skidded to a stop by the bed. "Are you OK?"

"I think so. Who screamed?"

Jenny stared at Libby, befuddled. "Lib, that was you!"

Libby swallowed. *"I screamed?"*

"Like a banshee. What were you dreaming?"

Libby felt her pounding heart gradually quieting. She recalled images of her mother lost in a swampy marsh and herself flailing around as patches of quicksand pulled at them both. *Symbolic, no doubt.*

Tia poked her head into the bedroom. "Looks like we're going to have a middle-of-the-night party," she informed them. "Your parents are awake. I told them I'd fix hot chocolate for them."

"We'll be right down." As Libby's equilibrium returned, she looked to Jenny. "Now what have I done?"

"In the scheme of things with your parents? Not much. They'll sleep late tomorrow and all will be well. With you? That's much more difficult to answer. You can't keep on this way, Lib. You aren't resting properly."

"And what am I supposed to do about that? I can't work any harder during the day or become any more exhausted—not without killing myself."

"Exactly my point. It's time to call in some outside help. There are excellent geriatric and Alzheimer's specialists here in Minneapolis. Talk to them. Dr. Hazard has encouraged you to do so. Interview a couple of homes. See what kinds of things can be done to help all of you."

"I don't want to put her in a home. Not now." *Not yet.*

"Talking to someone doesn't automatically lead to admission—or incarceration—as you call it."

"Jenny, my parents devoted themselves to me. Why can't I devote a little time to them?"

"If your mother could, what would she tell you about this situation?" Jenny asked.

Libby's expression softened. "To not be silly. To get help. To rely on God to guide me."

"Then maybe that's what you should do, Lib."

Libby sighed and stood up.

"Remember how scared we were at first to sit in that tree house your father built for us? Even though the tree was sturdy and huge, it moved in the wind. Sometimes we'd hang on to the planks and scream until your father rescued us."

"He used to say 'Don't worry,'" Libby recalled. "'It won't blow away. God designed trees to sway with the wind to be sure they wouldn't break.'"

"Pretty soon we got to *like* the feel of the wind in the tree," Jenny reminded her.

Libby closed her eyes. "It was like being on top of a big strong horse, rocking and swaying, moving with nature."

"Maybe that's what you need to do now, Lib. Learn to rock and sway with the ride life's giving you. And rely on God to keep you safe."

Libby scrubbed at her eyes and sighed. "I've never been much of an adventurer, Jenny. I don't like wild rides very much."

"No? Me either. Good thing we have a partner to take it with us." Jenny's smile dimpled her cheek. "And remember, God made both the tree and the wind. He's no stranger to adversity—or rescuing people from it."

"OK, God," Libby sighed. Then she turned her eyes heavenward. "I guess I'd better fasten my seat belt. I think we're in for a bumpy ride."

CHAPTER FOUR

*Broderie perse quilting involves cutting out and stitching
fabric motifs over larger pieces of cloth. First used
to make better use of scarce chintz fabric,
the technique is still used today.*

"I'm glad Luke is getting back from his trip today," Libby commented as she wiped a bead of sweat from her forehead and sent a cloud of ice crystals showering across her face. "I don't like shoveling snow."

"Who does?" Jenny leaned into her shovel and pushed it with her belly, inching it forward until she had a full scoop. "Mike has accused me more than once of marrying him for his snow shoveling abilities."

"And did you?"

Jenny waggled her eyebrows under the rim of her felt hat. "Of course. What else?" She propped herself on the shovel. "I've missed him so much. It won't feel right until both he and Luke are home."

"You love them a lot, don't you?"

"More than I ever dreamed possible. When Lee died, I thought my capacity for love had been reached and that I had no more to give. Now I know that I've surpassed that level a dozen times over. They opened my heart and showed me how much room there was inside."

"Amazing, isn't it, that something so tragic would ultimately bring you so much happiness?"

"A miracle," Jenny agreed.

They floundered to a small concrete lawn bench nearly buried in snow and sat down. The icy seat immediately began to radiate cold through their snow pants to the backs of their legs. Neither paid any attention.

"I pray every night that something equally good will come of my mother's illness," Libby said quietly. "But right now I can't see anything but heartache coming down the pike."

"*But,*" Jenny cautioned. "That's the word to get out of your vocabulary. I trust God *but* . . . I believe all things work together for those who love God *but* . . ."

"I get your meaning," Libby said, "but . . ."

They both burst out laughing. Libby rolled to her side and fell with a plop into the snow. She lay on the ground staring at the cathedral of sky and said, "Oh, Lord! Help my unbelief!"

"Amen!" With a thrust, Jenny launched herself across the snow to land by Libby. They both lay there making floppy snow angels and laughing until icy crystals crept down the necks of their parkas, inside their boots, and up the sleeves of their jackets. Still, they stayed there, marveling at the dramatic beauty of the day.

That was how Bill Reynolds found them—sprawled in the snow, like two of Jack Frost's mugging victims, covered with fluffy white.

"Excuse me . . ."

Libby scrambled to her feet first, her cheeks pink with cold and embarrassment.

Bill smiled and glanced at Jenny, who still struggled in the snow. "Do you ladies need any help?"

Libby giggled. "No. We were admiring the sky and got a little carried away."

Bill's eyes danced. "So I see. Reese and I were driving by and saw you out here. I have a pair of mittens and a blanket your party left behind after the sleigh ride."

Libby took the items Bill offered. "Would you and your brother like to come in for something warm to drink? Jenny and I are going to thaw out."

"Can we take a rain check? We're short of time this morning."

"Please do." Libby felt a flicker of disappointment that they couldn't stay.

"Those are two good-looking men," Jenny observed when they were inside warming their hands over the radiator.

"You're married. You aren't supposed to be noticing."

"Just because I'm on a diet doesn't mean I can't read the menu," Jenny said slyly. "I have single friends who obviously need help in the romance department."

She ducked when Libby launched a wet mitten at her head and added, "And talking about good-looking men reminds me that I've got to go home and put out the welcome mat for my guys."

"Kiss them both for me, will you?" Libby asked.

"Twice each." Jenny picked up her wet outer clothing. "Are you working tomorrow?"

"Are you kidding? During Tia's January clearance sale? She said death—my own—was the only excuse for staying home. She's had the battle plans laid for weeks. Tia doesn't like doing inventory. Therefore, she'd be happy if we'd sell the store back to the bare walls. I've already got my running shoes out for tomorrow."

"I'll stop by after work and see how you're doing," Jenny said. "If either of you isn't too tired to talk to me, that is."

....

"I think your daughter would love the pink throw. It's so soft," Libby said to her customer as she draped another lap blanket over the arm of the display's easy chair. She was beginning to wonder if Jenny's words were prophetic. Perhaps she *would* be too tired to speak by the time Jenny arrived. She'd already sold a half dozen of these today plus a myriad of other gifts.

"Aren't you Libby Morrison?" The lady whose arms were full to overflowing with colorful lap robes and candles peered over her cache at Libby.

"Yes . . ."

"My youngest daughter went to school with you. Do you remember Nancy Marin?"

"Of course I do! We ran in track together. How is she?"

"Just fine. Married with three little kids. She says that experience in track paid off because she has to go full speed all day now." Mrs. Marin studied Libby. "Our family followed your running career quite closely. You were a talented athlete. Didn't you receive a college scholarship in track?"

Libby flushed. It all seemed so long ago. "Yes, I did. I ran two years. Now I barely get around the lake for exercise."

"My daughter always admired you," the woman confided as Libby began to ring up her purchases. "You influenced her a great deal."

"I did?" Libby was surprised. Nancy had been a sweet girl, but they hadn't socialized much outside of bus trips and track meets.

"She became a Christian because of your influence, you know. She said you always behaved so generously and so kindly that she wanted to model herself after you. You probably don't remember, but once she mustered up the courage to ask you how you could remain so cool and collected when the coach was throwing towels and yelling."

"That happened often enough," Libby admitted. "What did I say?"

"That your peace and self-respect didn't come from outside yourself but from having Christ in your life. It made such an impression on her that she wanted to 'get some of that for herself.' You had a wonderful influence on our family, Libby. I'm glad I've gotten this opportunity to thank you."

Libby covered her mouth with her hand, and tears sprang to her eyes. "It wasn't my doing, you know."

"True. But you were the vessel."

That conversation lifted and carried Libby through the rest of the day. But by five o'clock even that couldn't push back her exhaustion.

"Tia, if I don't get to sit down soon, my feet are going to fall off."

"One more accessory to sell," Tia muttered. "Something for the person who has everything—human feet, ready to be shod—pumps, loafers, moccasins—whatever the room dictates. Set them by your bed, on your bathroom scale, stir up your conversation with feet sold by the foot. . . ."

"She's turned into a marketing maniac," Libby hissed as Jenny came upon the pair.

"Just maniac, I'd say. Do you sell something in a nice canvas straightjacket, size small?" Jenny looked relaxed and happy in a cherry red tunic and white turtleneck sweater.

"Looks like having your men back home has improved your disposition," Libby observed while Tia meandered off muttering something about overstocks in the resin Christmas ornament department.

"Look what Luke brought me." Jenny held out a pendant on a chain from her neck for Libby to see. "And see what's inside." She popped it open to reveal a photograph of her and Mike on one side and Luke and Spot on the other.

"Have you mentioned it to Luke yet that he and Spot are not actually brothers separated at birth?"

Jenny chuckled. "No, but it passed through my mind. Luke hardly looked at me until Spot had had the chance to slobber kisses all over his face."

"We know this child's priorities," Libby observed. She gave a gusty sigh of relief and sat down.

"Can you do that?" Jenny asked. "Aren't you afraid Tia will start selling off your parts?"

"Let her try. I'm whipped," Libby groaned. "Oh, how I dread the thought of going home to make supper!"

"Actually, that's why I stopped by. I have an entire pan of lasagna left over from a noon luncheon I catered. If you can stand the commotion, I'll bring my guys and the food to your house tonight."

"Are you talking food? Sustenance? Manna from heaven?"

"Lasagna. Libby's place. Seven o'clock. Be there or be square," Jenny ordered as Tia passed them carrying a box of Santa ornaments.

"Square? Did you say square? Libby, did we put those children's blocks on clearance? I have to make sure. See you at supper time, Jenny!"

"Who was that masked woman?" Libby said with a laugh.

"Maybe we'll find out if she shows up for dinner tonight."

....

"Mama, did you see that Spot wants to shake your hand? Mama?" Libby kneeled on the floor next to her mother's chair with Spot beside her. Spot sweetly laid a paw on Mrs. Morrison's lap next to a flaccid hand. His mouth was open and his tongue hanging out in his gleeful jester's grin.

The lasagna was long gone and the dishes done. Luke, Mike, and Mr. Morrison were lined up in front of the television watching the sports channel. Tia and Jenny sat in tense silence as Libby tried to rouse a response from her mother.

"Maybe she's just not feeling up to this tonight," Jenny suggested gently.

"She's never 'up to' things. We just have to work to find things that interest her, don't we, Mom?"

Mrs. Morrison continued to stare straight ahead.

A commotion erupted across the room as someone scored a basket on the television. Luke and Mike whooped like banshees. Mr. Morrison remained silent.

"Isn't your dad a Bulls fan?" Tia asked.

"Used to be. Now he sits in front of the television all day long and never seems to know who's playing."

"Mind candy," Tia muttered. "Airwave Prozac. Television, the great anesthetic. Makes people think they're doing something when all they're watching is predigested junk."

"Then what do you suggest I do with them?" Libby asked testily.

Jenny went to the bookcase and pulled out an oversized volume. "Let's look at old photos. Here you are, Libby, wearing nothing but a diaper and a pair of toy six-shooters."

"My cowgirl phase." Libby arranged chairs around her mother to include her in the activity. "I was quite attractive back then, if I do say so myself."

"If you call rolls of baby fat attractive." Tia leaned over the album. "Now here's someone who's obviously going to be stunning when she grows up. What a cute child!"

"That's you, Tia," Jenny said. "And you are wearing a mixing bowl on your head."

"Stylishly tipped to one side for a rakish appearance," Tia defended.

"At least it distracts from that ugly dress you're wearing," Libby said.

"Hey! Watch it! My mom made that dress." Tia studied the photo. "It is pretty bad, isn't it?"

Their laughter and running commentary eventually enticed the men to join them, and the group moved to the dining-room table, where the pictures could be laid out for all to see. As each picture was passed around, Libby made sure her silent mother saw it before handing it off to Mike, who sat next to her.

"Mr. Morrison," Tia asked, "are you all right?"

Libby looked up to see her father rubbing his temples.

"Just a little headache, that's all."

"Would you like an aspirin?"

"No, no. I hope I'm still a tougher man than that." He smiled. "Don't worry about me. I'm fine."

"Here's an album of photos taken when you were young, Daddy." Libby opened a leather-bound volume of pictures held in place with black paper photo corners.

"Cool car!" Luke gushed as he looked at the Packard in the photo. "Do you still have it?"

Mr. Morrison, finally showing genuine animation, chuckled. "That car would be nearly sixty years old by now."

"Wow!" Luke's eyes grew round. "That's really old."

"You don't have to be rude," Mike chastised his son.

"I'm not rude, Dad. Mr. Morrison is just plain old!"

When the laughter subsided, Tia opened the album to another page. There were photos of Mrs. Morrison as an infant and small child. On another page were the Morrisons' wedding pictures.

Libby stared at the pages while the others discussed changes in fashion and hairstyles.

"Lib? Are you OK? You're so quiet."

"I have so many questions. Where's Mom's wedding dress now? What did she like to do as a little girl? Did she have boyfriends other than Daddy? Why didn't I ask her when I had the chance?"

Tia snorted in a most unladylike fashion. "Have you tried?"

Libby looked at her mother, then at her friend. "Tia!"

"Well, have you?"

With a disgusted sigh, Libby took a wedding picture from the album and laid it in front of her mother. "Mama, do you remember this?" She struggled to keep the annoyance out of her tone. Couldn't they see . . .

Then Mrs. Morrison said in a clear, strong voice, "Of course I do."

"Mother?" Libby gasped.

"I made my own wedding dress," Mrs. Morrison continued, oblivious to the excitement she was causing. "I bought the sateen at Wilkins Department Store. Oh my, that was pretty fabric." Her voice grew soft and wistful. "I wish I'd saved the dress, but my cousin asked to borrow it for her wedding and she never gave it back."

"Is that what happened to the dress?" Libby's father fell eagerly into conversation with his too-often-silent wife.

"Hilda let her children wear it for a plaything," Mrs. Morrison said. "Such a shame." She skewered Libby with clear, bright eyes. "Don't lend things out to just anyone, dear. Be sure they're people who'll take care of possessions."

"What is going on?" Tia hissed to Jenny. "I thought she was . . . you know."

Jenny pulled Tia into the kitchen. "The doctor said Libby's mother might have some lucid moments. Apparently the photos triggered something in her memory that flipped a switch."

"You mean it might flip off again? Just like that?"

Jenny cocked her head to one side. "Are they singing in there?"

Indeed they were.

When Jenny and Tia reentered, the group was no longer at the dining-room table. They had congregated around the spinet piano in the living room, where Libby was plucking out familiar tunes and her parents, Mike, and Luke were warbling out the words. Spot punctuated the music with an occasional "woof."

"Shades of Lawrence Welk!" Tia breathed. "They're pretty good!"

Mr. and Mrs. Morrison, their old voices surprisingly clear and sweet, slid smoothly from one song to another as Libby played.

"Love and marriage, love and marriage, go together like a horse and carriage. . . .
"On the old rugged cross where the dearest and best . . .
"The old gray mare, she ain't what she used to be, ain't what she used to be . . ."

The songs seemed to foreshadow what was inevitably to come. For the moment, however, Libby's mother was more like her old self than any of them had seen her for some time.

Luke, losing interest in old-fashioned songs to which he didn't know the words, began to play with the toy airplane he carried in the pocket of his jeans. His guttural "varoom" sounds and dive-bombing movements caught Mrs. Morrison's attention.

"I rode in one of those, you know."

The plane paused midair. "You did?" Luke's eyes were wide and curious. "When?"

"When I was just a girl. With Martin McGregor. 'Last of the barnstormers,' that's what he called himself."

"What's a *barnstormer*?" Luke asked, his full attention on the old woman.

"Mother . . . ," Libby began.

"Hush, Libby. The boy asked a question." Mrs. Morrison's firm voice stopped Libby in her tracks. "A barnstormer is a pilot who does acrobatic tricks with his airplane. They got their names by flying right through open barn doors, in one side of the barn and out the other. I wish I'd flown with Martin when he did that. . . ."

"Now that's a little far-fetched . . . ," Libby began.

But her father shook his head. "She's telling the truth. I've heard about it many times. Your mother was quite a daredevil in her day."

"You mean she's not just wandering?"

Mr. Morrison looked at his wife with palpable love in his expression. "No. She rode horseback standing up like they do in the circus and kept up with her older brother and his friends no matter what kind of mischief they got into. Oh, what a lovely, exciting girl I married!"

With her now rapt audience, Mrs. Morrison left the topic of barnstorming and began to reminisce about her childhood and her mama.

"She was such a good mother to me, so kind, so warm, so lovely." She sighed. "I loved it when Mama took down her hair at night and let it ripple across her back like black, silky water. I'd run my fingers through her hair and ask if I could brush it. She'd let me if I promised not to pull it. She'd read her Bible while I brushed."

Tears rested on Mrs. Morrison's cheeks as she stared at a point somewhere beyond Luke's head. "Mama? Mama? Is that you? Can I brush your hair tonight?"

Luke turned to Libby, confusion written all over his young features. "I thought her mama was dead."

"She is, Luke."

"Sing for me, Mama. You know how much I like it when you sing. . . ."

"Now what's she talking about?" Luke looked frightened.

"Hymns. I like hymns."

"Luke, she's just gotten tired and mixed up. . . ."

"Is she OK?"

"On a hill far away, stood an old rugged cross. . . ."

"Hey, buddy, let's take Spot for a walk before he has an accident on Libby's carpet."

Libby looked gratefully to Mike for diverting the boy. When they had left the room, she turned to her friends. "Help me get her to bed, will you?"

"We're sorry, Libby."

"It comes and goes. Every time she remembers, I hope . . ."

"I have to go to the bathroom," Mrs. Morrison shrilled, pure child now, all the adult woman gone again.

Libby reached for her, and the old woman cried out. "Who are you? Why are you touching me?"

"I'll help you, Mom. Let me take you to the bathroom. . . ."

"Mama! I want Mama to take me!"

As quickly and unexpectedly as the clarity had come, it was gone. It left in its wake a rambling, fearful woman-child.

As they walked her mother to the bathroom, Libby felt the joy, hope, and vigor drain out of her. She'd allowed herself to be vulnerable, to hope even now, after all the days and nights of hope-dampening confusion, exhaustion, and chaos.

Just as Mrs. Morrison's clarity had disappeared like the click of a switch, so had the animation and the life in Libby's face. "Good night, Mother," she murmured wearily, after her mother returned from the bathroom.

"Read to me?" a small voice from the bed asked querulously.

"Let me do that." Jenny offered.

Libby pointed to a small devotional book on the bedside stand. "I read the day's devotion and the Bible verse."

Jenny nodded and sat down on the bed as Libby withdrew to the far corner of the room. Jenny began to read.

"'For I know the plans I have for you,' says the Lord. 'They are plans for good and not for disaster, to give you a future and a hope.'"

A future and a hope? Libby had always believed God had something planned for her. Was this it? A mother who didn't recognize her and a father dying by inches from terminal sadness? Libby had abandoned her own interests one by one until she could barely remember having had any at all. The life she'd loved had morphed into something harsh and difficult.

Lord, what is your will? Am I trying too hard to keep my parents at home? Am I actually fighting your will in my quest to follow it to the letter? Show me, Lord!

As she watched her mother's eyelids grow heavy and heard her breathing deepen in sleep, Libby felt an unaccountable lightness growing within her. It wasn't until she was preparing herself for bed and found herself humming that she realized God had given her the elusive peace for which she'd been yearning.

"How is she?" Mr. Morrison asked when his daughter descended the stairs. Their company had left and the house was quiet.

"The same." Libby folded into the sofa. "How do you do it, Daddy? How do you watch Mom disappear before your eyes?"

"I don't do it very well—not every day. And my good days, well, I have God to thank for them." He rubbed his chin, just as he had every time Libby had ever asked him a question that he felt required serious deliberation. "I remind myself how blessed I am. I have a wife who has been loyal and loving for nearly half a century. I have a bright, beautiful, generous daughter. I have my home and a million good memories. Really, how could a man have it any better? I give thanks to God for that every night. And when I do, the days seem easier."

"Dad, you are a saint!"

"I was born a sinner. But do you know what the good news is? God loves sinners. He just can't get enough of them!"

....

Libby hadn't had time to dwell on the prior evening before the rest of her life took an unexpected twist.

It started with a telephone call from Reese.

"Libby?" He sounded tentative, embarrassed.

"Yes. How are you?" She felt as though her cheeks were on fire, something that hadn't occurred since ninth grade when her first crush had mustered up the nerve to ask her to help him with his homework.

"Are you going to be home today?"

Silly question. Where would I go? "Yes, I am. Why?"

He cleared his throat as if words had become stuck there. "I can't even figure out why I'm calling, but I have to be in your neighborhood. Bill and Annie's son is playing basketball over there, and I promised I'd catch part of his game. I thought maybe—"

"Come for coffee," Libby interjected, hoping to calm his unease. "Please?"

"I didn't mean to intrude—"

"You won't."

"Game starts at two o'clock."

"Then I'll see you at one."

Reese arrived promptly. From the window, Libby watched him maneuver his wheelchair out of the specially equipped van and lock it with his remote. His arms were amazingly muscular, she noted as he wheeled himself up the sidewalk, as was the rest of his upper body. His legs were surprisingly strong-looking too, thanks, no doubt, to regular physical therapy. He was a spectacular specimen of a man. Except, of course, for the grim look on his face.

She opened the door and he rolled inside. She was grateful for the small ramp they'd installed to make it easier for her mother to navigate. In the foyer he paused, looking to her for direction.

"Ahhh . . . living room?" Libby asked, sounding as if she didn't know the answer. Her composure had abdicated, and she felt utterly exposed and ill at ease.

His lip twisted in a half grin. "Sure."

Now that she had him in her living room, Libby had no idea what to do with him. Her parents were at the Senior Center so she couldn't even make cursory introductions. She was on her own with a man for the first time since . . . she couldn't remember when.

"Coffee?"

He glanced around the room. "Are your parents here?"

"No. The center called this morning and offered to pick them up for a special-events day. Mother seemed eager to go."

"So you're alone?"

"Yes . . ." Libby felt like a schoolgirl and hated herself for it. She'd never cultivated "cool" and had never regretted it until now.

"Then you could go to the game with me."

Libby's shoulders sagged with relief. *Sports.* That she could handle.

"Shoot! Shoot! Watch out! Ohhhh . . . off the rim." Libby dropped back onto the edge of the bleacher. "He should have had that one. Bummer."

Reese chuckled. "You're quite a sports fan, I see." They'd seen his nephew play and watched well into the following game.

"A remnant from my past." Libby's cheeks turned pink.

"Mine, too," he said softly. It occurred to Libby that it must be painful for Reese to watch all these healthy, mobile children and to be reminded of what he'd lost.

But Reese rallied to add, "How about that coffee now? I saw a Starbucks just a block from here."

Amazingly, Libby realized, as she carried their orders from the pickup counter, she'd hardly thought about the fact that Reese was in a wheelchair. His personality was so strong and dynamic that the chair seemed incidental to the rest of him. Unless, of course, he brought the subject up himself. Then a darkness overtook him that was startling in contrast to the rest of his demeanor.

"Quite a pair, aren't we?" Reese said as she returned with two double mochas and a biscotti to share. "The cripple and the caretaker."

Libby sat down across from him and stared at him until he lowered his eyes. "You aren't a cripple in my book, Reese."

"Then you're the only one. People see this chair long before they see me."

"How long have you . . . been there?"

"Does it matter?"

"It does to you. To your family. And to your friends."

He looked at her strangely, as if trying to decipher her intent.

What *did* she mean? Libby wondered. That she wanted to be included in that list?

"Two years this fall."

Before she could censor herself, she asked, "How did it happen? Illness? Car accident?"

"Gunshot."

The answer stopped Libby cold. "G-g-gunshot?"

"You've got it." He seemed to enjoy her discomfort, as if it served her right for being a supersnoop.

But Libby wasn't to be deterred. His gruff tough-guy act covered some real and terrible hurt. "I don't mean to pry, but . . ."

"But you're going to anyway." He sounded resigned, as if people poking and probing him, both emotionally and physically, were things he'd learned to bear.

Something bleak in his expression made her forge ahead. "Yes. Unless you tell me otherwise."

He gave a humorless laugh. "As if that would help."

Reese raked his fingers through his hair and stared at a point somewhere over Libby's left shoulder. He looked as if he'd slipped over a line into darkness. "I was a cop. It was a routine call—if domestic calls can ever be considered routine. Neighbors didn't like the yelling—even though they'd put up with it for months. When we arrived at the address, a little woman in a torn nightgown came running out of the house. Her nose was bloodied and she was screaming like demons were after her.

"Maybe they were." His eyes clouded. "One, at least. Her husband ran out after her with a gun. I took the bullet he'd meant for her."

His voice grew so soft that Libby had to strain to hear him. "I was barely out of the squad car. I'd turned sideways to talk to my partner when I heard the shot and felt this fire explode in the lower half of my body. Next thing I knew, Bill and Annie were hanging over the rails on my hospital bed bawling like babies. And it's been that way ever since."

"What way?"

"Baby in the house. I turned into *their* baby. In a second, I became as helpless as an infant." He gave another strangled laugh. "I went from being the macho big brother-cop-cowboy to poor, crippled Reese."

"You don't look so poor to me," Libby said boldly, wondering at her moxie. "You drive."

"Sure. A specially equipped van. My sports-car days are over."

"At least you *had* a 'sports-car day.' I'm still driving the car my father picked out—a big 'safe' car so far removed from sports cars as to be almost unrelated."

She saw him suppress a small smile. So he wasn't angry about her questions after all. Encouraged, she continued. "You seem to get around. Sleigh rides, basketball games . . ."

"Bill and Annie's ideas. Three years ago if someone had told me my big outings would be a ride in the back of a wagon or a junior high basketball game . . ."

"I take offense at that!" Libby retorted. "They're *my* big outings, too, you know!"

The mantle of bleakness settled more deeply over him. "I'm a joke now. Half a man. Relegated to a chair."

"You aren't half a man!" Libby was surprised by the vehemence in her words. "Not at all!"

Reese looked at her with derision. "No? If I'm not half a man, then why is it that the only way I can go back to the force is behind a desk pushing paper and answering phones? And why is it that I can't swing myself onto my own horses and ride? And, while you're at it, why don't you tell me why the women I used to date won't have anything to do with me now that I can't take them dancing or drive them around in one of my sports cars or carry them across a threshold? I'm half a man, all right, Libby. And more than once I've wished the other half of me had taken the bullet. Then I'd be dead right now."

"Oh, Reese . . ."

"We'd better go."

She stood up, feeling helpless. Words were useless. She put her hands on the back of his chair to roll it to the door.

"I can do it myself." Reese's words were sharp as shards of shattered glass. He nearly ran over Libby's toes leaving the room.

Libby watched Reese catapult himself across the parking lot—wide, muscular shoulders churning as he pumped the wheels, stiff-necked with anger and humiliation—and was reminded of her parents. There *were* things worse than growing old after a good life. As her father had said, he and Mother had had many fine, healthy years together.

It was another reminder, Libby thought, that she'd given God far too little praise for the blessings in her life and dwelt too much on the negative. She and God would have a talk about that tonight. Squaring her shoulders, she mustered up the courage to catch up with her unhappy companion.

Reese pulled up to Libby's front door and slammed on the brakes. He tapped his finger against the steering wheel and waited for her to get out.

Libby crossed her arms over her chest and settled deeper in the seat.

"Well? Aren't you getting out?"

"I don't think so. Not yet."

"Wha—"

"I'm not leaving until I believe you understand that the wheelchair doesn't matter to me—or a lot of other people. That's not the measure of a man."

"Yeah, right." He scowled so darkly that Libby longed to rub the deep creases out of his forehead and soothe away the pain.

"Surely you can't believe that you're judged only on your handicap!"

He glared at her. "No? It's certainly the *first* thing anyone sees about me."

"Anyone who stops with that isn't worth knowing."

"Listen, Libby, I know what you're doing and thanks. Now will you get out?"

"Don't go away mad, just go away?"

His lips tipped upward in a brief smile. "Something like that."

"Are you still angry?"

"It's hard to stay that way with you." His expression softened. "I know you don't have it easy right now either. Friends?"

Libby smiled brightly. "Friends." She slid out of the van and watched him drive away. As he turned the corner, she saw his hand come up in a wave. Hugging herself, she moved toward the house, feeling as though she were harboring a pleasant little secret. And a secret it would remain.

Libby didn't intend for her tentative friendship with this skittish man to be marred by her friends' inevitable speculation about a potential romantic relationship. They were two hurting people, nothing more. If they could possibly offer each other understanding and a sympathetic ear, it would be enough.

Mr. Sorenson was at the house when Libby arrived. He met her at the door.

"How nice of you to come to visit," she greeted him.

"Actually, your father called me. He had a little blackout and thought he might need some help."

Libby stepped forward, but the old man stopped her. He gestured toward the living room, where the Morrisons were watching the news. "He's fine now. He attributed it to stress."

"We know he's had enough of that lately," Libby muttered. "Thank you for coming. I'll mention it to his doctor."

One more thing to worry about, Libby mused. Fortunately, Jenny's sister-in-law from her first marriage knocked on the door.

"I've come to visit. Go out for an hour. Have some fun," Dorothy ordered as she bustled into the house swathed in the aroma of freshly baked cookies. "Scram. We're going to pig out on sweets while you are gone."

"I'm not sure how much fun I can manage in a hour," Libby said, "but I'm going to take you up on that offer."

Libby hadn't done anything impulsive in months, so she startled herself by turning into the drive of Fraiser Towers, an assisted-living and nursing-home facility less than a mile from her home. She parked in the visitor lot and stared at the brick-and-glass building. It looked more like an apartment building than the stereotyped image she'd constructed in her mind.

Almost of their own volition, her legs carried her to the front door.

"May I help you?" A kind-looking woman with a soft voice stepped out of an office.

"I . . . ah . . . no. I was just looking around." What was she thinking anyway?

"Certainly." The woman pointed toward the end of the hall. "That's our restaurant. It's filling up rather quickly tonight."

"Restaurant? Here?"

"Yes. We have two restaurants as well as a dining room. Residents who live in the apartments can eat in either restaurant or cook in their own kitchens. Most prefer to cook breakfast for themselves and eat out later in the day. Some choose to eat all their meals in one of the cafés. They can specify their preferences when they move in. Those who are in the portion of the building that provides nursing care eat in the dining room."

"It seems so . . . normal here," Libby managed.

"Well, I hope so! This is home to a lot of people. We try to make things more convenient for them with transportation, cleaning services, and the like, but we also want it to feel like a place where they want to live. Do you want to go upstairs to look at the rooms? They aren't apartments like the first levels, but the rooms are large and lovely. We have several couples living there. So nice they don't have to be separated when one of them becomes incapacitated . . ."

"Another time, maybe. Thanks so much." Libby beat a quick retreat to her car and sat staring at the hood of the automobile.

What did all this mean? Every barrier, every unpleasantness she'd imagined in her mind was in stark contrast with what she'd just seen.

I'm so mixed up, Father! I don't know what to do or what to think anymore. What's best for my parents . . . and for me?

She sat in the car with her eyes closed, listening with every fiber of her being. A single thought entered her mind. *Look to me.*

Slowly she began to relax. She didn't have to make a decision now, and she didn't have to do it alone. She'd fallen into an age-old trap by dwelling on the negative. When she did that, she had no eyes for God. Instead of looking down, she had to start looking up—to him. Only then could he move in and divert these attacks on her spirit and the bombardment of worries and fears. She had dwelled too long on her problems instead of on God, the solution. How many times did she have to stumble before she got it right? she wondered.

"Whatever you want," Libby murmured and felt at peace.

. . . .

The doorbell rang before breakfast the next morning. Libby glanced at her parents. They were both engrossed with their cereal.

When she opened the door, she was nearly knocked from her feet by a rocket of fur, feet, and dog drool.

"Hello, Spot. How nice of you to come by." She looked from the corner of her eye as she bent to pet the dog. "You, too, Jenny. Is there a special reason for this visit?"

"Dog therapy. Spot's making a house call." Jenny moved into the kitchen, poured two cups of coffee, kissed Mrs. Morrison on the top of the head, and signaled Libby to follow her into the living room. Spot she told to lie down at Mr. Morrison's feet beneath the table.

"Jenny, I'd love to pet-sit for you today but I just can't," Libby said as she followed her friend into the other room. "I've got my hands full as it is."

"Spot doesn't need pet-sitting. He's here to work. He's going to father-sit for you."

"And that means what?"

"Having a pet can lower blood pressure, lessen depression, and generally cheer a person. Spot and I discussed it. He's willing to do all this free of charge. He even brought his own dog food."

"And Luke agreed to this?"

"He suggested it, little sweetheart that he is. What do you think?"

"It's very kind of your family because I know how much you love Spot, but I just don't think it would help us. . . ." A chuckle from the kitchen interrupted her speech.

Laughter was an unfamiliar commodity around this household. Libby bolted out of her chair.

In the kitchen, both Mr. and Mrs. Morrison had pulled their chairs away from the table to watch the canine performance on the floor. Spot was doing rollovers. With his last, he lay sprawled at their feet on his back, legs falling open, long pink tongue lolling out of his mouth, eyes warm and begging for approval. Mrs. Morrison clapped as her husband tossed the dog a corner of toast.

Encouraged, Spot scrambled for footing on the tile, stood up, and laid his head on the woman's lap, soulful eyes gazing with affection into the woman's own.

As Mrs. Morrison petted the dog's shiny head, Mr. Morrison said, "Libby, maybe we should get a dog."

Jenny cleared her throat and looked smug. "Point made."

. . . .

By the next morning, Libby was in full agreement. She'd accomplished more in the past twenty-four hours than she had in some entire weeks. Her parents, enchanted with the dog's unflagging attention, had demanded less of her and seemed happier. They'd even eaten better—unless, Libby speculated, more food had been intentionally dropped for the four-footed scavenger beneath the table.

By the time Jenny and Mike arrived for an after-supper visit, a decision had been made.

"We're getting a dog!" Mr. Morrison announced. He'd moved from his usual chair to the couch so that Spot could stretch out and still have his head on the man's thigh. Mrs. Morrison, captivated by the dog's long scruffy toes, sat at the other end of the couch playing with Spot's feet. Spot, who thrived on human affection and attention, looked as though he'd dropped directly onto Planet Bliss.

"That was fast," Jenny commented as she, Mike, and Libby sat around the kitchen table. "Even for Spot."

"He's kept them entertained for hours!" Libby marveled. "I had no idea how much my parents craved stimulation. Spot played court jester all day. What's more, he seemed to sense when my parents were tired. When they laid down for their naps, he dozed at the foot of the bed."

Mike's eyebrow rose. "The *foot* of the bed?"

"And by the time I went in to check on them, he was stretched out down the center of the bed between them." Libby rolled her eyes. "Who'd have thought I'd allow a dog in my parents' bed? But each had a hand on him as if fearing he might vanish when they closed their eyes."

Libby felt tears welling. "It was so sweet, and they both looked so much more relaxed. I never imagined . . ."

"I'm free at three tomorrow," Jenny announced.

"For what?"

"The Humane Society, of course. Where else would you get a dog? Spot's a stray. I think some of those little creatures realize that they haven't got much hope left—and as a result, work hard to be loved."

"I work tomorrow. . . ."

"Tia can come, too. She wouldn't miss an event so monumental as this. Besides, she'll want to put her two cents in about which dog you pick."

Mike shook his head. "The Three Stooges Visit the Humane Society. I'm not sure you should go alone. I have visions of you emptying out the place and me building kennels and fences until I collapse."

"Thanks, Mike!" Libby patted his hand. "I accept your kind offer to build a fence and kennel for us."

He blinked. "Did I say that?"

"You did now, darling." Jenny pecked him on the cheek. "And we'll leave Spot here until his replacement arrives, OK?"

"OK," Mike sighed. "I've been caught in the Bermuda Triangle of human beings—Jenny, Libby, and Tia. The strangest things happen when I'm with you guys."

"And we're never going to let you escape." Jenny kissed him again.

Mike looked fondly at his wife and her friend. "It's a good thing I'm already hooked."

By the time they reached the Humane Society, Libby thought she was going to burst with excitement. It was the first time in months she'd felt this way and it was wonderful.

The building was gray block with a brick facing. From the entry they could hear barks and yips. Libby squeezed her arms over her belly, nervous. What if she didn't pick the right animal? What if there was only one Spot and this didn't work once she got the puppy home? What if, what if, what if . . .

"We'd like to get a dog, please," Tia said to the girl at the counter. "Where do we look?"

"How old a dog?"

Tia looked at Libby, who shrugged. "Maybe we'd better look at them all."

The girl looked surprised but pleased and led them down a hall. The noise increased as they neared the door at the end. She flung it open onto a vast bank of cages, each filled with a dog so excited to see a human that it looked as if it might explode with glee.

"Oh my . . . ," Libby breathed.

"I'll let you look around and then come back and answer your questions. Each animal's history is on its cage—if it is a stray or the reason it's being given away. Once you narrow it down to the ones you like best, I or one of the staff can give you more insights into that animal's personality. We have dog walkers who come in every day. They'd be of help to you, too."

Libby stared around, dumbfounded. "But I want them all!"

"That can be arranged, too," the girl said with a smile. "I'll be back in a bit." And she disappeared.

"Oh my, oh my, oh my . . ." Every dog seemed to vie for Libby's attention—big ones, small ones, mutts, purebreds.

"How did there ever get to be so many dogs that people don't want?"

"Irresponsible humans, that's how," Tia said, visibly upset. "People not neutering or spaying their pets, allowing them to have puppies, careless owners who disobey leash laws . . ."

"How do I choose?"

A big black Lab threw himself at the door to his cage and howled mournfully.

"He's trying to get your attention."

Libby kneeled at the door of the cage. The dog cocked his ears at the interest of this strange human. His tail wagged so hard his entire body shook. "Oh my . . . ," Libby moaned.

By the time the young woman returned, they'd narrowed the field to four dogs. Tia and Jenny had had to set some guidelines to prevent Libby from adopting them all. Determining that Spot was the "ideal" dog had focused Libby on the mutts in the bunch, those dogs with less chance of being adopted than the purebreds. She'd chosen three dogs of various sizes, shapes, and colors, all with more personality than good looks—and the black Lab who'd greeted her so effusively at the outset.

The staff person returned in the middle of a debate about the ideal size and weight of Libby's new dog to confuse the issue even further by asking, "Now would you like to see the puppies?"

An expression of pure terror crossed Libby's features. "You mean there are more? How will I ever decide?"

"Are we going to need a stretcher to carry you out of here?" Tia wondered after forty minutes in the puppy room. Libby was sitting on the floor petting a German shepherd-rottweiler cross puppy who was licking her as fast and furiously as he could. She'd been able to tune out all the other dogs, but this lone pup had gone right to her heart.

"I can't leave him."

"Then take him. That's what you are here for, to get a dog."

"But what about Inky and Puddles?"

"Who are they?"

"The dogs in the other room. The black Lab and that pitiful little mud brown thing that looks like it was put together by a committee."

"Libby, can you love a dog that ugly?"

"Spot looked pretty mangy when you got him," Libby reminded Jenny.

"Enough said. But you still can't get three dogs."

"And I'm not sure you have the stamina to train a puppy right now," Tia added.

Libby's mind was in a whirl. She was totally, unabashedly in love and was not going to leave without this puppy . . . or Inky . . . or mud-fence-ugly Puddles. But how?

The proverbial lightbulb went on in Libby's mind. "I think I know someone who might take the puppy."

"Libby, you can't just pick out a dog and hand it to someone!" Tia was appalled. "Are you nuts?"

"Maybe. Hand me your cell phone." And she dialed information for the number of Bill and Annie Reynolds.

CHAPTER FIVE

Quilts were used to help slaves in their flight to freedom
through the Underground Railroad during the Civil War.
A log cabin quilt with a black center was hung in a window to indicate
that the house was a safe house. This pattern became popular after the
death of Abraham Lincoln, who was called the "log cabin president."

"OK. Now I know what if feels like to tip over into true insanity," Tia announced. "And *get your tongue out of my ear!*"

As she pushed Puddles's head and lolling tongue away from her, Inky put a gigantic paw in her lap. "Jenny, drive faster!"

Libby giggled and buried her nose in the puppy's soft fur. It had taken until closing time to adopt the dogs, secure their inoculations, and do all that was necessary to bring them home.

"When I suggested a dog," Jenny said doubtfully, "I really meant only one. Don't you think you've gone overboard, Lib?"

"No. You see how well these guys get along. I knew immediately that Inky was my dog, but one look at Puddles and I knew that no one else in the whole world would want him."

"Amen to that," Tia muttered.

"And Annie thinks that it's a great idea to give Reese a dog—especially one that's part police dog."

"You aren't supposed to give pets as gifts," Tia muttered.

"That's what my store is for. I have ceramic dogs in every breed. No housebreaking necessary. Besides, what if he doesn't like the puppy?"

"Annie and Bill will take him. She said they'd been planning to go to the Humane Society to look for a puppy that had some German shepherd bloodlines. Annie is sure that if I like the puppy he'll be fine. They want a big dog to be outside in the barn. He'll have a great home at their place, whether Reese wants him or not."

"You hardly know this guy!" Tia yelped. Inky yawned, drooled all over her leg, and fell into a doze.

"I know. But I do know misery—up close and personal. And he's one miserable guy. If a dog can help my parents, maybe it can help Reese."

"I've created a monster," Jenny moaned. She pulled into the Morrison driveway. Mrs. Morrison was standing in the window, waiting for them. Her face lit at the sight of the car.

"I haven't seen her so animated in ages," Libby breathed. "She remembered that I said I was going to get a dog!"

"I hope," Tia said under her breath, as she curled her fingers beneath Inky's collar so as not to allow him to escape as she opened the door, "that this isn't opening a Pandora's box we can't close. Uh!" Inky jerked her nearly out of the car and to the pavement in his eagerness to follow Puddles and Jenny, Libby and the pup.

....

At 5 A.M. Libby tucked the puppy back into his kennel after an early morning stroll and stealthily climbed the stairs to her parents' room. Inside, her parents slept as they had since the day of their marriage, her mother on the left, her father on the right. But now a change had occurred. An ugly brown dog, far too thin and the color of mud, was curled blissfully between them, his head resting beneath her mother's fingertips. A smile tipped the older woman's lips in her sleep.

Inky had chosen to sleep on the rug next to the bed, his head on a pillow one of Libby's parents had put there for him.

Libby closed her eyes and sent up a prayer of thanks to God for blessings from unexpected places. Her mother had eaten supper with zest and been eager to get to her room. Her father claimed he was feeling wonderful—no dizzy spells or headaches. There had been no question that the dogs would sleep with them, Spot had seen to that. But her parents were genuinely pleased to have the dogs—almost as pleased as the dogs were to be in such posh surroundings.

She sighed as she crawled into her own bed. Now if only Reese Reynolds would agree that the puppy was a blessing. He obviously hadn't seen much of anything as a blessing for two years, and it was unlikely that he would start now. Still, Libby felt a compelling drive to try. She'd seen and felt enough hurt and frustration to last for a long time. Now she was filled with an unaccountable desire to allay it in someone else.

Libby's altruistic ideas were eroding by the time she reached Bill and Annie's place the next morning.

The dogs had, to her mother's delight and Libby's dismay, by 8 A.M. chased each other around the breakfast table, spilled a bucket of water, chewed three shoes, and licked clean all the dishes Libby was loading into the dishwasher. While she was chasing the big dogs, the puppy had piddled every two feet all around the kitchen, chewed the straw off a broom, and fallen asleep in his food dish. While Libby was tying Inky outside and settling Puddles and her mother in the living room, the pup had left Libby a rather unpleasant "gift" on the welcome mat at the back door.

She was glad to get into the car with just one dog, a kennel, and some peace and quiet.

Oh, Lord, she prayed as she navigated the driveway to the Reynolds' home, *help Reese to accept this meddling of mine in the spirit it is being given. I don't know why you've shown the pain in his heart to me, Father. I haven't got a clue how to help him, and I'm terrified that my impulsive move with this puppy is only going to make him more angry. Still, Lord, I felt as though you were telling me it was the right thing to do. Please use this pitiful vessel—me—to do what you want done. And don't let me mess up. Amen.*

She counted to ten, took a deep breath, took the puppy out of his carrying case, and began making plans to have her head examined as soon as possible.

"You brought me a *what?*" Reese wheeled his chair over to her when she'd pulled up in front of the barn and stared into the car as if it were filled with explosives. He was wearing jeans, a white shirt yoked at the front, and disreputable cowboy boots left over from another life.

"I'm sorry to be so presumptuous but I saw him and he just had your name written all over him."

"What? Idiot? Fool? Knucklehead?"

Libby gave a small smile. "Actually, Knucklehead wouldn't be a bad name for him right now. He's a little undisciplined."

"Of course he is." Reese took the puppy as Libby handed it to him. "No training, no care." Reese held the dog up to his face and stared into the intelligent brown eyes.

"He's mostly German shepherd and some rottweiler. He looked like a police dog to me, and . . ."

"Libby," Reese said with more patience in his voice than she'd expected, "I'm not a policeman anymore. I never will be again. What would I do with a dog like this?"

"Love him? Let him love you. Be companions. Isn't that enough?"

Reese stared at the dog. His fat little belly was pink and protruding and his tongue darted in and out of his mouth in a desperate attempt to lick Reese's face.

"Oh, for crying out loud. Come here, Knuckles." He tucked the pup beneath his chin and submitted himself to a tongue bath of enthusiastic proportions.

"What are Bill and Annie going to say about this?"

"They think it's a fine idea. I called them from the Humane Society before I adopted him. They said you'd all been wanting a dog for a long time."

"And you took it upon yourself to deliver one."

Libby's eyes filled. "I couldn't leave him. If I'd been able, I would have taken every dog they had. As it was, I took three."

"Three?"

"I couldn't choose between this black Lab retriever and a dog so ugly his mother wouldn't have him. And this pup . . . Knuckles . . ."

Reese shook his head in disbelief. "You don't even know me!"

"Maybe I know you better than you think." By this time Libby was leaning against the fender. Reese and his chair were almost touching her knee.

"Ha!"

"I don't know specifically about your situation but I do know about loss, frustration, anger, resentment . . . everything that happens when your life changes and you have nothing to say about it."

"And you've decided that when in doubt, adopt a dog?"

"Something like that."

"Well, I'm not going to thank you yet, Libby Morrison. This may be one gift I'll want to return."

Libby nodded but didn't believe a word of it. Knuckles had curled himself in Reese's lap for a snooze, and the man was unconsciously stroking its head and neck with movements so gentle Libby was surprised his large hands could make them.

She'd seen dog magic work for Jenny, for her own parents, and for her. Reese was no less susceptible to unconditional puppy love than the rest of them.

....

"Libby? Is that you?"

"Annie?" Libby felt a thrill of surprise. She hadn't heard from any of the Reynolds family for a long time. She didn't know if that was good or bad but was hanging on to the philosophy that no news was good news and that the puppy had wormed his way into the family's heart. At least Reese hadn't brought the dog back to her.

"Yes. How are you? I'm sorry I haven't called, but it's been crazy around here. The first mares started foaling March 1, and we all take turns sleeping in the office at the barn and watching the television for mares who go into labor."

"You see that on *television?*"

Annie laughed. "Sort of. The guys have a video camera rigged so they can see the mares from the warmth and comfort of a cot in the office. That way we can stay warm and still be on hand if any of them need assistance.

"But I didn't call to complain about sleepless nights. I was wondering if you'd come to dinner here on Saturday. The puppy is huge—all paws and legs. I thought you might like to see him."

"That would be great! I was afraid you weren't speaking to me anymore," Libby admitted.

"We love the dog, Libby. All of us. He and Reese are practically inseparable. Thanks to the pup's clownishness, we even get to see Reese smile occasionally."

"Oh, good." Libby gave a sigh of relief.

"Then you'll come?"

"I wouldn't miss it."

"Saturday at seven?"

"I'll be there."

....

Even knowing that the dog had been a success, Libby was nervous as she parked in the Reynolds' driveway.

Her apprehension was banished, however, by the warm greeting she received.

Annie, wiping her hands on the backside of her jeans, beamed when Libby entered. "I'm so glad you came!" She embraced Libby and then set her back at arm's length to study her. "You look tired but otherwise wonderful. How have you been?"

"Going day by day," Libby said evasively. *Moment by moment, more like it.*

"Well, you can kick back and relax here. Bill's in the living room. I'll be in as soon as I get the buns in the oven."

"Fresh bread?" Libby asked. "Yum."

"Nothing but the best for our friend."

Bill, half-glasses perched on his nose, was in the recliner reading the *Tribune*. He jumped to his feet when Libby entered. "Welcome, stranger!"

Libby's heart practically melted in gratitude. It was then that she noticed a small white-haired woman knitting placidly in the chair across from Bill.

"Libby, I'd like you to meet Annie's mom, Hilda Jenkins. Hilda, our friend, Libby."

"Hello, my dear."

Libby had never seen such a contented-looking woman. "Hello."

"Hilda, Libby is the one who brought us the puppy."

"You certainly brightened up this household, my dear," Hilda said with a chuckle. "Or contributed to the chaos."

Libby liked the woman immediately. "Do you live here in Minneapolis?"

"Indeed. At Fraiser Towers. Have you heard of it?"

Libby was surprised. "You?"

"Yes. I've lived there almost five years, ever since my husband passed away." Hilda laid down her knitting and beamed a high-watt smile on Libby. "It's a dandy place for an old woman like me."

"It is?"

"Oh my, yes! I've made such good friends there." Her eyes twinkled. "I may not look like it, but I play a wicked game of bridge."

Just then Annie entered the room. "Time to eat. Bill, where is Reese?"

"In the barn. I'll call him."

They were all seated at the kitchen table gazing hungrily at the roast chicken and vegetables, mashed potatoes, and fresh buns when the door flew open and a brown-and-black streak bolted into Libby's lap. She nearly fell backward in her chair as the dog laved her face with his huge pink tongue.

"Down, boy," Reese's voice held a note of command, and reluctantly the dog scrambled off her lap to a rug near the door.

Reese rolled his chair up to the table across from Libby. A small smile tipped one corner of his lip. "Serves you right, you know, for burdening us with that beast."

"As if you mean that," Annie retorted. "He and the dog are inseparable. They even sleep together." She didn't give Reese time to reply. Instead she said, "Let's pray."

It was Bill who spoke. "Dear heavenly Father, thank you for this food and this friendship. We thank you for bringing Libby into our lives. We ask your blessing on everyone here. May Hilda continue in good health and happiness. May our foaling season continue successfully. May Libby find whatever it is she needs in her life and Reese, too. Help us to remember how much you've blessed us. Amen."

Libby had, out of the corner of her eye, noticed that Reese had neither bowed his head nor joined the others in their enthusiastic amens.

The night flew by. Hilda, her competitive streak in full form, taught them to play dominoes, which were, according to her, "all the rage at Fraiser Towers." It was the truth, Libby decided, after Hilda defeated them in three consecutive games.

After dessert—strawberry shortcake and strong, dark coffee—Hilda excused herself. "I go to bed early, you know," she said as she trotted toward the stairs. "I get up for low-impact aerobics at home so I need to get my rest."

Annie and Bill waited until she'd disappeared to break into pleased laughter.

"We can't keep her here more than a day or two at a time anymore," Annie complained. "Then she's lonesome for her friends and her routine."

"No mother-in-law problems for me," Bill added.

"She really does like it there?"

"Best thing she ever did. She was sitting alone at home all day, getting depressed. Now she acts like she's twenty. She has new friends, new hobbies, everything we'd want for her."

"Really." Libby pondered this information, the wheels turning in her mind. She'd never considered that someone might actually *enjoy* being in a facility like Fraiser Towers. The knowledge pricked at her.

Suddenly, Bill looked at his watch and announced, "My turn. Excuse me, will you?"

Annie waved her hand in dismissal before turning to Libby. "We're still foaling and taking turns in the barn." She snapped her fingers. "I'd better make him some coffee for later. Excuse me, will you?"

That left Libby and Reese alone in the room in uncomfortable silence. Grudgingly, Reese finally spoke. "OK, so you were right. I like the dog. Thank you."

Libby's mouth dropped open in surprise. "You . . . you're welcome."

"This is the first year since the accident that I've taken my turn in the barn. The dog seems to have a sixth sense about those mares. I sleep all night and he wakes me when I'm needed." Reese almost smiled. "I haven't told Bill and Annie my secret. They think I'm staying up all night like they are."

The desultory conversation continued until Annie returned. Then Libby made her thanks and left. All the way home her mind whirred with new information. By the time she reached the house she had realized that, miraculously, God had cleared a path for her just when she least expected it.

....

"I have news," Libby announced a week later when she walked into the break room at Tia's store and found Tia and Jenny having tea.

"Good. This has been a very boring day," Tia said. "I hate boring."

"My parents are moving into Fraiser Towers this weekend."

Tia stared at Libby. "Just like that?"

"Just like that." Libby sat down and smiled at her friends. "I've been pounding my head on the wrong door. When I finally got to the right one, it fell right open for me."

Jenny's blue eyes grew wide. "I think you'd better explain."

Libby began with the night at the Reynolds' home and Annie's mother, Hilda. She explained the overwhelming sense she'd had that God had offered her respite in the place she'd least expected. And she admitted that it had taken much to overcome her doubts. "But God provided—full measure and shaken down. When I finally approached my parents they were willing to give it a try! Mom would do whatever Daddy did, and he was very excited about the move. I didn't realize how lonesome and isolated they'd become. Dad's always been a people person. One of his joys was getting out and helping others. Mom's illness took that away from him.

"I didn't give them much hope, telling them that they'd probably have to go on a waiting list *if* I found out that the facility fit my requirements." Libby looked sheepish. "I made up a list of must-haves before I went to the administration at Fraiser Towers. God was more than faithful. Not only did the Towers fill my requirements, they'd just had an opening for a small efficiency. They said that Mother could get all the treatment and physical therapy she needed. They'll have their own place and yet have access to every service—transportation, the restaurants, social activities, housecleaning, laundry service— everything!"

Libby shook her head in amazement. "I never dreamed it could be so easy—for all of us. I guess I didn't trust God enough."

"And when you really stepped out of the way and let him work, shazam! Miracles began to happen!" Tia concluded.

"Yes," Libby admitted in wonder. "Miracles."

. . . .

"You look swamped. Or is *doughed* a better word?"

Jenny piped one more stream of white frosting into place on the wedding cake she was decorating and laid down the pastry bag. "Business has been increasing exponentially. If this keeps up, I may have to move to bigger quarters."

"What's the big occasion now?" Tia picked up an éclair from the bakery case and bit into it with satisfaction.

"High school graduations. Weddings. It's a good thing Dorothy and Ellen have agreed to work more hours, or I'd never get it all done. Not everyone can decorate a cake the way I like it."

"Jenny's Signature Cake Collection," Tia intoned. "Don't Get Married without One."

"Remind me to hire you as my marketing person," Jenny retorted.

"So where's your help today?" Tia asked. There was a drip of vanilla filling on her chin.

"Libby's coming in. I have several birthday cakes to finish, three anniversary sheet cakes, and a cake shaped like a bowling ball for McQuire's Lanes' bowling banquet."

"Good. I hope she comes before I have to leave. I haven't talked to her since she moved her parents into their new place."

Before Jenny could comment, the chime rang on the back door.

"What are you guys staring at?" Libby demanded suspiciously.

The way her friends were observing her made the little hairs on the back of her neck bristle. She wished they would quit x-raying her with their eyes every time they saw her, reading her for hidden cracks and little pockets of weakness.

"You look awful!" Tia blurted. "Like death warmed over!"

"Thank you so much. I needed to hear that." Libby hung her jacket on a peg, put on her apron, and went to the sink to scrub.

"You were up all night. That much is obvious."

"I kept waking up thinking I'd heard Mom. Then I'd realize that she wasn't there and would feel this wave of loneliness crash over me. Thankfully, I had Inky and Puddles to keep me company. Ironic, isn't it? When I thought I'd finally get some rest . . ."

"How are your parents?"

"Much better than I am, actually. They have a beautiful corner room. Daddy's got his chair and ottoman; Mother, her rocker. I hung their favorite pictures, set up lamps from their bedroom, and displayed familiar rugs and mementos. It's very cozy. Dad says the food is fine, and he's already found a chess partner. Mom spends much of her day in the activity room, and it seems to entertain her."

Libby's eyes brimmed with tears. "All this time I thought I was sacrificing myself for them when really I was protecting *myself*."

Things certainly hadn't worked out the way she'd predicted they might. God had made it all so simple that there had been no doubt in Libby's mind that her parents' move was his will. The unanswered question now was, *What about her?*

"I know it hurts right now, but you're just going through a bad patch of road these days," Jenny soothed. "It will get better."

"Bad roads? What's that saying? Minnesota has two seasons—winter and road construction? I'd say I've been in both."

"Do I hear a bit of humor creeping through the gloom?" Tia teased.

Libby tugged at the hair casually twisted into a knot at the back of her head. "I guess. It's just that things are working out just as I prayed they would and I'm still not happy! What's wrong with me?"

"You're human?"

"Disgustingly so," Libby sighed. If it wasn't one thing, it was another.

More to talk about with you, Father.

"Here come the reinforcements," Dorothy announced cheerfully as she and Ellen entered the bakery. "Have frosting, will decorate."

Libby was glad for the diversion. This was a fresh wound and a chance to understand for herself what had happened, and to heal.

"You've drawn the short straw today, Dorothy. I have a huge party to cater tonight, and you get to do miniature cheesecakes."

Dorothy nodded briskly. "I'm on my way."

"I'll finish the cakes," Ellen offered.

"Then Tia and Libby can help with the deviled eggs," Jenny concluded. "Put on your hair nets, girls, the boiled eggs are waiting."

"I feel like I'm being watched," Tia complained as she studied the trays of hard-boiled eggs Libby had been slicing into halves. "By dozens of big, ugly yellow eyeballs. Gross."

"Quit trying to get out of work and keep peeling," Libby ordered.

"They do look like eyeballs, you know," Tia persisted. "How can people eat these things?"

Jenny, who was popping the yokes from the eggs into a huge mixing bowl, said calmly, "You've always liked deviled eggs."

"That was then and this is now. I don't think I'll ever eat another one. Look at them, crying out to me!"

"What are your eggballs, I mean, eyeballs, saying?" Jenny asked with a chuckle.

" 'Don't let that woman make my innards into mush! Don't make me go to a boring party and sit on a tray all evening drying out! Don't dress me up with paprika and a sprig of parsley! That's so uncool.' "

"Talkative little things, aren't they?" Libby felt herself growing more relaxed as the friendly banter about spring fashions, stock options, fat-free recipes, and the latest talk show scandals hummed around her.

"If all this yolk came out of these eggs, then why won't it all go back in?" Tia wielded a pastry bag filled with a mixture of egg yolk, mayonnaise, and spices.

"Tia, you're making a mess," Jenny chastised. "Can't you put a swirl of filling in each egg without analyzing it?"

"Guess not." Tia lumbered back to her station. "How can you guys do this all day long? Cook, make little sugar roses and canapés? Aren't you bored?"

"Not with you around," Jenny retorted cheerfully. "But things are progressing quite nicely in spite of that. We're going to be done early."

"Are you implying that I'm not helpful?" Tia held her hand to her chest and threw back her head in the mock sorrow of a theatrical French chef. "You stab me through the heart! You wound me to the quick! You cause me to die a thousand deaths!"

"Speaking of suffering and trauma," Jenny said, "Tia, isn't your birthday coming up soon?"

Tia bounced to her feet. "I thought you'd never ask!" She grabbed Libby and gave her a hug. "Don't be so down, darling. Keep your mind busy—plan a party for me!"

Libby couldn't help smiling. "You are incorrigible! I thought you might have grown up by now."

As a child, Tia had played the part of a prima donna for weeks prior to her birthday, holding it over everyone's heads that if they weren't nice to her, they wouldn't be invited to her party. One year she banished so many people from her inner circle that, if her mother hadn't intervened, Tia would have been alone with her birthday cake.

"Tia, it's harder to plan a party for you than for anyone else I know," Jenny commented.

"Why is that?" Dorothy asked.

"Because she loves presents," Libby said. "And with the store, she can buy anything she really wants. So she tells us not to buy her anything, and we end up making gifts. Do you remember the year we decided to make homemade paper and do a collage for her bedroom?"

"Ewww!" Jenny burst out laughing. "We didn't know how much scrap paper and fiber we'd need so we made an entire spaghetti pot full. I was cleaning that stuff off my floor for a week."

"And Dad built us a box screen to press the water out of our paper. The whole family got involved."

"I adore that collage." Tia's eyes grew misty. "It's my favorite piece of art. Except, of course, for those ceramic pigs you painted for my bathroom . . . and the flowers you dried and arranged for my kitchen table . . ."

"I see what you mean about Tia's birthday being a problem," Ellen said. "What do you ladies plan to do for her this year?"

"Good question!" Tia said enthusiastically. "Have you started making plans yet? I can give you a hint or two if you're stuck for a gift. I saw this cool life-size wooden carving of an antelope in a catalog. If either of you knows how to work a chain saw . . ."

Jenny and Libby looked at each other and burst out laughing.

Age was a mysterious thing. Libby's mother had regressed into a second childhood. Tia was determined never to leave her first.

....

After Tia and the others had left for the day, Libby and Jenny sat down to put their feet up. "I guess we'd better start planning a party. Doesn't sound like we'll get out of it this year either."

"I can't think of a thing. Tia loves theme parties, but we've covered almost every theme a birthday can justify."

"It would serve her right to make her think she wasn't getting a party this year," Libby muttered. "That would really get her upset!"

"That's it! We'll have a surprise party!"

"But Tia already assumes we're having a party."

"So if we act like we aren't having one because of my business and your family problems and that we just don't have time, it will really get to her."

"Ohhh. Diabolical, Jenny. Very diabolical."

"Thank you. Sometimes I even amaze myself. But we still need a theme for the party we aren't having."

"It had better be good if we're going to make her think we ignored her birthday," Libby warned. "Something to make up for all the worry that will cause her."

"I'm trying to remember her birthday parties as a little girl. Were there any favorites?"

"Only the one that never happened."

"What?"

"Remember the girl down the street who got to have a real live pony at her party every year? Everyone got rides and a souvenir cowgirl hat to wear home?"

"Oh yes! Tia begged for a pony for her party every year and never got one."

Libby straightened, the proverbial lightbulb glimmering in her mind. "We could give her a party with pony rides! A Western theme! Boots, hats, toy six-shooters, whatever. We could fulfill Tia's childhood birthday dream now. It would be easy to decorate with red-and-white checked tablecloths, a few hay bales, some lariats . . ."

"And just where do you plan to get the pony?"

"That's the easy part. We'll ask Bill and Reese Reynolds. I'm sure they'd have a horse to rent."

Hopefully Reese will still speak to me after the way I've meddled in his life.

Jenny nodded thoughtfully. "Not bad, Libby, old girl. Not bad at all. A Western theme would be easy—chili, biscuits, corn bread . . ."

They spent a few more minutes hatching plans before Libby gathered her things and left.

. . . .

"Hi, Mom, Dad." Libby poked her head into their room. "How's it going?"

"You're just in time, Libby," Mr. Morrison said, jumping up with more agility than he'd shown in a long time. "I'm going to watch the game on the big screen television in the recreation area. You can keep your mother company."

"Nice to see you too, Dad," Libby said with a chuckle as he disappeared through the door. She slipped a new tape into the cassette player, picked up a book, and sat down beside her mother.

"Hello, Libby." A woman her own age stepped into the room. "Hello, Mrs. Morrison. Are you ready to cook?"

"Looks like I came at the wrong time," Libby observed as an aide followed to spirit her mother off to a cooking demonstration in the activity room.

"Your parents are wonderful. They've adapted so well and take advantage of every activity. I'm sure you must be pleased."

"Yes. Pleased." Libby moved to the window and looked out over the pond below. Here she was again, alone. This wasn't at all what she'd expected—no, dreaded—when she considered the idea of her parents moving out of the house. It was becoming more and more obvious that she'd worried about the wrong person all along. Her mother and father were thriving in their new environment.

"Now me, Lord," she murmured. "All of a sudden *I'm* my biggest problem. Their lives are full and mine is empty." A tear slipped silently down Libby's cheek as she walked toward the elevator.

....

"What took you so long to answer the doorbell?" Jenny inquired as she stepped through Libby's doorway.

"I had to untangle myself from the mess I've created." Libby picked a long white thread from the leg of her black jeans.

"Now what?"

"I'm quilting again. I needed something to keep my mind occupied."

"I didn't know you still did that." Jenny walked into the kitchen and helped herself to a cup of coffee.

"I walked into Patty's fabric shop and saw all the beautiful colors and textures. Next thing I knew, I walked out with enough fabric to cover every bed in the house. It was too beautiful *not* to buy! Patty told me I had a good start on a new *stash*."

"Huh?" Jenny looked alarmed.

"That's what quilters call their unused fabric. Quilters like to purchase fabric as much as they like to sew it."

Jenny took off her coat and joined Libby at the table. "What are you making?"

"A log cabin quilt." Libby held up a brightly colored square of narrow strips of fabric fashioned in the traditional log cabin style. "See the red square in the middle? It stands for the heart of the home. The strips sewn around it represent the logs of the cabin. Cozy, huh?"

"I thought you'd given this up because you didn't have time to sew."

Libby looked at her friend sadly. "Not anymore. What else do I do with my spare time now? You know how active my social life is. The only man who ever comes to the house has a pouch on his back and *U.S. Mail* printed on the side of his truck."

"Are you lonesome, Libby?"

Libby saw the genuine concern and compassion in her friend's expression and knew that if anyone understood loneliness, it was Jenny. But she didn't want pity from her friends. Nor did she want the kind of extra attention it would generate. If Tia got wind of it, she would be bombarded with date prospects—which was ironic considering Tia was always "too busy" to go on dates of her own.

"My plate is too full to be lonesome. Just bored sometimes, but I shouldn't even be that now. I want to finish this quilt in time for Tia's birthday."

"You're making it for Tia? What a great gift!"

"I have great friends." Libby laid a hand over Jenny's. "Don't worry about me. My next project is the upcoming surprise party. . . ."

Jenny groaned. "Speaking of which, is Tia driving you crazy?"

"With what? The fifty phone calls a day reminding me that she'll be a year older soon? Or the casually dropped hints about the types of gifts she really likes to give *or receive?* Or the discussions of her favorite flavors of cake and frosting?"

"You mean she hasn't recounted the events of the day she was born or what the doctor said when he saw a baby with such a full head of black hair?"

"She spared me that one, thank goodness."

"She's getting worried, Libby. She thinks we aren't having a party for her."

"I know." Libby grinned evilly. "I made it worse by telling her that my parents were going to a party at their place this Saturday night and that the coordinator had asked me to help with games and refreshments."

"Are you?"

"Of course not. But there *is* a party. That's why I'm free. Mom and Dad will be too busy to want visitors."

"No wonder she's in such a panic." Jenny frowned. "Are we being too mean?"

"You could invite her for supper at your house that night. Tell her again about the party at Fraiser Towers. Don't lie to her. Just make her think I've said yes to volunteering. At least she'll think she has *something* to do."

"Tia won't be happy unless she thinks you'll be there, too."

"Then she'll have to be unhappy—at least until she sees what we've planned."

Jenny squared her slim shoulders and gave a resigned sigh. "OK. I hope I'm woman enough to hold Tia off until Saturday. She's one person who doesn't want anyone messing with her birthdays."

....

"Shhhh." Libby held her finger to her lips as she walked around Mike and Jenny's backyard quieting the crowd. The group was comprised of Jenny, Mike, Luke, and Spot, several women who worked with Tia at her store and their husbands, Jenny's former sister-in-law, Dorothy Matthews, and their friend Ellen. In addition, Bill, Annie, and Reese Reynolds were present with two palomino quarter horses, which were brushed, combed, and polished within an inch of their lives.

The horses, Barbie and Buster, had been shampooed, conditioned, and dried to a high gloss. Their ears were trimmed; their hooves polished to a gleaming black; and pink, white, and blue ribbons and tiny silk roses were woven through their manes. Saddled and bridled, they were ready for their starring role in Tia's birthday bash. They shifted restlessly from side to side under their saddles and looked with boredom at the cluster of humans gathered in ridiculous-looking Western garb.

"Last time I saw a horse gussied up that much, it was ten inches high and being played with by a five-year-old girl," Mike commented. Smile lines deepened around his eyes. He'd been smiling a lot ever since he'd married Jenny and made a real family for his young son.

"And last time I wore heels this high was as a bridesmaid in your wedding," Libby thrust her cowboy-boot-shod foot out for all to see. "I said then that I'd never wear heels again."

"Jenny, you'd better go inside and watch for Tia from the window. You said she would be over as soon as her parents called to wish her happy birthday. We don't want her hearing noise and coming around the house to see what's going on."

Jenny nodded. Tia was always careful to be considerate of her parents, particularly so after the death of her older sister some years ago. A car accident had left Tia the only child in her family. Tia's parents, however, were much younger and more active than Libby's were.

When Jenny had disappeared into the house, Libby turned to study the crowd. She had to work hard to keep from smiling.

Luke was wearing his 4-H riding clothes. He, his father, and Bill and Annie Reynolds looked at home in the cowboy world. The other couples had patched together whatever they could find to fit the theme including some garish straw hats that had no doubt been state fair purchases. Everyone wore jeans, belts, and long-sleeved shirts except for Ellen and Dorothy, who looked like escapees from a square dance convention in their full-skirted, minichecked, matching gingham dresses with petti-coats and ruffled sleeves.

"Those outfits won't get you out of riding the horses," Libby pointed out.

Dorothy's face dropped. "No? I'm not good with animals. If this were happening for anyone but Tia . . ."

"It will be fine. Bill assures me that these are his most well-broken horses. Anyone can ride them. . . ." Libby's voice drifted away. What Bill had actually said was, "These are Reese's horses. He used to spend hours with them, and he had a knack for train-ing. I trust them more with novices than any others we own."

Used to spend. Past tense. No longer spends time with the horses. Libby had wanted to ask more. But the pain in Bill's eyes had prevented her. This was a part of Reese's life that she hadn't dared broach.

Libby glanced toward the gazebo where Reese sat alone in the yard. Though she was sure he had Western garb that would have outshone any here, he was dressed in a pale blue shirt and deck shoes. Very preppy and rebellious, considering the party's theme.

Reese's anger and rebellion were always more apparent when horses were involved. Libby was surprised that he had actually come. She supposed it was because of the two lovely animals currently making rather nasty messes on Mike's perfectly groomed lawn. She grimaced. Tia had better be pleased about this party, or she was sure Mike would have her over here tomorrow to clean up.

"She's here!" Luke and Spot came dashing back from the post they'd taken at the side of the house. "And she looks sad!"

Everyone quieted. Soon Jenny's voice came through the screen door. "I thought we'd eat outside since it's so nice tonight."

"Are you *sure* Libby couldn't come? I thought that *tonight* of all nights . . ." Tia's tone was querulous and disappointed.

"Libby?" Jenny said lightly. "Why, Libby said to tell you . . ."

"Happy birthday!" they all chimed together.

Tia's jaw flopped open as she took in the banners and streamers strung through the trees and the hay bales, red-checkered tablecloths, lassos, and cowboy hats. Jenny nearly had to pick Tia's jaw off the grass when she saw the horses.

"Tia, are you *crying?*" Luke was the first to notice the tears in her eyes.

"You knew!" she blubbered, mascara running down her cheeks. "I always envied that little girl so much!"

Jenny and Libby moved to embrace her. "Best Friends Forever, that's us. We can't make all your dreams come true, but there are a few we can get a handle on," Jenny said.

Tia whipped a tissue out of her bag and wiped away the mascaraed tears. "I love it!" Then she looked down at her silk tunic and leggings. "And now I know why you told me to wear jeans. I thought you were just trying to let me know I shouldn't expect too much for my birthday."

"It's OK. We knew you wouldn't listen. I have a pair of my jeans and a shirt laid out on my bed. You can change before you ride."

"Then let the party begin!" Tia crowed, already recovered from her near miss with birthday disappointment.

When the food was gone, the coals dimmed to embers just right for roasting marshmallows, and Tia was taking her fourth ride on Barbie, Libby sank onto the grass next to Reese Reynold's wheelchair. Though Annie and Bill had barely had time to choke down a burger between socializing and supervising rides, Reese had kept even the friendliest away with his scowls.

Libby was annoyed by his attitude. Even though *he* wasn't Tia's friend, he could have at least been superficially cheerful for her party. He'd even turned away the virtually irresistible team of Luke and Spot when they'd attempted to engage him in a game of catch. What was with him tonight?

When Reese glared at her, Libby gave him her most endearing smile. "Need a thorn taken out of your paw?" she asked sweetly.

It amused her to see his face register shock.

"Whadayamean?" he growled.

"You look very stern. You must have a thorn pricking you somewhere. In the seat of your chair? In a shoe? Or is it poking you in the attitude?"

"You are pretty come-uppity for someone who is renting my horses," he pointed out gruffly, but Libby thought she saw a gleam of appreciation in his eyes at her bravery for approaching the disgruntled lion.

"They are so lovely," Libby said. "Thank you for sharing them with us."

"It's not exactly sharing when you charge by the hour."

"I believe it is. You could have kept them home and had Bill bring others. He said that you usually don't allow anyone to use Buster and Barbie."

"Maybe I should start. It's not like I ride them."

She studied him covertly from beneath her lashes. His hair was a dark blond with platinum highlights, chopped off carelessly and combed with rough fingers. Amazingly, the rugged cut suited him and perfectly framed the high cheekbones and the gray-green eyes fringed with thick dark lashes. Fine lines radiated from his eyes, hinting at the former man—one who spent his time smiling and his hours in the sun. His lips were stretched tight over even white teeth as if he'd had too little practice smiling of late. If he ever *did* smile, the effect would be devastating. Wheelchair or not, there was nothing prissy or weak about Reese Reynolds.

"Hi, Libby." Luke, Spot, and Inky materialized from behind a cluster of shrubs. Luke wore the expression of a child who'd eaten too many sweets. Even Spot and Inky looked as though they'd overdosed on junk food.

"How are my favorite guys?" Libby patted the ground, and

Luke sat down beside her. Spot wormed his way into the crevice between them. Inky, who'd immediately deferred to Spot as alpha-dog, settled at Libby's feet. Puddles was nowhere in sight.

"Pretty good." Luke looked at Reese. "Nice horses, mister."

Reese nodded a curt thanks.

"I've got a palomino too, you know. Sunshine. My 4-H horse."

For a long time Libby didn't think Reese would speak. When he did, it was in a strangled voice. "That's how I learned to ride, too."

"No kidding?" Luke was oblivious to the emotion behind the words. "Would you guys like to come to see Sunshine some-time?"

"That would be very nice, Luke. Thanks for asking." Libby answered quickly, afraid that Reese would hurt the child's feel-ings with a refusal.

She was surprised to hear him add, "Thanks, kid. Maybe I will sometime."

"Good. The barn Sunshine is boarded at isn't far from here." Then, with an attention span the length of a lightning bug's flicker, Luke changed the subject. "When are we gonna open the presents, Libby? I brought Tia a great present. I made her a calendar on the computer. It's got everybody's picture on it—even you. Mom took it at the store one day."

"I suppose it is that time. Tell everyone to gather around for gifts and cake." Libby stood up and turned to Reese. "May I push you closer to the group?"

"I didn't bring a present."

She could actually feel the resistance he radiated. "But you did. Yourself and the horses. Will you come? Please?"

He looked as happy as a root canal recipient, but he allowed Libby to maneuver him closer to the action.

"Time for presents," she announced.

"I thought you'd never ask!" Tia materialized beside the gifts before Libby could get there. "What do I get to open first?"

"Mine!" Luke chimed.

"And so it shall be," Tia said somberly. Then she tore into the first package like a toddler at Christmas.

By the time Tia was done admiring Luke's lovingly made calendar, the assortment of scarves, gloves, perfume, and candy from her employees, and the handwritten recipe journal into which Jenny had put all her favorite recipes, tears were flowing unabashedly down her cheeks.

She gave an unladylike snuffle as Luke handed her the last gift—a large box wrapped in gingham fabric and tied with a bright fabric bow. "More? I don't deserve it!"

"Is that Tia speaking?" Mike asked in mock surprise. "Tia I-Love-Presents Warden?"

"Hard to believe, I know," Tia admitted, "but I think you guys have finally done it. You created the birthday of my dreams. I don't need another one. This should hold me forever."

"Wow!" Jenny said. "Libby, did you get that on tape? Will you put it in writing, Tia?"

"Hush," Tia retorted, more interested in the package than declaring an end to future parties. "What could this be?"

A small gasp went up around the circle when she lifted a plump and cozy quilt from the box and it swelled across her lap in lush warmth. "How lovely!"

"Libby made it!" Luke crowed.

Tia looked up and stared at her friend. "You did? For me? How? When? You never have any time! There's no way you could have done this!"

Libby smiled serenely, delighted at Tia's response to this labor of love. She was completely unaware of the contemplative eyes of the man in the wheelchair upon her.

Annie, who had said little until now, came forward and picked up the edge of the quilt. "The craftsmanship is absolutely beautiful, Libby."

Libby blushed and hung back as the others forged ahead to see her handiwork. When the backs of her legs hit metal spokes, she nearly toppled over Reese's wheelchair.

"My sister-in-law is very fussy about things like that." His voice came out of the settling dusk. "If she said it was good, then it is."

"That's good to know. Thank you. I like quilting. It's like doing a fabric puzzle. My life has been quite a puzzle lately so it's rather appropriate that I've become interested in putting them in order.

"The quilt is a metaphor for my life right now," Libby continued more to herself than to Reese. "Complex. Challenging. Frustrating. A million unmatched pieces. Yet, if I really think about it, in many ways it is warm and cozy and satisfying. I'm not always as grateful as I should be for the good things I have been given."

She was about to apologize for sounding maudlin, but when she looked into his eyes, she knew that somehow, someway, tough-guy Reese Reynolds understood exactly what she was saying.

Libby was finishing up the dishes in the kitchen when Annie entered.

"Two more cups. They were hiding beneath all that wrapping paper." She leaned her hip against the counter and smiled engagingly at Libby. "You certainly know how to put on a party."

"Thanks in big part to you, Bill, and Reese."

"Our pleasure. Seeing a smile on Reese's face was worth providing horses for a hundred parties."

"You think he enjoyed himself?"

"There was more animation in his face today than there's been since the accident." Annie's eyes misted. "It was wonderful to see him smile."

Libby wiped her soapy hands on a dish towel and turned to Annie but didn't speak. Annie picked at a crumb on the counter before lifting her head to speak. "Reese is an entirely different person than he was before the accident. It's as if I've had two brothers-in-law. This Reese doesn't have anything to do with the man I knew before the accident."

Libby recognized Annie's need to talk. "How has he changed?"

"He was the most patient, compassionate man I'd ever met, even more so than Bill. I think Reese could have tamed a jack-rabbit or wild deer. Nothing rattled him. That's why Bill always preferred that Reese be the one to start our young horses. They came to Bill so tame and calm that getting in the saddle for the first time was nothing. Now Reese won't even go to the barn unless Bill forces him."

Annie scuffed her booted foot on the tile. "There used to be a spiritual quality about Reese that simply radiated from him— patience, kindness, goodness. Now he's usually hard, cynical, and angry. That's even more sad than losing the use of his legs."

"Is Reese a Christian?" Libby asked.

"Was. *Was* a Christian. He doesn't believe in much of anything anymore—if you hadn't noticed." She sighed. "But I've learned to be grateful for anything I can. Tonight I'm grateful that I saw him smile when Tia climbed on the horse. . . ."

". . . and would have fallen off the other side if Mike hadn't caught her?"

"Whatever works," Annie murmured. "Thanks for everything. Reese was on his way out to the van, and Bill was loading Buster and Barbie. I'd better go."

Libby opened her mouth to say something but closed it again. She had no words that could help.

CHAPTER SIX

*Women in the 1920s and 1930s were accustomed to making
something out of nothing. String quilting made use of scraps
of fabric of every size by sewing them onto a base of newspaper.
Then these strings of fabric could be pieced together in traditional
patterns. Today this technique is still used in paper piecing quilts.*

"Are you listening to me?" Luke glared at Libby, tapping one small booted foot, his arms crossed over his thin chest.

"Sorry, buddy. What did you say?"

"*I said* that this is the tack room and that's my saddle." His lower lip trembled. "I thought you *wanted* to see Sunshine and the stable!"

"Oh, honey, I do." She looked at the eager little face and could see Mike written all over it. "It's just that I was wondering how my parents are doing today. I'm sorry. That isn't fair of me. I am very happy to be here, and I want to see Sunshine."

"Then pay attention, please." Luke's worry slid away and a cloak of self-importance replaced it. "Come on."

Libby stifled a smile. The child had been hounding her ever since the day of Tia's party to visit the boarding stable. His persistence made her realize that she'd been ignoring her friends for the sake of family for far too long. She'd called Luke immediately and invited herself for a visit.

And, she had to admit, it was pretty wonderful here—fresh air, sunlight, beautiful animals, and one very enthusiastic young boy.

While Libby observed, Luke saddled Sunshine and lunged her in the round pen to take the edge off her energy before climbing aboard.

The boy was obviously a natural. He took Sunshine through her paces with ease. With each pass around Libby in the arena, she grew more and more wistful. It seemed so easy and so natural for him astride that huge bright horse. So free. Libby longed for whatever it was Luke experienced in that joining with the horse. His young face was relaxed and radiant.

"Want to ride her?"

"Oh, Luke, thank you, but I'm not an experienced rider. Can't you ruin a horse by putting someone inexperienced on her?"

"I'll tell you what to do. We'll just stay in the arena. It'll be OK."

Doubtfully, Libby acquiesced. The horse looked awfully high from ground level.

Luke tugged on her jacket. "Put your foot in the stirrup."

Libby tried. Oh, did she try. Finally, in desperation, she snagged the hem of her jeans with her hand and manually shoved her foot into the stirrup. Trouble was, she still had to propel herself into the saddle. Luke's little hands on her rear were not enough to shove her into place.

"Bounce a little. On your last big bounce, swing your leg over."

The voice of one of the adult riders at the stable rattled Libby so that she pulled her foot out of the stirrup and staggered around to get her balance. Luke covered his mouth to prevent her from hearing him giggle.

Libby dusted her hands on the front of her pants legs. "Guess I'll save a ride for some time when I've done my stretching exercises and put on my loosest jeans." She glanced longingly at the horse. Why was everything she wanted just inches out of her reach these days?

"Now what?" Luke asked as they climbed into Libby's car for the trip home.

"Any ideas?"

"Ice cream?"

"Why not?"

"And could we look at the pet store while we eat it?"

Libby drove to the closest mall.

She was eating her ice cream outside the pet store while Luke studied the variety of rabbits on display when she saw a familiar face shooting toward her.

Reese Reynolds looked as though he wanted to kill someone. He rolled his chair down the tiled aisle, his shoulders pumping, his face flushed, his forehead damp. His eyes were flinty and furious.

"Have you seen that idiot brother of mine?" he rasped.

"B-B-Bill?"

"That's the idiot."

"No. Should I have? Did he come by here?"

"I don't know. He just took off." Reese's flushed face was a canvas of annoyance, anger, and frustration. "We were at the sporting goods store when he decided to fly the coop."

"Wasn't he feeling well?" Libby asked.

"I guess not. He said I made him sick." Reese almost appeared to enjoy her discomfort.

"Wha-what happened?" she stammered.

"He's always lording it over me that I can't hunt anymore by looking at new guns or gear. He could save it for a time when I'm not with him, but no . . ."

"That doesn't seem so awful," Libby ventured.

Reese glared at her. "No? Then you try sitting in this chair and having everything you've ever enjoyed taken away from you. And once you're here, have your family and friends try to make you act like everything is the same as it's always been when strangers even talk louder when I'm around—like my legs have affected my hearing! As if I'd be interested in hunting now . . ." The bitterness in his voice was threaded with anguish.

"Were you a good hunter?" Libby asked.

He hadn't expected that question. Reese looked confused for a moment. "Me? Sure. Of course."

"Well, not everyone is," Libby reminded him.

He actually gave a stiff little smile, and she was reminded of how handsome he could be if he'd ever relax.

"True. But I was good." His eyes darkened. "I've had a lot of experience with firearms."

Before Libby could ask more, Bill Reynolds appeared, his face red, his hands buried deep in his pockets. "I see you found someone you know." The big man looked miserable as his brother glared at him.

Reese shrugged. His expression was cold. Libby felt the tension between them growing thicker.

"Maybe we'd better go now," Bill suggested.

"Do I have a choice?"

"What do you mean?"

"I'm a cripple, remember? I depend on you for everything, right?"

"Knock it off, Reese. You drove your van today. You could have left anytime you wanted."

"Just like I could go hunting?"

"I'd take you. I told you that. We could set you up in a blind . . ."

"Sounds fun. While the rest of you walk off, I could sit there and hope something wanders by. What would I shoot? Another crippled creature like myself?"

Libby could see Bill plucking the tattered strands of his patience together before he spoke. "I didn't mean it like that. I thought you might enjoy it."

"Thanks, but I think I'll take up basket weaving instead."

Fortunately, Luke chose that moment to arrive. "Libby, come

see this big lop-eared rabbit! He's great! Do you think Mom and Dad would let me have him? The store owner said he'd sell him to me cheap!"

"If you'll excuse me . . ."

Libby stood up. The brothers hardly noticed. She could see them arguing quietly as Bill pushed Reese's chair toward the exit doors.

....

Libby made it a point to have dinner with her parents in the dining room at their new home at least once a week. It was a joy to see her father fully engaged in life once again. He'd begun leading an adult Bible study and joined a table tennis group—two of his all-time favorite pursuits. Her mother seemed comforted by the simple routine of life at the Towers and appeared content most of the time.

"You're quiet," Libby's father observed as they ate supper that evening.

Libby took another spoonful of beef stew and spread it over the biscuit on her plate. "Sorry. I saw something today that troubled me, and I can't get it out of my mind."

"Mother and I are fine," Mr. Morrison assured her. "I haven't had a dizzy spell for some time now. In fact, I'm feeling better than I have in a long while."

"Oh, it wasn't you, Daddy. It was someone at the mall. He was very angry."

"About what?"

"Life, I guess. He's confined to a wheelchair, and he doesn't accept it very well. He takes his frustration out on others."

"A young man?"

"My age."

"No wonder he's angry." Mr. Morrison glanced at his wife. She was eating quietly. "I get upset sometimes, and I have to remind myself what a good life I've had. I was an old man before my troubles started. It would have been a real struggle to accept a loss that large at your age."

He stirred his tea. "What happened to him?"

"He's a policeman shot in the line of duty. He's like a lion with a thorn in every paw."

"Then you'd better start praying that God will send him someone to pluck them out."

"Me?"

"Why not you? You see his problem. That makes it your responsibility to pray for a solution. We're all God's children. You see someone hurting. The least you can do is pray for him. Seems to me it's yours to do."

Mine to do. Libby turned that over in her mind for the rest of the evening—as she swept the kitchen floor and as she put the finishing touches on a quilt Tia had asked her to make to sell in the shop.

It was after midnight when she finally retired. The bed looked oh so tempting, but Libby felt a weight on her heart that wouldn't go away, one she knew would keep her awake if she didn't do something about it. So she dropped to her knees beside her bed and cradled her forehead in the palms of her hands and prayed.

Dear heavenly Father, I ask that you will comfort and heal Reese Reynolds. He's so miserably unhappy, Lord, and he's lashing out at everyone around him. I don't even know what to ask for, Lord, but you do. Provide that, whatever it might be. And give his family the strength and patience to see him through this. I don't know if he's right with you, Lord. He believed in you once. Help him to do so again. Amen.

"Luke had a wonderful time with you on Saturday," were Jenny's words of greeting.

"He's a sweetheart," Libby said. "We had a nice time together at the stable."

"So he said." Jenny motioned Libby into the house and moved toward the kitchen, where she had tea already brewing. "Are you planning to visit again?"

"I'd like that."

"How about this Saturday?"

Libby frowned. "Oh, Jen, I'd love to, but you know how little time I have right now."

"All the more reason to do it. Plan on Saturday. It will be fun. That's the day families come out. It's amazing to see the young children ride."

"No fair, Jenny."

Jenny looked up, her face a mask of innocence. "What?"

"Bribing me with children. You know I'm a sucker for little kids."

"Then you'll go?"

"I can't." Libby picked up a sugar lump, dipped it with her fingers into her tea, and sucked the sweet juice from it until it crumbled between her lips. "Mom and Dad have a luncheon event at their place, and I promised I'd be there."

Jenny's slender fingers curled and uncurled the edge of the place mat in front of her as she contemplated the floral rose pattern of the fabric. It was a long time before she spoke. "Libby, what is your passion?"

Libby finished pouring herself another cup of tea, settled the pot beneath its cozy, and stared at her friend. "Passion? For what?"

"Anything. What do you care about? What, if you had all the time in the world, would you do?"

Libby stared at her. "I . . . I don't know."

"There must be something."

Libby felt strangely empty, as if when looking inside herself for an answer, she'd discovered the well was dry.

"Right now it's my family?" Libby's tone rose in question.

"Tell me, don't ask me," Jenny chided. "What is your passion?"

"The Lord." That was one thing that wasn't in doubt. Maybe now Jenny would quit pestering her.

"Of course. That's a given," Jenny said complacently. "What else?"

"What do you mean, what else? What are you getting at?" Libby allowed her annoyance to show.

Jenny tucked her feet underneath her on the chair and looked at Libby intently with those piercing blue eyes. "If you could design a dream life, Libby, what would it be? What would you include in a life that was totally fulfilling to you?"

"I've said it already. God and my family and friends."

"There are a lot of hours in a day. If you had just a few to spend on yourself, what would you spend them doing?"

Libby stared openmouthed at her friend. "I don't know."

She stared down at her fingernails and thought about what she'd just said. "Jenny, I actually *don't know!*"

"Then isn't it time you found out?"

The question cut Libby to the quick. She'd been so sure that she was getting everything under control now. Her parents were happy in their new home. She'd been making it to work at both of her jobs on time. And just when she'd convinced herself that things were at least OK, Jenny made her feel that they were anything but that. It shook Libby to her core.

It had been a long time since Libby had examined her own dreams. So long, in fact, that there didn't seem to be any left.

Jenny, seeing the expression on Libby's face, said gently, "Think about it. What are two or three things you'd really love to do or to have in your life?"

Libby felt all trembly and nervous inside. *Design a dream life? How?*

"God wants us to have good in our lives, Libby. He doesn't expect us to be dreary and work worn. What do you want in yours?"

"Can I get back to you on that?" she asked weakly.

Jenny grinned. "You bet. And in the meantime, plan to come with us to the stable. It will be fun."

It seemed the more she tried to drive that conversation with Jenny out of her mind, the more it stuck there. Libby could only compare it to a Chinese finger puzzle, the kind that stuck on a finger of each hand. The more Libby tugged and squirmed to free herself, the more trapped she became. And every time she decided never to think about Jenny's question again, it came popping into her mind in ever larger neon letters, flashing and blinking until she could see nothing else.

What *was* her dream, her passion? Had she ever had one? She supposed so, but it all seemed so long ago and so distant compared to the urgent needs of her family.

There was a time, Libby acknowledged, that she'd assumed that someday she'd have a husband and a family. She'd never dwelled much on the husband part of the equation, feeling that God would provide that on his own schedule. But she had fantasized about children.

She'd always loved them. She was the most popular, in-demand baby-sitter in the neighborhood. Tia, who jokingly maintained that the words *child* and *rugrat* were synonyms, forwarded every baby-sitting request that she received on to Libby.

But children weren't something she could casually design into her "dream life." They were the culmination of a loving, honest, value-sharing relationship between two people who wanted to spend a lifetime together.

Libby moved restlessly around the living room, mentally berating Jenny for pushing whatever button had started her on this internal journey. She picked up a travel magazine that her father had requested and fanned through the pages.

How ironic. Here Dad was, as stranded as a shipwreck survivor on an island, exhibiting glaring signs of frailty, still thinking about places he might go or things he might see. She sank into his chair and studied the glossy photos.

The magazine fell open to the first page of an article about rodeos and horse shows in Wyoming. One page featured Western Pleasure competitors, another, a clown decked out in ragged jeans and a padded barrel. Libby didn't spend much time looking at the subjects of the photos, rather she stared past them into the sea of faces in the audience beyond. Everyone, it seemed, was smiling.

As she looked up, her gaze snagged on an old framed photograph of herself, Tia, and Jenny at the water park. There they were, three scrawny children laughing into the camera with such joyous abandon that she could still feel it from across the room.

"What a lot of fun we had back then," she murmured. "Plain old, unadulterated *fun*. What happened?"

What indeed?

The Best Friends Forever had been a playful lot. Some of that playfulness had been chipped away by responsibility, obligation, death, and now, by Libby's mother's disease. Play had been sacrificed for the burden of responsible adulthood. Why did that have to happen?

Or did it *have* to happen? Had they missed something important by bowing totally to the responsibility of adulthood?

Libby sat straight up and stared at the photo. Then she got up, went to the mantel, and took it down. An idea began to form in her head. Still nebulous and without shape, it clung to her consciousness just as Jenny's question had.

What was her passion? If she was to design a "dream" of a life, what would it be? Though Libby didn't have an answer, at least she was beginning to understand the question.

....

"What's wrong with you?" Tia asked Libby when she walked into the bakery where Jenny was decorating an anniversary cake.

Libby sat on a stool, hands clasped and hanging between her knees, a befuddled expression on her features.

"I think Jenny's trying to drive me crazy by asking me too many questions."

"What on earth is she talking about?" Tia asked Jenny. "Sounds to me like she's several fries short of a Happy Meal today."

Jenny smiled. "I think she's talking about her lifelong dreams."

"Oh, that." Tia dismantled the frosting bag she'd picked up to eat the frosting bit by bit. "That's easy. Mine is to be a successful businesswoman who is loved by all." She looked up and grinned. "How am I doing so far?"

"You are a *very* successful businesswoman, dear."

Tia made a face at Jenny and turned to Libby. "So what are you going to be when you grow up?"

Libby gnawed at her upper lip. "When Jenny asked me what my passions were, I didn't have an answer. My emotions, my desires, my wishes, and my dreams were all on hold while I cared for my parents. I'd assumed that my life would be one-dimensional until I no longer had responsibility for my parents. But now I am free to do what I want, and I don't know what that is. I believe life for a Christian should be full and rewarding. If that's true, then God must have plans for me that I'm ignoring. I've been asking myself what else is calling to me, pulling me in new directions."

"My, my, I didn't realize that Jenny could inspire so much thought." Tia winked at Jenny. "What pursuits have risen to the top of your list?"

"I just don't know. The only time I'm happier than I've been in years is when I'm around horses. I had a wonderful day with Luke and Sunshine." Libby lifted her shoulders helplessly and gave her friends a sheepish smile. "I also like dogs and kids. What good is that?"

"Libby, when I asked you to think about what your interests were, I didn't mean to upset you," Jenny said.

"I'm not upset. You made me start thinking and praying. I've asked God to show me what's next for me."

"God works in mysterious ways," Tia observed. "Go with it."

"But how, exactly, am I supposed to do that?"

"If it's God's plan, he'll get you there." Tia shrugged. "You know how God is—a big-picture sort of guy—he knows what he's doing. Your job is to trust him and to go along for the ride." Tia's dark eyes brightened. "Get it? Go along for the ride? Horses? Ride? Maybe I could be a stand-up comedian!"

Jenny ignored Tia. "I agree that if you've been seeking God's will and this is what you've been given, you have to stay open to it."

"I can't remember that you liked horses all that well as a kid," Tia mused. "You did read *Black Beauty* about three million times, but other than that . . ."

"Did you ever want a real horse?" Jenny asked.

"What good would it have done if I had? I live in a neighborhood that doesn't exactly welcome horses."

"Kids make sense," Tia mused, ignoring Libby's annoyance. "You are probably the most maternal person I've ever met."

"How can you tell? I've never been a mother."

"Because you mother everyone else, of course! Look at me. I'd be a mess without you. Who puts homemade TV dinners in my freezer and takes out my garbage when it's stacked thigh high in the garage? Who made me a quilt, and then after my birthday was over, added pillow shams? Who tells me when my skirts are too short and my music is too loud? Libby the Maternal. That's who."

"Not a very attractive picture," Libby muttered. "A single woman of my age would probably rather be called brilliant, enticing, or enchanting."

"It's not a put-down. Everybody loves you. You nurture anyone who needs it. You have a heart of mush where children are concerned."

Libby couldn't contradict that. She was a marshmallow in

human form where little ones were involved. Always had been. Always would be.

"Do you remember how Libby used to cry when those Feed the Children commercials came on television?" Tia asked. "Once, at my house, I went out for sodas and when I came back, Libby was sobbing her heart out. I thought she was crying over *The Brady Bunch* when really it was the commercial that got her waterworks going!"

"And the phone company ads," Jenny reminded Tia. "They were almost as bad."

"OK, OK. You've made your point. I'm a sucker for kids and animals. What's God going to do with that? Have me run a combination day care and pet-boarding facility?"

"It's not a bad idea," Tia mused. "I think with some clever marketing we could make that work. . . ." She snapped her fingers. "How about something like Rocking Horse Ranch—a place to round up all your little cowboys and their critters."

"Get out of your corporate mode, Tia. I'm not going into business." Libby hesitated. "I don't think."

Who really knows with God in the driver's seat?

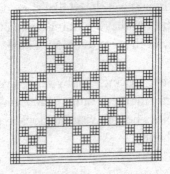

CHAPTER SEVEN

*The nine patch quilt is a simple design. Nine small fabric
squares are sewn into larger squares. These multifabric squares are
then interspersed with solid quilt blocks. It is a good quilt project for the
beginner, though accuracy in both cutting and sewing is required.*

"Party time!" Jenny burst into Libby's house, her arms filled with
trays and boxes. Tia was behind her with more boxes. Mike and
Luke brought up the rear with a cooler and a bag of disposable
cups.

"Sounds like you started the party without us," Mike
commented at the sound of music blaring through the house
from the living room. "What's up?"

Libby beamed. "Dance hour. I've been trying to get Mother
and Dad to exercise and haven't had much luck until now.
Instead of unfamiliar movements, I've begun playing music like
the rest home does and they dance. Go take a peek."

Jenny returned to the kitchen laughing. "Now that's a Kodak
moment if I've ever seen one!"

"What are they doing?" Libby arranged goodies on her own
ceramic trays.

"Your mother and Inky are doing the two-step. He's on his

hind legs with his paws on her shoulders, and she's swaying back and forth with her eyes closed like she's dancing with Cary Grant. Your dad and Puddles are doing some little swing-and-step thing that they both seem to enjoy. Come. You have to see this."

"As long as they are moving," Libby said. "I've seen a significant difference in my mother's range of motion and strength. Now, when she comes here to visit the dogs it is always party time. Everyone is happy."

Including me.

The music swelled throughout the living room, but Inky lost interest in dancing when he saw Spot. He squirmed out of Mrs. Morrison's clutches to investigate the other dog.

Smoothly, Mike stepped in. "May I have this dance?"

To Libby's astonishment, Mrs. Morrison looked him straight in the eye and said, "Yes, young man, you may." She stepped into his arms like a young girl.

They swayed to the music until Mrs. Morrison's steps began to falter. Then Mike led her to the piano, where Jenny was plucking out tunes.

"Amazing grace! how sweet the sound—" Mr. Morrison warbled. "That saved a wretch like me!"

"I once was lost but now am found," Mrs. Morrison joined in, sparkling in one of her infrequent moments of clarity.

Libby wiped a tear off her cheek as she watched and listened. It was a gift, this moment—her parents, her friends, the dogs—a tableau of warmth and normalcy. Libby closed her eyes tight and embedded the scene in her mind.

Later, as she served ice cream and hot fudge sauce to accompany Jenny's baked goods, she savored the laughter around the table. She felt her father's hand brush against her wrist as she reached across the table.

"It's a nice night isn't it, honey?" His eyes gleamed with happiness. "Like old times."

"The best, Dad. I never thought we'd have another like it."

He chuckled. "The dogs were a bit of genius. Your mother has always loved animals. She used to rescue birds that fell out of nests and stray kittens that wandered into the yard. She told me once that if she'd been born later, when women were more likely to have careers, she would have been a veterinarian."

"I didn't know that!"

"Oh yes. Quite a nurturer, your mother." He looked at Libby. "A lot like you, my dear."

Then he pushed away from the table. "It's time for us to go soon, Mother," he announced. "The van will be coming to get us."

His wife pushed back from the table and waited for him to help her from her chair. Holding hands, they made their way to the front of the house, three dogs trailing loyally behind.

....

At 6 A.M. the next morning, Tia's telephone rang.

"Whatdayawant? It better be good," was Tia's muffled greeting.

"It's me, Jenny."

"Do you know what time it is?" Tia peered blearily at her alarm clock. "This is my day off. I was planning to sleep in."

"Plans have changed. Get dressed and meet me at the hospital."

Tia was suddenly wide awake. "What's wrong?"

"Libby is with the doctor right now."

"Her mother?"

Jenny sighed. "No. Her father had a stroke in the night."

Tia found Jenny in the waiting room with Libby.

"Oh, Lib . . ." Tia embraced her in a bear hug.

"It's OK, Tia."

"OK?"

Libby smiled wanly. "At least as OK as it can be."

"Your mother?"

"Someone from Fraiser Towers brought her here. She's holding his hand."

"And his prognosis?"

"They won't say. Dr. Hazard did tell me that it was a good thing that someone discovered him right away. There were things they could do for him that they couldn't have done later."

"Then what did they give you?" Tia demanded.

Libby and Jenny both stared at her.

"Look at you! You're so calm! If I were you I'd be bouncing off the walls right now!"

"No medication, if that's what you mean. What I got was God given." Libby smiled at Tia's puzzled expression. She sighed. "As I sat in the ER with Dad, I did again what I've been struggling to do all along—give it to God."

"You look so calm."

"I gave it *all* to him. We're in more desperate straights than we've ever been before." Libby paused to gather her composure. "He doesn't need my help to manage our lives."

A smile flickered on her features. "It's his alone now, and I feel like the weight of a concrete building has been lifted from my shoulders."

The hospital chaplain arrived, an older man, balding, with kind eyes behind wire-rimmed glasses. He looked rumpled, as if he'd slept in his black trousers and knit sweater.

Libby made the introductions between Pastor Merlin and her friends and then said, "I'm trying to explain to my friends why I'm not a blathering bowl of jelly sitting in a corner somewhere."

"The peace that passes understanding," he murmured. "Hard to understand if you haven't experienced it."

"I have," Jenny volunteered. "There came a point after my husband died that I finally let God take over and . . . wow. It's a miracle that is difficult to explain."

"Exactly. But when God is fully engaged and invited into a

situation, then we are blessed with a calm that penetrates all the way to the soul. A miracle indeed."

"How does he *do* that?" Tia mused.

"We'll probably know someday, but for now all we can do is recognize his ability." The chaplain turned to Libby. "Having our feet knocked out from under us might not be such a bad thing once in a while. That's when we discover what is really firm foundation beneath us and what is merely shifting sand."

"Take nothing for granted," Jenny murmured. "Embrace each moment because things never stay the same."

"Except God," the chaplain interjected.

"Except God," Jenny echoed.

"Live in the moment." Libby's thoughts flew back to the evening before—her parents dancing around the room with the dogs, their voices raised in song, their hands linked together in love. She *had* been in the moment then, so happy that her parents were experiencing a slice of the normalcy that others took for granted. She'd known it couldn't last. She just hadn't expected it to be her father who stumbled first. And once she'd turned this totally, 100 percent, utterly, and without reservation to her heavenly Father, she'd realized what a gift it was that they had all been so absorbed in that moment in time that neither the past nor the present had intruded to mar its beauty.

Libby gave a loud snuffle.

"Want a tissue? A shoulder to cry on?" Tia offered.

"It's OK. Really. I'm just so grateful that my parents had last night and that I did, too. It will make whatever happens next a little easier."

Living one day, one hour at a time. That's the only way I can live anymore. It is the way I've struggled to live all along—not worrying about the future or rehashing the past.

Father, thank you for all you've taught me in these past months! I think I get it now. Finally. Fortunately.

"Lib?" Tia peered into her eyes.

"I was just thinking about living in the past instead of the present, wishing for the way things used to be. It's a little like confessed sin, isn't it?'

Tia's puzzled expression egged Libby on.

"Once we confess a sin to God, it's gone from his mind," Libby explained. "Poof. Vanished. To be held against us no more. But we keep dredging up our old sins and replaying them to a chorus of 'if onlys.' God doesn't do that. Just us."

"And your point would be . . ."

"The past is the same way. Over. Done. Gone. Yet we still mourn for it and try to recapture it rather than look ahead for the blessings yet to come. God doesn't dwell on our confessed sins or the pasts we've put behind us so why should we?

"Why is it that we can't quite believe that he wants only good for us? That we have that future and a hope he talks about?

"We can't bring back the past and we shouldn't want to do so. Christ bought us back from our sin. Our slates are clean. My parents are in God's hands, and he has a future and a hope for them, too."

Libby paused to take a deep breath. "Don't you see? If Dad had been at home and had this stroke things might have been far different. God knew what was coming and made sure that Daddy was where he needed to be. We were in God's hands all the time!"

She gave her friends a wobbly smile. "And when I start feeling sorry for myself, it's your job to remind me of that!"

"Gotcha," Tia said. Jenny merely put her arm around Libby's shoulder.

"Libby?" Dr. Hazard was standing nearby.

"Yes? Dad . . ."

"Is stable. We're out of the woods."

"And Mom?"

"She says she wants to go home. Something about a dog."

Dr. Hazard looked puzzled when all three of them burst out laughing.

Judy Baer

"Then let's take her home," Jenny suggested. "Doctors Inky and Puddles are both on call today. She should be in the best of hands . . . er . . . paws."

"Puppies?" Mrs. Morrison asked for the hundredth time as they turned into the driveway.

"They're here, Mom. See?" Libby pointed to the front window, where two eager faces peeked out. There was slobber all over the window as high as the dogs could reach with their wet tongues and cold noses.

"Puppies." The relief was evident in her voice, like that of a child who'd feared she'd misplaced her favorite toy.

"Do you want us to come in?" Tia and Jenny had accompanied Libby to the house.

"Not now. I'm going to spend some quiet time with Mom and the dogs before I take her back to Fraiser Towers."

The dogs greeted them as if they'd been gone for months instead of hours. Libby noticed the visible relaxing of her mother's shoulders as she petted Inky. She gave thanks again for whatever had possessed her to adopt the dogs.

The ritual of bathing; having her hair washed, dried, and set; and slipping into bed for a nap soothed Mrs. Morrison even more. Still, as she laid her head on the pillow, her hand snaked over to her husband's side of the bed and searched vainly for his presence.

"Daddy's not here right now," Libby soothed, running a gentle hand over her mother's forehead. "You've been up a long time. You'll feel better after a nap."

"What's wrong, Libby?"

Libby was startled by her mother's question. Everything was wrong. Everything and nothing. Life was just unfolding in ways they couldn't understand.

"What's wrong with *me?*"

Even now, her mother was not so deep into senility that she didn't realize that something was deeply wrong.

"Oh, Mama," Libby laid her head on her mother's shoulder and longed for the time when she'd been the child and her mother the parent. But that was the past. It was the present now and everything had changed.

"You are still the most wonderful, loving, sweet woman you've always been. You've just started forgetting some things." *Like my name sometimes. And your name, too.*

"I'm scared, Libby."

Libby gathered her mother in her arms and cradled her, rocking her as she might a child.

"Oh, Mama, I'm scared, too."

....

Libby suspected Spot's arrival when her doorbell chimed in one continuous ring. Her suspicions were confirmed when she opened the door and saw Spot, his paw resting on the bell, his goofy, tongue-lolling grin near her face.

"Tell Luke he could teach his dog something other than how to ring doorbells," she said by way of greeting as Jenny entered.

"He has. How to catch table scraps on the fly. How to take over two-thirds of a double bed. And, the *pièce de résistance*, how to dominate a conversation without saying a word."

"At least he's nurturing this multitalented animal. Come in and explain the reason for this visit."

"Since you decided to keep your mom overnight instead of taking her back to Fraiser Towers, Spot's come to stay over, too. I've got his suitcase in the car."

"Jenny, don't you think we have quite enough dogs in this household already?"

"I don't see any." She looked around.

"They're upstairs with Mom. She had a long nap but wanted to go back to bed after supper. She's exhausted. She won't sleep without the pups, however, and they don't seem to mind a bit.

Puddles saw us start for the stairs and was in her bed by the time we reached the top."

"Exactly. Puddles and Inky have to sleep with your mother. There is no one to comfort you. Hence, Spot. Fortunately, it's spring and only a one-dog night."

"Huh?" Libby paused in her tea preparations to stare at Jenny.

"Old Eskimo thing. When the night isn't too cold, you only need one dog in bed with you to keep you warm. Colder and you'd need a second. Really cold? A third. Hence the term *three-dog night.*"

Libby smiled wanly and put the teapot in front of Jenny. "Cute. Thanks."

She sighed as she sat down. "It's been a two-dog night every night lately for me. And probably will be for a long time to come."

"What do you mean?" Jenny dumped extra fortifying sugar into Libby's tea.

"I mean that Inky, Puddles, and I are a threesome. Now there is absolutely no question that my parents are best off where they are. Or that I've somehow misplaced my own life and am not sure how to get it back."

Jenny reached across the table and put her hand on Libby's slender wrist. "Nothing has really changed, my friend. You're just facing what's been there all along. Of course you'll get your life back!"

"I know, I know. You and Tia have been trying to prepare me. I just haven't wanted to listen."

"Death is something that happens to people, Libby. No matter how hard we fight to save them, it happens anyway."

"But I'm not ready yet!"

"It's not about you. It's about them. They both know the Lord as their personal Savior and that's what matters."

"I'm so sorry, Jenny," Libby blurted.

"About what?"

"For not understanding—not truly—what you went through when Lee died. I thought I understood, but I see now that you can't fully understand until you face it yourself. I was so good at giving advice. 'Snap out of it.' 'God loves you.' Platitudes, all of them. I had no real idea what you were going through."

"Don't be so hard on yourself. You gave me the right advice whether you understood 100 percent or not."

"Then it was God talking, not me."

"And you are apologizing for that?"

"I read to Mom before she fell asleep. Somehow I got into Matthew 12:3: 'And I tell you this, that you must give an account on judgment day of every idle word you speak.' When I read that I got chills. How many times have I let my mouth run ahead of my mind? Of prayerful responses? Too many to count!

"It's ironic, isn't it? People want to give advice the most when they get a situation the least."

"Don't be so hard on yourself, Libby. It's true that all the well-intentioned but misguided advice in the world won't help. But understanding, listening, loving, and being there for someone will work wonders. I know. You did it for me. Now I want to give some of that gift back to you."

"How did you cope with it all?" Libby wondered.

"God. My friends. Taking it one day at a time. Living in the moment. And it helped me a great deal to realize that there are no coincidences in life. I know now that nothing happens without reason and that there is no situation God cannot turn from something bad into something good."

"God-incidences, huh?" Libby smiled.

Jenny studied her friend with utter gentleness in her expression. "And now what?"

Libby knew the answer. It was time for her. God had been prodding her to grow, but she'd been resisting, afraid of what might await her. She'd been guilty—again—of not trusting fully.

Simon Peter had nothing on her. They were both habitual offenders.

This was the jumping-off point into her new life, Libby realized. God had promised never to leave her alone, so she might as well hold her nose, close her eyes, and jump into the deep end of the pool. After all, her lifeguard had assured her that he wouldn't let her drown.

CHAPTER EIGHT

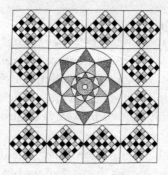

Quilting was introduced to Native Americans by settlers and missionaries. Native Americans quickly found ways to make quilts with their own cultural designs. The Morning Star pattern represents Venus— a single, large, eight-pointed star the size of an entire quilt top.

Tia arrived at Libby's covered in packing dust and strands of orange hay.

"What have you been doing?" Jenny asked, as Libby made more tea and brought out a mug for Tia.

"Unpacking Halloween decorations! Can you believe it?"

"Halloween? Shouldn't we celebrate the Fourth of July first?"

"That was celebrated before the last snow melted. In retail terms, at least."

"Time passes too quickly as it is," Jenny complained, "without you store owners rushing it even more."

"I remember my grandmother patting me on the head and saying I was growing up too fast," Libby admitted. "Now I do the same to the children I know!"

"As guilty as I am of season jumping, it still creeps me out." Tia rubbed her arms as gooseflesh stood out on her pale skin.

Libby tossed her a sweater. "Why the strong reaction?"

"I'm not ready to grow up yet! I don't want to be the older generation."

"Hello, Peter Pan."

"What's so bad about wanting to stay young? Look at Libby's folks. They're proof that the last part of life can be the hardest of all. I'd like to keep working at something I love forever."

"I've been thinking a lot about staying young versus being ware-housed with the old," Libby admitted. "For obvious reasons."

"But life must come full circle," Jenny pointed out.

"And that's another thing I don't like!" Tia fumed. "We're born babies—wrinkled, helpless, fussy. And we turn into babies again—old babies, *ancient* ones, who need help to be fed, to keep ourselves clean, to be entertained . . . ugh!"

She jammed a spoon into the sugar bowl so hard it bent. "How did we start this depressing conversation anyway? Surely some-one else has something more interesting to talk about."

"Not really. I have a dentist appointment tomorrow," Jenny said. "Thrilling, right?"

"I'm getting my eyes checked," Tia added. "How about you, Libby? Don't tell us you're getting fitted for lifts in your shoes or a hearing aid!"

Libby chuckled. "Almost as exciting. A trip to the hospital. Dad and Mom are both scheduled for tests."

"Boring," Tia said with a yawn. "Somehow we have to get some action and excitement in your life."

As it turned out, the excitement Libby found *was* at the hospital. She nearly tripped over Reese on her way into the lobby.

"What are you doing here?" she blurted unceremoniously. Except for the mall, she hadn't heard from him since their dinner at Bill and Annie's.

"Isn't this where guys in wheelchairs hang out?"

"Quit playing poor me for once, will you?" Immediately, Libby wanted to slap her own face. What possessed her to be so rude?

But he didn't seem offended. "Spunky little meddler, aren't you?"

"So my reputation precedes me." She didn't know whether to be relieved or embarrassed.

He smiled and Libby was startled at the wide, supple mouth and even teeth. When he was relaxed and smiling, Reese was one devastatingly handsome man.

"How is the pup?"

She was overjoyed to see that no matter how hard he tried, he couldn't keep the pleasure out of his expression.

"Cutest little troublemaker I've ever seen. Except, maybe, you. He changes every day. It took a lot of guts to bring him out, Libby."

Libby took that as a backhanded compliment.

"He had your name written all over him. Besides, Annie and Bill wanted him even if you didn't. I'm not a complete fool."

"I worked with police dogs for part of the time I was on the force. It was my favorite stint."

"I didn't know that!"

"You didn't?" He looked genuinely surprised. "I thought that was why . . ."

"No. I just knew what Jenny's mongrel did for my family and thought it couldn't hurt to try with yours."

"Unconditional love," Reese murmured. "Even when it comes from something that springs a leak every half hour and whines all night, we all still need it."

"There are other places to get unconditional love, too, you know." Libby wasn't much at sermonettes. It was easy to talk about her faith with Tia and Jenny, but she hardly knew Reese. Still, she felt compelled to continue.

"You aren't going to talk religion, are you?" Reese scowled. "I've been down that road. I knew God. Look where that got me."

A pang reverberated through Libby's heart. "He didn't put you there. A bullet did."

"But if he were there, why didn't he let it miss me—or kill me."

He is serious! "God is about good, Reese, not evil."

"So I was told. So I even believed—once. I prayed for a long time, Libby. I petitioned to the guy upstairs but nobody was home."

Reese's anger was palpable. Libby backed off from his intensity. "You didn't tell me why you were here."

"Routine stuff." He eyed her speculatively.

"Annie told me about your dad's stroke." Reese's voice softened. "That's tough, Libby. I'm sorry."

"Thank you. I'm OK with it now." Since she'd quit playing her usual game of catch with God, giving him her problems and then taking them back, she'd experienced such peace that she knew she'd been a fool not to trust completely from the start.

"Coffee shop isn't too bad," Reese pointed out gently. "Good caramel rolls. I've eaten plenty of them in the past. Want to try one?"

Libby followed him to the cafeteria, watching his strong arms and shoulders propel the chair. His hair was longer since they'd first met and it curled softly at the nape of his neck.

She was embarrassed to realize how engrossed she'd been in the look of him when she ran into his chair as he stopped at the cafeteria door. Self-consciously, she followed him inside.

"So you *really* aren't angry with me about the puppy?" she asked as she buttered her roll at the table.

His grin was lopsided. "He's great, Libby. I didn't realize how much I'd missed a dog." His eyes shadowed and he disappeared into his own thoughts. "Or a lot of other things for that matter."

"Do you still call him Knuckles?"

"Actually, we had to change his name to suit his actions."

"What is his name now?"

"Rin Tin Tinkle."

She nearly choked on her coffee. "Poor thing!"

"Hopefully he'll grow out of it. Then we'll call him Ranger."

"I can't tell you how pleased I am that you didn't take little Rin Tin Tinkle and shove him down my throat," Libby admitted. "It took a lot of moxie to do what I did. I'm sorry. I don't know what got into me, but for some reason, I just *knew* you had to have that dog."

"It's one of the most perceptive things anyone has done for me in a long time," he admitted. "I think Bill and Annie were giving up on me."

"How so?"

"Annie says they don't know how to make me laugh. Or to help me want to get up in the morning."

"And Rin Tin Tinkle, I mean, Ranger, does that?"

"Yes. Or he wets my bed."

Libby giggled. It felt wonderful. How long had it been since *she* had really laughed either?

"How are your parents?"

"Dad is regaining his physical strength. Fortunately, his mind and speech were not severely affected." She stirred the liquid thoughtfully.

"Reese, did you and your family ever consider that you might have to live in a nursing home after the accident?" Though she'd made peace with the concept, it was still much on her mind.

His face contorted and Libby yearned to retract the question. "I'm sorry, I didn't mean to . . ."

"It's OK. I understand. Some mouths need a bridle instead of a spur, that's all," he said darkly and swilled down some coffee before continuing. "It was assumed that I'd be in one. No one thought I'd be able to manage on my own."

"But you did."

"Sort of. I can drive the specially equipped van and live in my own apartment at Bill and Annie's. Since I helped them with foaling, they now assume I'll be training and doing ground work next. They won't accept that it's not like it was." A faint, humorless smile flickered on his lips. "Of course, some might say that's not all bad. I was a wild son of a gun at one time. I'm certainly not that anymore."

"How did you manage?"

"One grueling day at a time. My motivation was the thought of being institutionalized, of living my days out in a nursing home. It terrified me into not giving up entirely."

"So dreading a nursing facility made you strong?"

He read her mind then, as if her thoughts were typed on her forehead. "For *me*, Libby. Me. You can't put me into the same category as your parents. You aren't feeling guilty now, are you? It's good for them to be where they are, you know."

"If it's so plain then, what I'm thinking?"

"I can read your thoughts like an open book."

"Then I'd better learn to close it."

"Please don't. That's one of the things I like about you."

Suddenly, they were both embarrassed.

"Tell me about yourself," she said, hoping to fill the awkward silence.

"Me? A standard story. Grew up on a farm. Lived on the back of a horse named Cocoa. Even ate my meals on her when I could. Mom said I would have slept on her if she'd have let me take a sleeping bag to the barn. Went to community college for two years and then finished my degree at the university. Joined the air force and became a flyboy. Acted up. Got in trouble. Got out again. You know the story."

"When did you meet God?"

Reese snorted. "I stumbled over him just before I joined the police force. He tripped me, I think. But he couldn't hang on to me after some of the messes I saw on the job. Molestations. Murders. Drugs. Far as I can tell, he abandoned the scene and left the police to clean up the mess."

"Oh, Reese . . ."

"Don't 'Oh, Reese' me. I saw what I saw. I learned what I learned. And that was that God took a powder and left." He gestured at his chair. "Proof positive, right here."

"I don't think God left just because my parents are in the conditions they are in."

"Good for you. Deluded, but good. I'm more of a realist than you are, Libby." Then he reached out and put his hand over hers. "But I am thankful that you are impulsive. Otherwise Ranger . . . Rin Tin Tinkle . . . and I might never have met."

Libby withdrew her hand and leaned her elbows on the table. "I've been thinking about the way God works, Reese. It seems to me that sometimes God holds back in certain situations to force us to take the next step."

"Well, he's stepped out of the building as far as I'm concerned."

No use beating her head against a wall, Libby concluded. Deftly, she changed the subject. "You said you liked cars, right?"

"Yeah. So?" His eyes narrowed suspiciously.

"I've decided to trade my tank in for something sporty."

Then she put her mouth in gear before her mind. "Maybe you could help me . . . ah, give me some advice . . . show me what's good . . . or, oh, never mind!"

"Car shopping? It's the least I can do for the meddling female who dumped Rin Tin Tinkle on me."

"Vengeance is mine," says the Lord, Libby thought wildly. She hoped Reese wouldn't try to exact vengeance on her for Rin Tin Tinkle.

"So what are you doing this afternoon?"

"Today?" She couldn't hide her surprise.

"That's when this afternoon usually comes."

"Why, yes . . . I guess . . . oh, why not!" Feeling her face redden, she forged on. "When and where?"

And how and why? What had she been thinking of?

"I like this one." Libby peered into a sporty red two-door.

"Too many miles. It's probably been driven hard. How about that sweet little convertible we looked at first?"

"Reese, a Miata convertible? In Minnesota? Did you forget the five months of winter we have every year?"

"I thought you wanted the antithesis of practical this time. Besides, you'd look good in yellow."

Libby looked longingly in the direction of the car. "I know, I know. But I guess the apple doesn't fall far from the tree. As much as I want to break out, I can't justify a car that only has room for two people and a suitcase the size of a purse."

"You have to make up your own mind. Just remember, big old tank of a car or flashy sports car, it doesn't matter—as long as you have the ability to climb in and drive. There was a time when I didn't realize how much freedom that was. It's one of those things that you don't appreciate until you've lost it."

The longing in his voice tore at her heart. "Reese, I didn't mean to upset you by asking you to come here. . . ."

"It's OK. I'll never get to pick out another sports car for myself but I can live vicariously through you."

She didn't know how to respond or even what she should respond to—his sadness, his anger and resentment, his bitterness, or his pain. They were all wrapped together in his tone.

"Maybe *you* have to start living again, too, Reese." She ignored his derogatory snort. "I put my life on hold because I wanted to do what was best for my family. Yours was put on hold for you. But now it's time for both of us to pick up the pieces of who we were before and start living again."

Reese stared into space just over her right shoulder for a long moment before speaking. "But you have something to pick up. Is there anything you can't do now that you could do five years ago?"

"No, but . . ."

"I was a cop and a pilot. Now all I can do at work is answer telephones or push papers around a desk. I used to do some car racing. Now I drive a full-size, handicap-equipped van with less get-up-and-go than a Model T. I used to ride. I rodeoed, roped calves, rode broncs, showed horses, you name it. Now I can sit in the barn and watch for foaling mares because they aren't going anywhere anyway. There aren't any pieces for me to pick up,

Libby. They've all been blown away. And," he added at the look on her face, "I'm not playing poor me either. Those are the facts, and the sooner I learn to accept them, the easier it will be for me."

His eyes closed for a moment. "Trouble is, accepting it is even harder than living it."

She leaned against the nearest car, crossed her arms over her chest, and prayed for the right words to come.

"Believe it or not, I do understand. Not fully, of course, but in little ways. I woke up one day and realized that I had to get a life, to do whatever it was Libby did. And I didn't know what that was. I ran smack-dab into a wall. Here I am a grown woman only starting to discover the person I've become. I used to read articles in women's magazines about coming of age in midlife. And I was always glad they weren't talking about *me*.

"Then one day they were. And all the rules had changed. I was metaphorically let out of prison with a new suit of clothes and fifty bucks in my pocket. All I could ask was 'Now what?' I'm *still* asking it!

"It's the same for you, Reese. The old rules, the past, don't apply anymore. But that doesn't mean that we don't have a future."

"You can do anything you want. You just have to decide what that is. I can't."

"So start thinking outside the envelope! Some doors are closed to you, but God always opens others."

"Don't bring him into this."

"I bring him to everything in my life."

Reese stared sadly at her. "I envy you that, Lib. Life is much simpler when you think there is someone out there helping you."

"He's there for you, too."

Reese's eyes darkened. "I wish I believed that, I really do."

Libby changed the subject. "If you can't be a cop on the street, could you be a detective? They investigate crimes, don't they?"

"Special circumstances, Libby. I'm not trained. . . ."

"Then *get* trained if that's what you want to do. I know your passion for horses. Bill and Annie told me that you are the best trainer of young horses that they've ever seen. Bill said you wouldn't have to get on a horse to do the ground work."

"It kills me to work with horses when I can't get on one."

"Then figure a way to do it!"

Reese looked at her pityingly. "You don't get it at all, do you?"

"But . . ."

"There's no point in subjecting either of us to more of this conversation." Reese gave the wheels of his chair a forceful spin. "Give it up, Libby. You can't fix me and I can't fix me either."

"Ha!" she yelled to his retreating back. "You're a smart guy. You can find a way!"

He didn't look back.

As she got into her car, Libby laid her arms on the wheel and lowered her head. "Big mouth. Huge mouth. *Enormous* mouth. Why don't I just shut up? What business do I have telling Reese he can pull it together, when I don't even know what *I'm* going to do?"

Lord, show us a way. Help us to find what it is we're supposed to be doing now. And help Reese to find you.

"Why the long face?" Tia inquired when Libby slunk into the shop. "You look like you lost your best friend. Cheer up! I'm still here."

"I think I made an enemy."

"You? Impossible."

"Possible. Very possible." Libby told her what had transpired between her and Reese.

"He was really angry, Tia. Hurt, offended, indignant, frustrated. What was I thinking, telling him how to run his life when I can't run my own?"

"Angry like you won't ever see him again?"

"I think so."

"Wow. I didn't think you had it in you."

"There's a big, meddling mouth under this quiet exterior." Libby flung herself into a chair. "I'm so angry with myself!"

"Then you need a distraction," Tia concluded calmly. "And I have just the thing."

Libby eyed her suspiciously. "What?"

"You need a date."

"Oh, for goodness sake! I need another man to offend like I need a new hole in my head."

"My cousin from Boston is coming on Thursday. Some sort of medical convention he's attending." Tia waggled her eyebrows. "He's a doctor. Cute. Nice. Everything a distraction should be."

"No dates, Tia. I don't want to drag anyone into this morass I'm making for myself."

"He needs a date for the banquet on Saturday night. He called and asked me to go with him." Tia's mental wheels were turning. It showed in her eyes. "And now it seems that I'm busy but my dear friend Libby is available, and . . ."

"No way!"

"Ah, come on, be a sport."

"Tia, I don't see a man in *your* life. If they are the cure for all problems, then either you don't have any problems or you don't practice what you preach."

"I don't have time. You know that. I'm terrible on a date. I'm always reaching for my planner to write down an idea or I'm making phone calls. My work *is* my date these days."

"You weren't that way in high school," Libby reminded her, hoping to divert her. "I remember the night you accepted three dates."

Tia rolled her eyes. "That was horrible! I played tennis and ate supper with Ted, went to an early movie with Billy, and then after Billy brought me home, I went to the drive-in with Eddy. By midnight I was *exhausted!*"

"And you weren't allowed to go to the drive-in, if I remember correctly."

"Oh, that. I was young and dumb. Actually, I fell asleep. When I woke up, the movie was almost over and Eddy was sitting in the back of a pickup truck with some buddies. I could never see the dangers in drive-ins that my parents seemed to find."

"Your mother always said you were her 'little challenge.' I guess that was an understatement."

"Fine. Fine. Now about my cousin . . ."

"Lay off, Tia. No blind dates. No sighted dates. No dates at all. I need to find myself before I go out looking for a man." Libby toyed with a fruit-filled candle from the nearest display. "I'm not convinced that a man is the answer to everything—or to *anything*, for that matter. The only one I need to turn myself over to right now is God."

"I agree, that's your first and most important step." Tia paused. "But my cousin will be back again in August."

Tia ducked as Libby feigned a candle toss at her head.

....

Libby couldn't get her father out of her mind. What was it he'd said about Reese and his problems? Because she knew of them, because she'd been shown his need, she should pray for him— simply *because it was hers to do*. Her heart grew heavy every time she remembered Reese's bitter rejection of God.

There had been a time in Libby's life when she had not been highly motivated to talk about her faith. That had changed in the last few years and most particularly in recent months. For reasons known only by God, she felt an urgency where Reese was concerned.

But his heart was hard as stone and his head totally disinterested in hearing anything she had to say. Now what?

Soften his head and his heart, that's what!

Libby gathered her jacket, her Bible, and a study guide and strode purposefully out her front door. Maybe she alone couldn't do much about Reese, but she knew a group of prayer warriors that, if banded together in a single purpose, could certainly knock loudly on the gates of heaven and, as a result, on Reese Reynolds' heart.

"It's good to see you, Libby," Ellen said upon opening the front door. She gestured Libby into the sunroom. "Everyone else is here already except Tia. She's held up at the store."

"Hi, all," Libby said as she entered the bright room. Jenny gave a wave. Dorothy, Jenny's former sister-in-law, did the same. Patty, her friend from the fabric shop, and six others, all of whom had been doing Bible studies together for years, sat around the table, Bibles open.

"We're discussing which study we should do next, Lib. Any ideas?" Ellen handed Libby a glass of juice.

"Actually, I do." Libby scrambled to organize the thoughts whirling through her head. "How about something on intercessory prayer?"

"I like the idea," Dorothy said. "We haven't done that before."

"We always ask for prayer requests to continue in our personal time. I think it would be a great help."

"Matthew 6:6," Jenny murmured. "'But when you pray, go away by yourself, shut the door behind you, and pray to your Father secretly. Then your Father, who knows all secrets, will reward you.'"

"It's a great idea," Beth Marvin said. "I think we should learn everything we can about tapping into that power."

Libby looked across the table to Jo Nivens, the newest member of their group and a baby Christian. "What's wrong, Jo? You don't look as if you like the idea."

"Other than conversing with God, what good does our prayer really do? Hasn't God already got it all figured out? Why should we try to change something that can't be changed? I thought that nothing happened that God hadn't already planned to happen.

So really, what's the use? I don't want us wasting our time on something we can't do anything about."

Debbie Cash, wife of the youth pastor at the church Libby attended, said mildly, "God didn't create us to be powerless puppets pulled along at the end of a string. He really wants us to be partners with him. He didn't say it's hopeless to pray because everything is already a done deal. God *told* us to pray. He *wants* us to be active in his kingdom."

"So *I* could ask him to change his mind?" Jo sounded shocked.

"Why not? Moses did. God was ready to turn the Israelites into toast. He would have, too, if Moses hadn't pleaded for his people. I'm not saying it was easy, but I am saying it's possible and the power is within us to do it. Moses prayed before God for forty days. God heard him and decided not to fry the Israelites."

"Wow," Jo breathed. "I had no idea. . . ."

Listening to the conversation, Libby felt a surge of excitement and encouragement. She could *pray* Reese into a different attitude, one open to God's promises.

Awesome. Definitely awesome.

Look out, Reese. You think God doesn't act in the world today? Just wait and see.

CHAPTER NINE

"Crazies," as Victorian crazy quilts were called, were occasionally used as fund-raisers for admirable causes. This was especially successful if someone famous were to give the makers a piece of clothing to incorporate into the quilt.

Libby hummed as she emptied the dishwasher. She'd had her morning coffee on the porch in her favorite rocker, watched a squirrel in a tree, and listened to a symphony of birds in the distance. Bliss. Sheer bliss.

A twinge of guilt pricked at her conscience but she banished it immediately. Her parents were fine, happier than they'd been since the beginning of her mother's illness. The unvarying routine of their new home had given her mother a pleasant structure for her life. And when Mother was happy, Dad was happy, too.

The past few days Libby had experienced a sense of being freed from a velvet prison—but a prison nonetheless. Now her time was her own.

There was an urgency that gnawed at her, a compulsion to make up for lost time—for trips not taken, for laughter not shared, for service to God not yet rendered. Freedom was a double-edged sword. Too much freedom could make her lazy and complacent. What Libby needed now was a purpose.

Get a life, Libby old girl!

But what might that be?

Frustrated with the asking and still at a loss for the answer, Libby finished the dishes, picked up her keys and billfold, and headed for the car.

She rolled the top down, turned the music up, and let the wind whip her hair around her face all the way to the shopping mall.

Libby spent a full hour in the sporting goods store trying on running shoes before she chose a pair. Then she began to wander through the mall.

Never vain or self-concerned, Libby had no interest in the clothing and cosmetic shops, Italian shoes, or designer leather handbags. She had plenty of T-shirts, more books than she could read in a year, and no gifts to buy. Libby studied the window of the specialty chocolate shop, almost stepped in and then changed her mind. She was finally recapturing some of the physical energy she'd lost in the months past. She didn't want to blow that now.

She wandered aimlessly until a beautiful hand-tooled leather saddle in a Western shop window caught her eye. Libby stepped inside.

She drew a deep breath and relished the fragrant smell of new leather. Her gaze moved over racks of boots, a display of jackets and dusters, and the jewelry case full of huge belt buckles, Western ties, and broaches of bucking broncos. Strangely, she felt right at home.

"Can I help you?" A polite, almost courtly, voice inquired. Libby turned to see a gray-haired gentleman in tight jeans and a turquoise-and-pink shirt with a gray felt Stetson on his head.

"I . . . I don't know. I just wandered in here and now that I'm here, I like it."

"You have horses?"

"No." Libby looked longingly at the wall display of bridles and bits. "I wouldn't mind having one, but my neighborhood isn't exactly set up for that."

The man chuckled. "That happens in the city. But there are ways to be around horses anyway."

"I really couldn't afford to board one right now."

"Wouldn't have to. C'mere, I want to show you something."

She followed him to the desk, where he laid out several posters, flyers, and brochures. On them were photos of children in riding helmets sitting on horses. They had pure joy on their faces.

"This is the place I spend my time." He pointed to the name emblazoned on the poster—Reach Out Ranch.

"It's a nonprofit, volunteer-operated ranch that provides equine-facilitated therapy." He smiled at Libby's blank look. "We provide horse therapy for children and adults with handicaps."

"*Horse* therapy? What do the horses do? Say 'please lay down on my couch of straw and tell me what's been happening in your life'?"

"Something better. We put people with handicaps on horses and give them the opportunity to feel normal. Take a person—adult or child—who's wheelchair bound, always looking into people's belt buckles and never into someone's eyes, and put them on a horse. They feel like they are flying. For once they can look down at people, not up. Can you imagine what that would do for someone who'd always felt like an outsider of the human race?

"It's an amazing process. I've seen breakthroughs with children who hadn't spoken in years. Suddenly, with a horse under him and the reins in his hand, a life-long wound breaks open and a pocket of pus pours out. Healing can finally begin. He speaks. Maybe not to the handlers or therapists right away. But the clients speak to their horses. Once that door has opened, we're on our way to bigger and better opportunities for healing and for self-respect." The man's face glowed with excitement.

"All that—from a horse?"

"Our horses are the sweetest, most well broken, patient, loving creatures on earth. They are great healers." The man chuckled. "Sometimes I see our clients sitting in the box stalls having a heart-to-heart with the horse they've ridden. And I swear those horses listen. I know for sure they can love."

"You're very enthused about this, Mr. . . ."

"Rollie Weatherspoon. Call me Rollie. And I am enthused. This is the most exciting thing I've ever done. The most fulfilling and the happiest." He looked her over. "And you could, too."

Libby cleared her throat nervously. His enthusiasm was almost overwhelming. It was one thing to admire horses from afar, but . . . "What is your job in all of this?"

"I was a volunteer for a few years, just on weekends. The longer I worked with people with handicaps and the horses, the more I saw that this was more than a hobby for me. It's a calling." He appeared amused at Libby's puzzlement. "God works in mysterious ways. Who'd have thought he could use an old cowboy like me and a bunch of mild-mannered horses to work miracles?

"Anyway, I started hiring help for the store and spending more time at Reach Out Ranch. Now I only work here when some-body's on vacation, and I'm full-time at the ranch. I train horses, oversee the book work, and coordinate therapy sessions. In my *spare* time I do public speaking and bush-beating to let people know about the program and how they can help. And, of course, I still spend as much time as I can in the arena, helping riders."

Libby had never seen a man's eyes sparkle like those of Rollie Weatherspoon. They brimmed with pure, unadulterated joy.

"I'm impressed. I wish I could find something to do that was so wonderful."

He gave a snort that sounded a great deal like the whinny of a horse. "You can! I'll tell you how."

And that was how Libby found herself having lunch in the

mall's food court with a man she'd only known for fifteen minutes—and wondering if, through this chance meeting, he would be the one to help her discover herself and what God had in store for her. One thing Libby had learned through the wrenching process of moving her parents out of their home was to look for God in all the odd places. He had a way of using the lowly and the unexpected to move in people's lives.

She was fascinated by the man across from her. His enthusiasm was catching. It made Libby long for that kind of genuine excitement in her own life. Flattened and battered by the recent convolutions of her life, she was ready for renewed energy and passion.

Libby picked at her steak fries and asked, "How long have horses been used in therapy?"

"Probably since man crawled on a horse's back. Unfortunately, animals are often abused by ignorant people who don't understand them. But we're moving forward to remedy that. People don't 'break' horses in the literal sense much anymore—unless they've had their head in the sand. In the 1960s doctors began to recognize what horses could do for them. The North American Riding for the Handicapped Association—the NARHA—came into being in the late sixties and we've been growing ever since."

Libby felt a twinge of doubt. It was hard to imagine that this therapy would provide any more than a little pleasure. "What kinds of handicaps does horse therapy treat?"

"You name it, we see it. Autism, multiple sclerosis, accident victims, emotional and learning problems, anything you can think of. It rebuilds confidence and self-esteem."

"Sounds like a wonder drug with no side effects," Libby observed.

"You might say that." Rollie sat back in his chair, crossed his arms over his chest, and grinned. "Yessir, I think that's right. And it works for any age, too! I try hard to get a good fit between horse and rider—temperament, size, stride, even personality."

"But I don't see how. . . ."

Rollie read her mind. "When you're riding a horse, it's not so different from walking. The body performs many of the same movements. Since many of our clients *can't* walk, this gives them the opportunity to exercise their 'walking' muscles. When you're in the saddle, a horse feels a little like a boat on the water. You're moving forward, but at the same time swaying from side to side as the horse takes his leads and changes gaits. Add to that the fact that you are bouncing along—sometimes with your seat slapping so hard against the saddle that you wonder why your teeth aren't rattling—and you have no choice but to be aware of and react to your mount's every move."

"So the rider develops better balance?"

"Sure. And muscle strength. Everyone wants to stay on board, you know. Eventually those stiff, unused limbs start to loosen up. Stretching spastic muscles is a big benefit of hippotherapy. Sitting astride a horse stretches the adductor muscles in the thighs. That's why we start out slowly at first—making sure the client is warmed up and—" Rollie chuckled—"riding a thin horse. It doesn't hurt either if the client can feel the warmth of the horse's body. Warmth aids relaxation.

"The therapists say hippotherapy is good for sensory integration, too. That's a fancy term for touching the horse, feeling it move, hearing it nicker. The riders can see the world pass by as they ride, smelling hay, manure, and the distinctively sweet and dusty smell of a horse. Best of all, it's a lot more fun than a workout with a physical therapist."

Sight, smell, sound, touch, and maybe even taste. All five senses from one hair-and-hoof-wrapped package.

"So," Rollie said, "when are you coming out to visit us?"

Libby searched for reasons why she shouldn't visit the facility. She found none. "I suppose I could, but wouldn't it be pointless? There's nothing I could do. . . ."

"Ha!" Rollie roared so loudly that the people at the tables

around them stared. "Don't you see what I'm getting at? Keeping someone who has no muscle control or has rigidity or balance problems on a horse *requires* a group of people. We call them 'walkers' or 'sidewalkers.' That pretty much explains it—people on the ground who lead the horse, walk at both sides of the rider, and bring up the rear to make sure each ride is safe and successful."

"Don't you need special training for that?"

"We'll teach you everything you need to know. We've got a lot of new clients and are sadly short of walkers. When can you start?"

"But I haven't even seen how it works!"

"Then come to the ranch on Sunday afternoon. We're having a picnic. It's an opportunity for clients to get to know each other and the people who work there and vice versa. We try to create a happy, family-like atmosphere. Of course, that isn't hard with horses."

"I suppose it couldn't hurt. . . ." The man was head over heels in love with his work, with his clients, and probably most of all, with the horses. Libby felt a little as though she'd been rolled over by a piece of paving equipment.

Rollie whipped a card out of his pocket. "Noon on Sunday. I'll be watching for you. Now I'd better get back to the store and give my employee his lunch break."

What's this all about, God?

Libby believed that everything in life happened for a purpose—that God was in the small things in her life as well as the big ones.

And when did God get so interested in horses?

"You're going to do *what?*" Tia lounged on Libby's couch, feet up in the air, a box of chocolates resting on her stomach. "And *why?*"

"Rollie was so enthusiastic that I couldn't resist. Besides, it's not like I signed my life away. I'm just going out there to look around. It might be fun."

"It might be smelly," Tia observed. "Whew! Like a barn."

"I *liked* the smell of Reese's horses when he brought them for your birthday. They smelled earthy and sweet—like fresh air and hay."

"The earth mother has really done it this time," Tia moaned to Jenny, who sat nearby paging through a photo album. "This is as earthy as it's going to get. Tell me, Libby, who cleans up the droppings horses leave? The newest volunteer, I presume."

"You can't talk me out of it." Tia's response made Libby even more determined to go to the ranch. It *couldn't* be as bad as Tia wanted her to think. "You can go with me."

"Oh, no. Not me. I have something important to do tomorrow. Nap . . . no, a crossword puzzle. And I have to floss my teeth and clean my toilets. I have enough fun planned for one day!"

"I'd go with you, Libby, but we're invited to Dorothy's for lunch. Maybe another time?"

"Don't humor her, Jenny. She might get some weird idea in her head to become a cowgirl." Tia began humming the theme song from *Rawhide*.

"I'm glad she's found something that interests her. Leave her alone. Besides," Jenny added, "you like animals. You only *talk* like you don't."

Tia harrumphed and put a pillow over her face. A muffled voice wafted out from beneath it. "Don't say I didn't warn you. When a horse steps on your toe or bites your arm or drools on your shoes, it's not my fault."

"Shoes!" Libby straightened in the easy chair in which she'd been slouching. "I'd better make sure I have boots. And jeans. I wonder if a sweatshirt would be OK. . . ."

"I can hardly wait to see your fashion statement, Libby." Tia held out the box of candy she'd been hoarding. "Have a choco-late?"

．．．

Sunday morning Libby hurried home from church and donned the clothing she'd laid out the night before. Then she downed a glass of milk to settle her nervous stomach and went to her car, eager to get going before she chickened out.

The Reach Out Ranch was on the western edge of the city, where many hobby farmers and horse owners were located. She got lost twice before finding the sign that pointed her toward the ranch.

Rollie practically fell on her as she climbed out of her car. "You came! All righty, then! We've already started dishing up so get in line." He took her by the hand and led her into the throng, introducing her to everyone they passed.

By the time she got to the front of the line, Libby's head was swimming with names and faces. Even more indelibly printed on her mind, however, were the handicaps with which these people lived. The littlest people seemed lost in their wheelchairs, surrounded by metal. One girl kept her head down, her eyes on the ground, the entire time Libby observed her.

"She's mute," Rollie whispered in Libby's ear. "Traumatized by abuse. Her name is Jessica." He pointed to a teenager wearing Western garb and a protective helmet. "That's Joel. He didn't talk when he came here either. Now we can't get him to shut up! There are a hundred stories here."

Rollie gave Libby an encouraging shove. "Dish up. There's plenty. We'll sit at the far table."

"Hiya, Rollie! Who's this?"

Libby looked up from her potato salad to see a man in his late twenties or early thirties beaming down at her. It was immediately apparent that he had Down's syndrome.

"Frankie, this is our newest helper. Her name is Libby."

"But I'm not . . ." Libby's voice trailed off. A protest wasn't going to quench Rollie's ebullient attitude.

"Frankie started out here a few years back as a client," Rollie continued. "He's done so well that now he's one of our walkers. He's here every day, aren't you, Frankie?"

The man nodded with obvious satisfaction. "'Cause I can tell the little kids not to be scared."

"Were you scared once, Frankie?" Libby asked.

He nodded so hard she thought his head might snap off. "I thought my horse would run away and I'd fall off." He grinned. "So I held my breath and grabbed the reins so hard that my knuckles turned white."

"And now he's our right-hand man." Rollie clapped Frankie on the back, "Now he's learning to ride English and to jump horses."

Libby was impressed. What a wonderful program this must be to give this young man such a sense of purpose and meaning for his life.

"What are you doing, Frankie?" Rollie inquired as Frankie pulled away.

"Trying to get the new ones to eat. Gotta go. Bye." And he strode off like a man on a mission.

"Some of our newest clients have poor appetites," Rollie said by way of explanation as they sat down. "They need better nutrition than they're getting, so Frankie has decided that, until they've been riding awhile, it's his job to see that they eat."

"What does riding have to do with appetite?"

"See those kids over there?"

Libby looked to a table of children who were wolfing down their food and asking for more.

"Those kids have been with us awhile. We began to get reports from their families of how much better they're eating since they've been coming to our ranch. Makes sense, of course, because riding stimulates the appetite and the digestive tract. These kids began to enjoy their food more, fill out, and have more color in their cheeks. Soon they are more robust in every way."

"Amazing!" Libby felt her enthusiasm grow. How appropriate that one of God's creatures, the horse, could be used to heal another of God's own. "I had no idea. . . ."

"Of course you didn't. That's why you had to come out here to see for yourself." Rollie wore a triumphant, I-told-you-so expression.

"I only see a few adult riders here."

"We have several in the program but the picnics draw primarily children and their families. Occasionally adults resent being here." Rollie chuckled. "But we ride that out of them sooner or later."

Libby pushed her plate away. "Would you mind if I wandered around?"

"Go ahead. When you're done, come to the arena to see one of our riders in action."

Libby walked across the immaculate lawn to the barns. A gentle breeze ruffled her hair; the sun warmed her shoulders and relaxed her limbs. The air smelled of freshly cut grass. She'd never been in a place so serene and restful.

The inside of one of the barns was as immaculate as the outside. Box stalls lined each side of the wide walkway. The tack room—equipped with saddles, bridles, bits, and blankets—was pristine. A grizzled horse stuck her nose out of the stall and whinnied welcomely at Libby.

"Hi, old girl. Aren't you sweet?" Libby touched the horse's forelock. When the horse didn't back away, Libby extended the back of her hand palm down for the horse to smell. When its nose brushed Libby's wrist, she succumbed to the temptation to rub a finger across the horse's nose.

It felt like warm velvet. Libby had the urge to plant a big kiss on that soft nose and might have done so, if she hadn't heard someone enter the barn.

She turned slowly, so as not to startle the horse, and her jaw dropped in shock and amazement. "Reese?"

He looked up as surprised as she. "What are you doing here?" he growled, the least welcoming person she'd met in this adventurous foray of hers.

"Rollie invited me. What are *you* doing here?"

"Bill and Annie. Who else? They found out that my doctor suggested this program to see if there were any way for me to get on a horse again. As if that were possible." The scorn in his voice was heavy.

"It could help, couldn't it? It has helped others."

"Get real, Libby. Getting me on one of these animals is a major production. Staying there is another."

"How . . . ?"

"I've always had slight feeling in my legs. Since that has increased in the past few months, my family got excited, thinking this program might help me." He plowed his fingers through his hair in frustration. "Riding a horse is something I've done all my life, and now . . ."

Libby tried to imagine how it might be not to jog or play tennis whenever she wished, how difficult it would be to do nothing more than crawl when she'd known how to soar. Her heart ached for him. It was no wonder that Reese Reynolds was the most gruff, unsociable, bad-tempered, and bitter man she'd ever met.

But it doesn't have to be that way. God can sweeten even the harshest situations if he is given a chance. Unfortunately, Reese doesn't appear to be giving God any chances.

"Maybe if . . ."

"No ifs or maybes. I'm here because the doctor and my brother forced me into it. I'll come for the prescribed time just to get them off my back. Then they'll know for sure that it won't work and leave me alone."

"Good attitude. Very enthusiastic and positive. Glad to hear you're open to possibilities and change. Your optimism should make a real difference."

"No sarcasm, Libby. You don't understand. You aren't trapped in one of these." He took a swipe at his chair.

"No, but I do know that even if you are stuck in that chair forever, your life will be much smoother and more joyful if you can heal your attitude. That wasn't irreparably damaged." Whatever button Reese pushed in Libby, she always found herself being uncharacteristically blunt.

"Are you on a mission from God to save poor, crippled Reese from himself? If that's what you're thinking, forget it. I'm not interested and I'm not savable either. So get that out of your pretty little head and leave me alone."

As he turned to leave, Libby stepped in front of his chair. "Wait just a minute, buddy." She couldn't believe she was hearing herself *say* these things. "Quit deciding for me what I'm thinking. Go ahead and plan your pity party. Just don't expect me to turn tail and run. Rollie says miracles happen here and I believe him."

Then she amazed herself by adding, "I'm going to volunteer out here no matter how stupid or useless you think this is. It is neither stupid nor useless. But you have to give it a chance." She looked him over from head to toe. "I didn't realize you were inclined to sit around and pout."

Her face was beet red and she was breathless when she finished. She started to close her eyes, raise her hands, and deflect the blow she was sure Reese wanted to send her way. Instead, she heard him chuckle.

Opening one eye, Libby saw him looking at her with something akin to admiration.

"Spunky little meddler, aren't you?"

"You aren't mad?"

"I'm furious. That doesn't mean I can't appreciate feistiness in someone. I knew you were a busybody, but even I didn't expect this!"

"I'm sorry. You just make me so angry. . . ."

"Forget it. You didn't tell me anything that I haven't already heard from my brother or sister-in-law."

"Then why don't you *listen?* Surely you aren't totally thick-headed. . . ." She blushed. "I didn't mean that. It sounded so rude. Well, I *did* mean it but not quite that way . . . oh . . ."

Libby sat down on a hay bale and put her head in her hands. "You bring out the worst in me!"

"And you in me. We're a matched set."

"Then you will continue to come here and try to put some heart into it?"

"I didn't say that."

"If you are going to be here anyway, at least *try!* Think of it as an experiment. Give it a chance. If it doesn't work, what have you lost? Nothing. And if it does . . ."

"Don't turn Pollyannaish on me."

"Then don't come on like Scrooge to me!"

Reese sighed. "OK. I know enough not to butt heads with a battering ram. Truce?"

Libby smiled and reached out to shake his hand. "Truce."

Now all she had to do was figure out how to tell Jenny and Tia what she'd gotten herself into.

CHAPTER TEN

*Few Civil War quilts survived the ravages of war, yet we remember
and use patterns of that era. This is proof that beauty
can persevere through darkness.*

"You did *what?*" Tia, sleek, glossy, the perfect businesswoman,
was seated behind her desk, aghast. Jenny, the exact opposite, in
dusty jeans and a cotton shirt, straight from her garden, also
appeared astounded at Libby's announcement.

"You mean you actually *want* to spend your free time at this
ranch?" It was more than Tia could fathom.

"I really do." Libby marveled at it herself. She'd carefully omit-
ted Reese from her explanation, however. There was nothing to
tell; but Tia, ear to the ground for the sound of approaching
men, would worry that subject to the bone. Libby didn't care to
explain the disagreement she'd had with Reese or their wary
truce. She needed to sort that out in her own mind before Tia
got wind of it.

"It's really wonderful clean air and sunshine. The clients are
eager to come and reluctant to leave. Everyone has a good time.
What could be better?"

"I'm sure it's great," Jenny said supportively. "Maybe we can come out and see it sometime. I'll bet my guys would enjoy it, too."

"Speak for yourself." Tia punched a pen into a cup full of them and pushed her chair away from the desk. "Bugs, sunburn, odors, wild animals. Yuck."

"Those horses aren't wild. They are the gentlest creatures I've ever seen. They know instinctively how fragile and precious their riders are."

"Whatever." Tia waved a hand in dismissal, her mind already spinning onto a new track. "How about going to that new Chinese place for dinner?"

Over hot-and-sour soup, vegetable lo mein, baby shrimp with cashews, General Tso's chicken, and sweet-and-sour pork, Libby couldn't contain herself. "There are horses of all sizes—wide and thin, short and tall. . . ."

Tia rolled her eyes.

Jenny, however, was genuinely interested. "How do they choose these horses?"

Libby was itching to answer. It was something she'd learned only this week. "Some are gifts to the ranch; Rollie buys others. He's very fussy. He likes a horse to be—"

"How long do they live, anyway?" Tia popped a bit of pork in her mouth and dabbed at her lips with her napkin.

"They can live twenty-five years or more. An older horse is more mature and calmer than a young one. Not so much surprises them anymore."

"Hmmmm. Just like us."

"He wants them healthy and tolerant and to have a personality that mixes well with people."

"Not bad characteristics for human friends either. Where does he find these guys?"

Libby ignored Tia and continued. "He looks for animals who have been in the showring—horses that 4-H kids have raised, like Luke's horse Sunshine, or that have been in a horse club—reliable horses. Rollie doesn't want horses with bad habits that need to be retrained. Their riders are fragile packages."

Libby leaned over her plate, and Jenny whisked Libby's sleeve out of the sweet-and-sour sauce. "Rollie likes foundation quarter horses because they are steady and dependable, but there are some beautiful Arabs and Thoroughbreds that have performed very well for the ranch, too.

"Horse people have distinct preferences for certain breeds, and no one will ever convince them that the breed they like isn't the very best in the world."

"She's already beginning to sound like she owns the place," Tia muttered.

"Volunteers ride the horses to get them accustomed to ramps, wheelchairs, walkers, and canes before the clients even see the animals." Everything about the ranch was a thrill to Libby.

When the waiter brought their bill and a pile of fortune cookies to the table, Tia made a lunge for the plate. "I'm buying. And everyone has to read their fortune cookie out loud. Jenny, you first."

Obediently she cracked the cookie and pulled out the tiny white slip of paper. "'It is wise to prepare for the unexpected.' No kidding! My life is the perfect example of that."

"Do you still feel the need to be prepared for the unexpected, Jenny, now that Mike and Luke are in your life?" Libby asked.

"Yes and no. I'm fully aware that life is unpredictable. Yet I am more confident than ever that whatever happens, God knows all and is in the midst of my life. As long as I remember, no matter *what* is going on, to ask myself the question, 'Where is God in this?' I'm OK. Once I start to look around in times of trouble I always discover that he is there—somewhere, someway, somehow. If I find what I'm supposed to learn from life's current lesson and acknowledge that God is trying to teach me something in the middle of the uproar, I'm at peace."

Tia tore at the wrapper on her cookie. "Now me. 'Be your own boss. Resist the temptation to follow the leader.'"

"You do that already," Libby said dryly. "Have you read that cookie before?"

"I guess I'm as wise as a sage Chinese scholar."

"It only means," Libby said, "that you are as wise as whoever writes these dumb fortunes."

"Party pooper," Tia said with a grin. "Now read yours."

Libby unfolded her slip of paper slowly. As she read it, one eyebrow quirked upward and an amused smile lit her face. "Well, at least it's good news. 'You will have exciting news to share with your friends.'"

"Hmmm, a new boyfriend, I'll bet."

"I'm not so sure Libby would think that was great news, Tia."

"Actually, getting my car loan paid off sounds like great news to me."

"Plebeian," Tia accused. "You two are so boring. Why do I have to provide all the stimulation for this group?"

"Because you are all the stimulation we can stand," Jenny said. "Let's go. If we hurry, we can catch a movie."

Their fanciful fortunes were immediately forgotten.

....

Libby hadn't seen Reese for two weeks. She'd almost forgotten that he even came to Reach Out Ranch. She was involved with too many others to spend time dwelling on him. Most of her waking and sleeping hours were occupied by one of the children who came to the ranch.

Robert was a shy, silent child who avoided eye contact at all costs. He'd been removed from his abusive home and put into foster care. Fortunately for him, his foster parents were familiar with the ranch and had enrolled him immediately. Although he had ridden for several sessions, Robert had never uttered a word.

Heartbreaking was the only word Libby could use to describe him. He was a beautiful child with haunting eyes shadowed too deeply. His black eyelashes matched thick soft hair that crowned at the top of his head in a cowlick whorl. His porcelain skin proved without a doubt that Robert had not had enough sun for a very long time.

Because Libby was so sensitive, it seemed perfectly natural that Robert had become her pet project.

"How is it going for you two?" Rollie's voice boomed from the door of the tack room, where Libby was attempting to teach Robert the basics of cleaning a saddle. It was a little like the blind leading the blind, considering that she had just learned the basics herself the week before.

"Robert had a great ride today," Libby said with pride. "Now we're working on tack. Tell Rollie what you did today, Robert."

She continued the conversation as if the child had actually spoken. "Now he knows where his bit and bridle are stored. Pretty soon he'll be tacking up by himself!"

Rollie reached out to stop another volunteer as she walked by. "Would you finish up with Robert? I'd like to talk to Libby for a minute."

Libby ruffled Robert's hair affectionately before following Rollie to the other end of the barn.

"Is something wrong?"

"No. And yes." A somber expression marred Rollie's usually jolly features. "I've got someone in the program who is a real challenge—and it takes some work to be considered a challenge around here since many of our clients can't walk, speak, or hear. But they usually have their attitudes going for them. I'm worried about this one."

"I wish I could help, but—"

"You'd help?" Rollie clapped her on the back, and Libby realized that this had been his intention all along. "I was hoping you'd say that! You have a way with people. We have loving, generous volunteers, but there is something about you that is, well, special." He studied her as if attempting to puzzle out what this mysterious something was. "You glow sometimes, like you are lit by an inner light. There is a tranquil expression in your eyes that I envy. And you never get upset or angry. Whatever it is you've got, Libby, we should all have it."

God.

"This client is out back looking at his horse. He comes here madder than hops and leaves that way, too. I thought maybe . . . if you would . . . could you take him on for me, Libby? He needs Reach Out Ranch more than any other person I've ever seen— and resists it more, too."

"I don't know how I could help if others have tried and failed. I'm much less experienced."

"It has to do with that inner glow of yours. You calm people down. I can't tell you why, but you do. Will you give it a try? A month or two. OK?"

"A *month?* That's a long time if things aren't going well."

"We'll break through to him." Rollie patted her arm. "Thanks, Libby, I owe you one. Just so you know, this client hasn't been on a horse yet but I'm bringing him up next."

"I'll be there," Libby said with more confidence than she felt.

Rollie walked away, and Libby turned to stare out the open barn door. She took a deep breath and steeled herself. Look how far even Robert had come, she told herself. There couldn't be a case much harder than his.

But when she walked out of the barn and into the sunshine, she knew she'd been wrong.

Reese scowled at her. It was obvious that he was thinking the same about her.

Rollie, you can't do this to me! I could handle a child, but not him!

But Rollie had extracted a promise from her to give her best effort for a client. Even if it killed her. And by the look of Reese's glowering features, it very well might.

"Hello, Reese." Her mouth was dry and her tongue thick. It was all she could do to get the words out. Her instinct was to close her eyes and cover her head.

"What the . . . what are *you* doing here?" If he'd been miserable before, now he was both miserable and annoyed.

She could hardly blame him. She was feeling fairly wretched herself. She was totally out of her element on this one.

"Rollie asked me to help with a special client," she said honestly. "I assumed he meant a child, someone even more inexperienced than I. I never imagined it would be you."

"Did Bill and Annie *plan* this?"

"I doubt it. Rollie shoots straight from the hip. He wouldn't get involved in subterfuge. And if he did, he would have told me. This is just a coincidence."

Or a God-incidence.

But what could she do for Reese? His family and doctors couldn't help him. She didn't hold out even a flicker of optimism. Still, she'd promised Rollie she'd take on his special project, and she prided herself on always carrying out her promises.

"Don't worry. You'll like the program. You'll never be alone with me when you are riding. One of the trainers is in charge. The rest of us walk along, making sure you're safe."

She knew it was a poor choice of words as it left her lips.

"It would be terrible if I got hurt, wouldn't it? Maybe I wouldn't be able to walk anymore. Or maybe I'd just fall down and die. That might be the best solution for all of us." He challenged her with his glare.

"Oh, snap out of it, will you?" Libby wondered if any of the glow Rollie had mentioned was shining through now. But it was no use pussyfooting around Reese. He saw right through that. "Your mount is ready."

He gave her a withering look. "And just how do you propose that I get on?"

"I'm sure Rollie has something worked out. Would you like me to push your chair or would you rather do it yourself?"

He nearly ran over her toes as he spun by.

When she caught up, Reese was staring in pure horror at what was before him.

A black-and-white quarter horse, with patient and long-suffering brown eyes, stood beside a mounting ramp. On her back was a saddle obviously designed for riders who were unable to straddle a horse.

"No way. Uh-uh. There is no way you're going to get me to sit on that horse like that. I refuse to ride sidesaddle!"

Because you think that's for ladies and sissies, Libby thought darkly.

Rollie held a riding helmet out to Reese. "If it goes all right today and if we are sure we can help you into a Western saddle, we will. But in order to do that, we have to start with this."

"Forget it."

"No helmet, no horse. Safety reasons. Here, put it on."

Libby ached for Reese. She couldn't imagine the humiliation and frustration he was experiencing. A man who once lived on a horse, reduced to this.

She couldn't allow her sympathy to interfere with the business at hand, however. She leaned over and whispered in Reese's ear, "I'll bet you are scared to do it."

That was the red flag she'd been seeking. She'd just made the bull furious.

He slapped the helmet on his head and slipped the straps into place. "Then let's get it over with."

Rollie gave her a thumbs-up as they maneuvered Reese onto the horse. It wasn't as difficult as she feared. The staff had had years of experience and Reese had excellent upper-body strength, making the job much easier.

A trainer moved to the front of the horse, and walkers flanked him to help Reese keep his balance.

As Libby took her position at Reese's side, what she noticed wrenched at her. His hands were trembling as he took the reins in one hand and the saddle horn in the other. The horse started smoothly at a signal to make a trip around the arena. As the horse took her first steps, Reese began to sway in the saddle. He caught his balance by clutching at the horn.

It had been a long time since he'd felt a horse step out beneath him.

As they walked, Libby attuned herself to Reese, trying, as she always did, to be mentally one step ahead of the horse and rider in case something were to go wrong. But there was little chance of that.

The longer he rode, the more relaxed Reese became. Even in this condition it was obvious that he'd been a skilled horseman. Somehow he and the horse—Smokey—had joined in spirit. Reese seemed to be reading Smokey's mind—and vice versa.

When they stopped, a new man came down from that horse. The frown lines and those etched by pain had vanished. His eyes gleamed with a gentle affection for Smokey.

"Good girl. Nice girl. You did a good job." Reese stroked the horse from his chair, thanking her for what she'd done. Smokey nickered a reply.

When the others moved away, Libby put her hands on the grips of his chair. "Want to go for a walk?"

This time he allowed her to push him. They moved through the yards, around the barns, paddocks, and round pen and finally stopped at the fence bordering a small pasture where several horses grazed.

"You did very well."

Reese bobbed his head. "I should have. Been riding since I was three. Didn't have much more control than I do now."

"How did it feel?"

"Great. Like I was flying. I'd forgotten how good it felt. And I didn't realize how much I've hated looking at everyone and

seeing them at chest height. I'm tired of buttons. I've been cran-
ing my head to look at people ever since I got into this chair.
Today I was higher than everyone else."

Libby squatted on her haunches in front of him to look at him
eye to eye. "I didn't realize. . . ."

"It's something you have to experience to know."

"Will you do it again?"

"Do I have to ride sidesaddle?"

"Maybe for a while. It depends on how you progress."

He didn't like the answer but he didn't argue. "I'll even wear
that danged plastic hat to get another chance at the horse."

Libby saw in his expression some of the former man. She
hoped against hope that Reese could experience that kind of joy
in other parts of his life.

....

"What do you suppose Tia is up to now?" Libby and Jenny were
driving toward Tia's after being summoned there like serfs to a
queen.

"She said she needs us to help her make some decisions,"
Jenny said.

"That's new. Tia usually decides everything for herself—and
for us, too, if we let her."

Tia lived in a town home not far from her store. The house was
dramatic—like Tia herself.

She met them at the front door with her garage-door opener in
hand. "You've got to see this." She pressed a button and the door
rolled upward. The garage was filled with empty tables.

"Very nice," Libby said. "You're going to serve a sit-down
dinner for thirty in your garage. Why didn't I think of that?"

"Don't be ridiculous."

"Then what?" Jenny asked.

"Come into my kitchen and I'll show you."

Tia's white kitchen with dramatic black accents looked as though it had experienced an explosion. Every cupboard was open. Pots and pans, mixing bowls and appliances, dishes, flatware, and every kind of kitchen gadget ever created were sitting in the middle of the floor.

Tia held up a garlic press. "Do you think I need this?"

"Do you ever cook with garlic?"

"I don't even *like* garlic."

"Then the answer is no."

"So I don't suppose I need a clay garlic baker either?"

"Not unless your taste buds change."

"How about this?" Tia held up a corkscrew.

"Have you ever used it?"

"No." Tia threw it in the box with the garlic press.

"And this! Isn't it cute? A mini deep-fat fryer. Look how compact it is."

"Do you deep fry food?"

"Too many fats and calories." Tia sighed and relegated the fryer to the box.

"This is wonderful fun," Jenny said, "but it would be even more enjoyable if we knew what we were doing."

"I'm getting ready for a rummage sale. I decided yesterday that my cupboards are full and I'm never home to cook. In that box over there—" she pointed to a pyramid of boxes stacked against a wall—"I have a yogurt maker, a malt mixer, a dehydrator, a juicer, and some little sandwich-making thingy that I never figured out how to work."

"But what are we here for?"

"To help me decide what to get rid of, of course! No one knows me better than you two. Besides, you can both cook and I can't. You can tell me what I really need if I get hungry."

"A bowl, a spoon, a box of cereal, a toaster, and a loaf of bread. That should do it."

"Don't be sarcastic, Libby. You're too sweet for that." Tia ran her fingers through her hair until it stood straight up in black bunches. Her eyes brightened. "I already have something done. I made signs. Do you want to see them?"

Jenny, who'd already started dividing the wheat from the chaff in Tia's kitchen, looked up. "Sure."

Tia reached behind the table and pulled out large sheets of cardboard. "Ta-daa . . ."

Libby and Jenny burst out laughing.

In large stenciled letters and embellished with stick-on flowers were the words:

> The I'm-Not-Martha Stewart-Sale
> Saturday Noon Till Six
> 400 Oak Terrace
> Be There Or Be Square

"Do you think it will catch anyone's eye?"

"Just anyone who reads it."

"Good. Now help me finish sorting in the kitchen so we can go through my closets next."

At supper time Jenny ordered pizzas and had one delivered to Tia's and another to Mike and Luke. The threesome sat in a circle on the floor and devoured a large sausage and mushroom before speaking.

Libby waited until they were done eating to drop her bombshell. She picked at the mozzarella on the cardboard circle inside the pizza box and said casually, "I'm going to help Reese Reynolds learn to ride again."

Jenny looked puzzled, as if she didn't comprehend what Libby was saying. Tia, however, responded immediately.

"Are you *nuts?*"

"Not that I know of."

"*You* don't even ride! How do you plan to get a two-hundred pound paraplegic on a horse?"

"I'm not doing it alone. It's my assignment from the director of Reach Out Ranch."

"Mission impossible, if you ask me."

"Don't be too sure of that. The people there are accustomed to clients who can't ride horses in traditional ways. Some ride side-saddle or facing backward. I saw a child riding while laying down on the horse's back because his physical condition didn't permit him to do it in a more traditional way. There's both a mystery and a miracle in the experiences people have with the horses."

Tia rolled her eyes. "A mystery, a miracle, and a mess, if you ask me. What else happens up there, high tea?"

"We played catch and a couple of relay games today."

"Anyone hit a home run or make a field goal?"

Libby smiled patiently. "Oh, ye of little faith! Those activities help to improve balance."

"And hand-eye coordination, I would imagine," Jenny added.

"Exactly. The clients are in intense therapy while they are riding, but they're having so much fun that they don't even real-ize that their limbs are being stretched and exercised or that they are doing things they would never attempt in a hospital setting. They think all they're doing is having fun.

"Even the therapists at Reach Out Ranch have a great time. It doesn't seem like work to any of them and yet they are reaping astounding results."

"You sound like a smoker who's seen the light and had her last puff," Tia grumbled. "A born-again horse person."

"Hardly," Libby said mildly, "but I am thrilled that something so simple and straightforward could do so much in a person's life.

"Imagine if you felt, for the very first time, that you had some control over your life! Wouldn't your self-confidence soar? And, in a life of doctors, hospitals, and surgeries, you found some fun? If, for perhaps the first time in your life you felt normal?"

"And that's how Reese is feeling now?" Tia still sounded doubtful.

"He's had a taste of it, I think. He once lived, breathed, and slept horses. He misses them more than any of us can imagine. It has to feel good to be around them—and on them—again."

Libby recalled the excitement and satisfaction she'd experienced at the ranch. "I want to devote a portion of my life to this, to helping people who'd given up ever being helped."

"But how?" Jenny rolled a soda can between the palms of her hands and frowned.

Libby rubbed her hands on her knees. "I've been thinking of approaching Rollie about having a fund-raiser for the ranch, something to get the word out about this therapy and raise some money besides. Imagine how wonderful it would be to provide scholarships or reduced cost to the people who need it most. Helping the helpless, loving the unlovely, serving others—isn't that what God wants us to do?"

"You've got that right."

"I feel so fortunate to have come upon this opportunity to serve others. These people need me." Tears gleamed in Libby's eyes. "When my parents were at home they needed me, but no more than I needed them. They were my opportunity at servanthood, at honoring family. But I held on to them too long. God helped me get them to the place they needed to be just in time. They're happy and busy and as healthy as can be expected.

"And now I think I've found a way to serve again." Libby beamed at her friends.

"We didn't realize. . . ."

"How could you, Jenny? Our lives are a journey we each have to travel alone. Fortunately, we have a traveling companion to read the map."

"So are you going to do this full-time or what?" Tia was ever practical.

"I'd like to but I've got two jobs to attend to and I have to start taking better care of myself. That means daily jogging and working out. It means more time set aside for Bible study and prayer. And it means releasing some of my creative side by making quilts. It's relaxing for me. . . ." Libby was quiet for a moment, then the proverbial lightbulb seemed to switch on in her head. "That's it! I could make quilts for the ranch! They could be sold or raffled or given to donors who contribute significant amounts of money! We could have the Boots-and-Spurs-level contributors and Bits-and-Bridles. . . ."

"And the Saddle Club for the big-time donors. They should be the ones who get your quilts, Libby." Tia was immediately enthusiastic. "They are truly pieces of art. I could do a display for you in the window of the store explaining the program and letting people know how they can get involved. We could put a rainbow of quilts out for everyone to see. Why, you'd probably have donors coming out of your ears!"

"Once you come around to an idea, you come all the way, don't you, Tia?"

"Sure, sure." Tia dismissed Libby's observation. "If you have quilts to me by the middle of next month and information about the ranch, I'll pull it together. You can direct, of course. Something in a Western motif maybe." She tapped her chin for a moment. "We'll take pictures of the clients and blow them up to show them riding. They should be laughing. Will it be hard to get photos of them laughing?"

"You'd have more trouble finding someone frowning."

It wasn't until later that another thought occurred to Libby. *We'll have to avoid Reese if we want only happy pictures.*

The following Saturday as Libby was working with a group of children, she had a brainstorm concerning Reese and his surliness around the ranch.

As he propelled his wheelchair in her direction, his sour expression marred his classic features and good looks.

"You're finally here!" she greeted him. Her heart was in her throat, but she forged ahead anyway. "We've been waiting. I have a job for you."

Both Reese and the children looked surprised but Libby soldiered on. "We are learning the parts of a horse. They've got the head and tail down pat, but there are a few things in between that they still need to learn. I'm almost as green at this as they are so we need an experienced horseman like you to teach them."

"Wha . . ." He scowled. "I haven't got all day."

But he *did* have all day and Libby knew it. And she knew *he* knew it, too. Libby blundered on. "Tell them about this!" She randomly stuck out her hand and pointed at a spot on the long-forbearing horse.

"That's his mane, Libby."

The children giggled but she persisted. "And this?"

"His withers."

"This?"

"Throatlatch. Coronet. Fetlock. Pastern. Tail," Reese spit out. But his annoyance evaporated slightly, and by the time Libby was pointing to the cannon on the horse's hind leg, he was overtly amused.

The children caught the spirit of the game, giggled at the strange labels, and nearly doubled over when they realized how many body parts they shared with the horse.

"Knee. Thigh. Buttocks. Shoulder. Forehead. Eye. Nostril." As Libby's hand moved over the creature, Reese shared from his treasure trove of information.

CHAPTER ELEVEN

Native Americans are generous givers of gifts.
One of the most popular gifts given at powwows or
baby-naming ceremonies is the quilt.

Rollie was at the door of Libby's car as soon as she drove into the yard, his grin as wide as a slice of watermelon on the Fourth of July. "I'm not sure you have time to be here. You should be home making quilts."

"*More donors?* Rollie, I'm going to need some help. I can't sew a quilt overnight, you know. Especially when each one is so personalized." Libby had been appliquéing her own special designs on the quilts. It had been a big success—so much so that she was falling behind.

"Not yet, but there's going to be!"

"What idea are you hatching under that hat now?" Libby marveled at the man's creativity and enthusiasm—and hoped she could be so productive at his age.

"A loudspeaker system!"

"What on earth for?"

"One of the therapists suggested it. She thought that some

music in the arena might be beneficial. Horse therapy and music therapy all rolled into one!"

"It's a good idea, Rollie, but how much will it cost?"

"Just two or three quilts to two or three generous donors. And then a few more for the people who want to buy a carriage. We've been getting calls from families of children who have too many physical disabilities to ride a horse. They've heard about the good things going on at the ranch and want to know what we offer them."

"And carriages are the answer?"

"If you can't ride a horse, clients would still get great benefit from driving one. We'll have to design something adapted to our special-needs children. It shouldn't be too hard." Rollie took off his cowboy hat and scratched his balding head.

"Maybe I'll ask Reese to draw something up. He's had enough experience with horses to have an answer for me."

Rollie paused to study Libby, who, hair shining in the sun, bronzed skin gleaming, and strong, supple body relaxed in the warmth of the day, looked incredibly healthy and happy. "I have to thank you. You got Reese to help the little ones. Now he's been one of our best volunteers. And he's popular. The kids are fascinated by all he knows about horses. It's been good for everyone."

"I'm glad," Libby said simply. She seldom saw Reese. He came in early most days, while Libby seldom arrived until late afternoon. She always knew he'd been there, however. By comical drawings of cartoon horses on the chalkboard inside the barn. He used them to illustrate points he was making for the children. Today she'd noticed a drawing of two horses standing on their hind feet doing the two-step. She had no idea what Reese was trying to get across with that one.

"He's riding more himself, too." Rollie tried not to look proud and failed miserably. "His doctor says he's regained most of his preaccident strength, and Reese admitted to me that he's had increased sensation in his legs lately."

"Really?" As much as Libby believed in the program, she was still surprised.

"His brother told me that they'd expected he'd eventually regain feeling, and they are pleased that it's finally happening."

"So his spinal cord wasn't severed by the gunshot?"

"Apparently not. We can't heal him but we *can* help him, Libby. I just know it."

"You have already. He's a different person than when I first met him."

She watched Reese from a distance whenever she could. He had charm enough to fill a water tank to overflowing and a smile bright enough to light a room when he was talking to the children. The transformation was amazing. Unfortunately, it hadn't carried over to the adults in his life. He was still cautious, wary of letting down his guard and having someone pity him. Reese didn't want pity, and he didn't get it from the kids. He was safe with them.

For a while she'd hoped that they could develop a real friendship but they were still just guarded acquaintances. Even the horses couldn't change that.

"Reese and Bill are giving the ranch some horses," Rollie continued. "Every one handpicked and trained. They are giving us the smartest and the calmest of the lot."

"How nice." Libby felt strangely empty as she walked away after the conversation. Reese was making great strides. It would have been nice had he mentioned the horses to her. . . .

As if there is any reason to tell me about his gifts to the ranch!

Her emptiness didn't last long, however, for she saw Robert wheeling his way across the drive toward her, his smile so big and wide it nearly split his face in two.

"Hi, buddy. How's it going?"

"Good. I get to start coming twice a week!" His small, pinched face beamed. Not once had Libby heard the child complain about anything. Since he'd begun involving himself and making the effort to speak, he'd found his whole world fascinating. How a small, parentless boy in a wheelchair could view life as such an adventure, Libby couldn't imagine.

"Good deal. Who arranged that?"

"My foster mother and my therapist decided I was pro . . . progres . . . progressing and that I should ride more often." His brown eyes lit with delight. "Will you push me over to see the new colt?"

Libby willingly obliged. While Robert kept up a running commentary about the other children in his foster home, a bug he'd seen squashed on the grill of Rollie's car, and his new summer clothes, Libby's mind took its own path.

She'd learned as much as she could about this child. Born with a birth defect that left him unable to walk, Robert had been given up for adoption by his birth parents—young, unmarried students who had no means or desire to struggle with such a burden. Considered "undesirable" because of his handicap, Robert had grown up in a series of foster homes, sometimes enduring terrible abuse. The last two years, however, he had been placed with a loving and dedicated family who had taken the initiative to find this hippotherapy program and make sure he was able to attend.

"It was my birthday yesterday, Libby," Robert confided. "Did you know that?"

"No, honey, I didn't. How old are you?"

"Nine."

"Did you have a party?"

Robert shrugged thin shoulders. "Sort of."

"How do you sort of have a party?" Libby stopped by the fence and gazed in at the gangly little filly sticking close to its mother.

"No one was home but Nana and me." *Nana* was what Robert called his foster mother. "So we made our own party. Nana blew up balloons and played the birthday song."

He grinned. "I sang 'Happy Birthday' to *me!*"

Something inside Libby's heart twisted. A little boy content singing happy birthday to himself . . .

"Nana gave me new shoes. See?" Robert pointed at his feet.

"Did you get any other presents?" Libby asked.

"No." A small cloud flickered across his features but he brightened. "But I *really* like my shoes!"

Libby felt a lump gathering at the back of her throat. She'd felt sorry for herself when her parents moved into Fraiser Towers! She'd felt abandoned. How weak she was compared to this child who, without a living relative to remember his birthday, could be so overjoyed by a pair of shoes!

"What's wrong?" Libby blinked and found Robert staring worriedly into her face. "Are you crying?"

Perhaps she was—crying inside—for all this child had missed.

Robert, however, did not dwell on the sparseness of his day. He clapped his hands together and called out to the mare and her filly. Then he turned in his chair and said, "Me and the little horse have the same birthday, don't we?"

"I suppose you could say that. . . ."

"Then *that's* my present, too!"

A physical therapist walked up to them at the fence and put her hands on Robert's chair. "We're ready for you now, big guy."

Libby watched them move toward the barn before sinking onto a nearby bench and putting her head in her hands.

Father, she prayed, *forgive me for my selfishness and my self-centeredness. My problems are so insignificant compared to those of that child, and yet he knows how to enjoy the everyday blessings you provide. I pray that someone will come along who will love Robert and make a home for him. I pray that not all his birthdays will go unnoticed. Send someone to be his father and mother, Lord.*

Libby lifted her head and saw Robert riding in a circle in the arena, his face shining with joy. If anyone deserved a blessing it was Robert.

....

"You have *got* to be kidding!"

Everyone was at Jenny and Mike's for dinner. The meal was over, and Luke had already left the table to take the dogs for a run, leaving the adults to finish their coffee. Libby had decided it was as good a time as any to run her latest idea up the flagpole and test the response.

Tia was holding her cup in midair as if she'd forgotten she even had it in her hand. "You? Adopt a child? A handicapped child? Really, Libby . . ."

"Don't you think I'd be a good mother?"

"Of course, but to do it alone? And a child with special needs? Isn't that biting off more than you can chew?"

"Did you just decide this on a whim?"

"Of course not!" Libby said indignantly. "It might have started that way, but . . ."

"Oh?" Tia was giving her an X-ray stare. "A whim?"

Libby expelled a gusty breath. "If you'll be patient, I'll explain! It's just hard to know where to start. . . ."

So she began at the beginning, with Robert's health and family situation, his aloneness in the world, his bubbly, joyous personality, and the intense desire to have a "real" family that he'd confided to Libby.

"Just because he wants a family doesn't mean you have to try to provide it for him," Tia said gently.

"I know that." Libby scraped her fingers through her hair. "I've surprised myself but it's been a little like . . . falling in love."

"Someone your own age would be nice."

"You know what I mean. The more I fight my feelings for him, the stronger they grow. It took a long time on my knees with God before I began to see what was happening."

"Do tell." Tia was still a skeptic but willing to listen.

"I think God put Robert and me together." She took a deep

breath. "I didn't see it at first, but everywhere I was, there was Robert with his unflagging zest for life and his unmet needs. It was as though God kept shoving him in my face until I finally realized what God was doing.

"I was trying to protect myself from more responsibility and more heartache. I thought getting involved with this small boy could only lead to more work, more expense, and more danger of having my heart broken. I was being very selfish."

"And now?" Jenny asked softly.

"Now I believe Robert is a gift God has put in front of me, and it is up to me to decide what to do about it." Libby played with her dessert fork. "I've been praying every waking moment, asking what God wants me to do. And slowly I've come to see the answer."

"Adoption?"

"Yes. But not because it will be easy or free of headaches and heartaches."

"Why then?"

"Because it's God's will. I've asked enough times and his answer never changes. Robert came into my life for a reason. Robert has very little future without me. He won't be adopted now. He's too old. I can do something for this child. I can love him.

"His biggest need is to have a family. I can be that. He'd have a grandpa and a grandma, even if she didn't always know who he was. And he'd have two adopted aunts, an uncle, and a cousin— you, Jenny, Mike, and Luke. And he'd have more dogs than he's ever seen in his life. What could be better than that?"

"It just seems so . . . *hard.*"

"It's not hard to love, Tia."

"Wouldn't you like a child of your own someday?"

Libby made a show of lifting her arm to study her wristwatch. "My biological clock is ticking. It's so loud that sometimes it drowns out the television. But in order to have a child of my own, I need a husband, which I obviously don't have. I *can* have a son. Why wait when I know that I have enough love for Robert *right now*."

"Think carefully before you act. It's a big decision."

"I have been, believe me. That's why I'd like tomorrow off." Libby looked hopefully at Tia. "I need to talk to some profession- als."

"Only if I can go with you. You'll need someone *sensible* along. All the nurturing hormones or cells or whatever might block your thinking. There's no danger of that with me."

Jenny chuckled softly. "Tia, your bark has always been worse than your bite."

Tia scowled. "No dog analogies with me, ladies. I'm the busi- nesswoman in this group."

"My bakery and Libby's work don't count?"

"Hey, you two have a life. My business *is* my life."

"Maybe you need a date," Libby murmured.

She grinned widely when Tia glared at her. "Just a taste of your own medicine, my dear."

Tia snorted rudely. "The only men in your life have four feet. I don't think I'd trust you to pick someone out for me!"

Coffee spewed out of Jenny's mouth and across the table.

Mike handed her a napkjn and inquired, "What's that all about?"

"I just had this image of Tia and Libby out on a double date— two ladies in a buggy with two four-footed Romeos pulling the cart." She began to sing. "Love and marriage, love and marriage, go together like a horse and carriage. . . ."

Mike shook his head and stood up. "I'm getting out of here." He kissed his wife on the top of her head. "Send Luke outside when he gets back. He can help me in the garden."

When he'd gone, Jenny sat back in her chair and studied her friend. "So, Libby, you want to be a mother."

A roller coaster of emotion rocketed through Libby's body. It sounded so permanent, so real when Jenny said it. *A mother.* But she wasn't scared. God had brought little Robert into her life for a reason and she had to follow his guiding.

"I'll pick you up at ten tomorrow, Tia," Libby said. "I've already got appointments with foster care, the adoption agency, and a social worker."

"Ten it is." Tia fingered her water goblet. "By the way, what do little boys like for Christmas? I have a salesman coming on Wednesday and I think I'd better stock up."

....

"Hi, Daddy."

Joe Morrison looked up from the church bulletin he was studying and his eyes brightened. "Libby! I didn't expect you here this morning. It's very early." He waved the folded paper in his hand. Libby noticed the scribbled words in the margins. "I was rereading Sunday's Scripture. Had a couple of things I wanted to ask the pastor about next week."

"Do you like going to church here at Fraiser Towers?" Libby took the easy chair across from him. "Or would you rather take the bus to our home church?"

"This is fine. Easier on your mother. And the fellow who comes is one sharp cookie. He doesn't seem to mind old duffers like me." Mr. Morrison eyed Libby. "But you didn't come to hear me give a sermon review. What's on your mind?"

"Is it so obvious?"

"Honey, I've been able to read you since you were six months old. You have the most open, expressive features I've ever seen. You are debating something momentous."

"I've decided to do something big, Dad. Huge. Enormous. Life altering!"

"Then it's a good thing you came to me," her father chuckled. "I'd hate to be left out of such a significant event."

Libby told him about Robert, his handicaps, his upbeat

outlook on his not very upbeat life, his sweetness, and his need. And her desperate desire to adopt him.

"What do you think, Dad? Am I out of my mind?"

"What's God been saying?"

"He's the one encouraging the idea."

"Then what are you waiting for?"

"But I'm a single woman! Robert won't have a father. I'll need to work to support us. He'll be a latchkey kid. . . ."

"Who's loved?"

"Well, yes."

"And wanted?"

"Of course."

"And who will be fed and clothed and taught about God?"

"Sure."

"Then what's the problem?"

Libby looked at her father in amazement. "That's *it?* No more questions?"

"If you've invited God into the equation and he says go for it, who am I to quibble? I'll pray about it, just like you have been. And I'll support you in whatever you decide."

Joe Morrison looked at his daughter with love glowing in his eyes. "Libby, you were my gift from God. Maybe he's got an equally special one planned for you."

Libby stood up and embraced her father. Words were far too shallow for a moment such as this.

As she left for her appointment with the adoption agency, her step was light. She threw her shoulders back and allowed her hair to brush across her back.

If God is for me, who can be against me?

It was almost noon when Libby and Tia picked up Jenny for lunch.

"How did it go?"

"Fine. My head is swimming with information." Libby's eyes

misted. "It's sad that people are waiting to adopt babies when there are so many older children who would love a home."

"Not everyone is able to open their hearts and homes like you are," Jenny murmured.

"'When you did it to one of the least of these my brothers and sisters, you were doing it to me!'" Libby quoted. "I want to be obedient to God's wishes and, for me, this is the way. Now I'm sure of it."

No one spoke until Libby said, "Should we run through a fast-food drive-in and pick up something to eat? We could drive out to the ranch. There are picnic tables to eat at and you could watch the riders."

"I'd like that," Jenny said.

"We'd better thoroughly check things out," Tia agreed. "Since you seem to be so smitten with the whole idea."

"Good." Libby felt her heart lift. She couldn't think of a single place she'd rather be on this gloriously sunny day.

"Wow!" was Tia's first comment as they drove through the ranch gates. "Cool."

"It is, isn't it?" Libby pulled into a parking spot. They looked across the lawn to the barn and arena, which were humming with activity. The horses, groomed within an inch of their lives by the eager riders, shimmered in the sunlight. Several children were mounted and circling the arena. Others waited patiently for their turns.

"Oh, look! There's Robert!" Libby pointed to the button of a child in a wheelchair careening toward them. His riding helmet tipped forward until it practically obscured his vision. The smile beneath was radiant.

"Hi, Libby!" The boy shoved back his helmet to reveal a thatch of dark sweaty hair. "Did you come to see me ride?"

"We came out here to eat lunch. Robert, I'd like you to meet my friends Tia and Jenny."

The boy solemnly studied the women, as if gauging them to

determine whether or not they were proper friends for someone so wonderful as Libby. When he finally smiled, it was as though there were two suns in the sky. "Hiya."

"Hiya, yourself, big guy. What's this?" Tia pointed at his chest.

"Binoculars. Rollie gave them to me. There are lots of birds to watch out here—especially down by the stream. Want to come bird-watching with me?"

"Can we take a rain check?" Libby asked. "I'd like to do it when I have more time."

Robert's bright eyes lifted from Libby's face to the sky. "A hawk! Do you see it?" Without a good-bye, the boy darted between them and in the direction the hawk was soaring.

"He's good with that chair," Tia commented. "He nearly took my knees off when he left."

"Reese has been teaching him about birds. Next time I come out, I think I'll bring one of Dad's old bird books."

"Well, well, look who's here." The odd tone in Jenny's voice made Libby turn.

Reese was behind her, aboard an impressive black-and-white paint.

Tia's jaw dropped. "Well, look at you!"

"I graduated to a real seat."

"Don't you need people with you?" Jenny asked. "What if you fall . . . ?"

"I'm considered an advanced rider. Basically, I'm strong enough to hang on to the saddle horn to help keep my balance and old enough to sign a paper saying I won't hold the ranch responsible if I fall off. I suppose I should be glad I have full use of my upper body." He didn't *look* glad as he tipped his cowboy-hatted head toward a group of riders lining up near the barn. "I can trail ride now. At least that's something."

Something? When I met you, you were curled up in the back of a sleigh feeling sorry for yourself! And look at you now!

Aloud Libby said, "You've made a lot of progress since I last saw you." She was so happy for him she thought her heart might burst.

"Good balance from riding bareback half my life," he said shortly. "It's not where I was and it's not where I want to be but it's where I am."

He looked to the horizon over their heads. "At least I feel an inch or two closer to normal up here."

They all turned as one of the therapists called Robert's name.

"Have you seen him?" Reese asked. "It's his turn to ride."

"He was here a minute ago. He took off at warp speed after a hawk."

"That kid is bird crazy." Reese scanned the horizon. "Which direction did he go?"

"That way." Jenny pointed to the east.

Reese frowned. "Are you sure?"

"Pretty sure."

At that moment Rollie came huffing and puffing beside them. "Have you seen Robert? He never misses a chance to ride."

"I can't find him anywhere, sir." A boy in his late teens came running up to them with a look of alarm on his features. Libby recognized him as Robert's foster brother. "I was supposed to watch him. I just went in to look at the new colt, and . . ."

"They say he went east chasing a hawk."

"These kids aren't to be left alone for a minute!" Rollie growled. "Get my horse. There's a creek at the bottom of the slope. If he gets too close to the incline, there's no way he could control his chair. He'd shoot right down to the rocks on the creek."

"I've been riding alone," Reese said crisply. "I can keep up with you."

The teenager returned with Rollie's horse. "Everybody is fanning out to look," he panted.

Rollie swung into the saddle. He gave Reese a cursory, weighing glance and made a decision. "Come on." They moved off together.

Even in her agitated state, Libby observed how natural Reese looked in the saddle. How beautiful it must have been for him before the gunshot. Like music, no doubt, the horse and man as in sync as the left hand to the right on the piano.

"Let's follow them." Libby started after the riders.

Robert's name echoed around the buildings and into the air. No Robert appeared.

Libby was growing truly alarmed. "He's the most reliable little guy," she told her friends. "He's *never* late for his ride. Something must have happened to him."

The men on horseback had forged ahead, Rollie and Reese staying together and scanning the horizon close to where the land sloped toward the creek.

Libby heard Reese give a bark of recognition just as they disappeared over the embankment. She started to run. Tia and Jenny followed.

When they got to the top of the slope, Libby gasped at the sight before her. Rollie's fear had become reality. Robert's chair lay tipped sideways at the edge of the water. The momentum of the roll had thrust Robert forward into the creek. He was lying on his side clinging to a large rock, fighting to keep his head out of the water, one thin arm flailing wildly.

Oh, Lord, he's not strong enough to save himself! Help him!

Momentarily paralyzed, the threesome saw a dramatic scene unfold before them.

Reese edged his mount toward the creek's edge. His horse, ears back, indicated his displeasure. Only because his rider was experienced did he obey.

Rollie slid down from his mount and headed toward Robert on foot. Then, as if in slow motion, his knee buckled and the older man went down hard, falling at the edge of the water.

From their vantage point, the women could see the look of horror on Reese's face as the older man fell. As Rollie struggled, Reese became the man in charge.

"Robert's slipping!" Libby screamed. "What if Reese can't catch him?" And she took off at a dead run.

Tia, keeping cool, ran back toward the barn, yelling for reinforcements. Jenny, in her skirt and heels, scrambled after Libby.

By the time Libby reached Rollie, he was clutching at a rock to hold himself up. "My knee went out. Help Reese with the kid. Robert isn't strong enough to keep his head up much longer."

Her feet slipping on smooth river stones, Libby raced toward Reese's horse. The animal was reluctantly approaching the water, protesting by throwing his head back and showing the whites of his eyes all around. His ears were back. But he was listening to the man who knew horses.

"Come on, boy. You can do it. Just a bit more, old man. You'll be fine. You'll be fine."

Libby didn't know if Reese was talking to the horse or to himself.

Robert was losing ground fast. His slender fingers scratched at the muddy bank. The terror in his eyes tore at Libby's heart. The binoculars were still bobbing around his neck, and the hawk circled above them.

Libby waded into the water and was shocked by its coldness and its depth.

"Can you get to him?" Reese's tone was clipped and businesslike.

"I think so. But I'm not sure I can carry him out." The water slapped at her hips, and mud and weeds sucked at her feet.

Reese was now so close to the boy that, had the child had the strength, he could have wrapped his arms around one of the animal's great legs and been carried to dry ground.

She could see Reese struggling with his balance. Without the use of his legs to steady himself, Reese couldn't lean far enough forward to grab the boy's upraised hand. He gripped the saddle horn so tightly that his knuckles were white against his tan. The

sweat of exertion had broken out on his forehead. He was liter-
ally holding himself on the horse with one hand.

"If you can push him far enough out of the water for me to
catch his hand, I'll pull him up." Reese's words came through
gritted teeth. "I can't bend any farther or I might take a header
into the water with him and you'd have two of us to save."

"I'll try."

With Herculean effort, Libby lunged toward the child. He was
crying, choking, and spitting water from his mouth. His hair was
plastered to his head, and weeds were groping at his limbs. Pasty
white and terrified, he was a pitiful sight. "Help me!"

Libby squatted in the water by the boy and managed to wedge
her shoulder beneath him. The creek bed was rough and etched
with drop-offs. She felt her foot slide into one of them and
Robert's body slip away.

He went fully under and Libby heard a scream. It was her own
voice, she realized.

Reese was totally silent, busy with the effort of keeping the
horse calm and maintaining his own balance. Libby grabbed
Robert's arm, pushed herself once again under his body, and
thrust upward.

She could see sweat pouring down Reese's face with the exertion of leaning forward, hand extended to the child.

*Can he do it? I have four healthy limbs and I can't keep my own
balance!*

"Higher, Lib, I can't bend anymore or I'll topple off." His voice
was a rough gasp from deep in his throat. Libby saw his hand
quiver.

She pressed down on her feet, solidly putting her strength
against the creek bottom and straightened her knees. Robert's
body rose slightly from the water.

"Again." Reese was drenched in his own sweat. Every fiber of
his body was trembling, threatening to give way. He needed
every bit of strength he had and more.

"Huhhh . . ." Libby expelled a breath, closed her eyes, and strained.

Then, suddenly, she felt the weight against her shoulder lighten and disappear. When she stood up, Reese had Robert by the arm, suspended in midair.

Tia and Jenny waded into the water and lifted the child high enough for Reese to pull him across the horse's withers and drape him there, unceremoniously, facedown. Clucking softly and pulling and releasing on the reins, Reese backed the horse out of the water.

Tia and Jenny pushed the wheelchair back onto the bank, while Libby went to Rollie. Leaning heavily on her shoulder, Rollie staggered with Libby onto dry ground where Rollie collapsed in a heap, tears streaming down his withered cheeks.

Reese turned the horse around and met the first of the other would-be rescuers coming down the hill. "It will be easier if I take Robert up to the barn and we lift him off there. Otherwise you'll have to carry him. And someone better call a doctor." Reese, the paint, and the limp body of the boy led the parade to the barn.

By the time Libby, Rollie, Tia, and Jenny arrived, Robert and Reese were both on the ground. Reese, wet and weary, sat in his chair with the boy on his lap. Robert sobbed and hung on to Reese's shirt, fingers wound so deeply into the fabric that they looked as though they'd never come out.

"You saved him!" were the first words out of Rollie's mouth.

"Libby saved him," was Reese's quiet answer.

"Not me, you. It couldn't have happened without you." Libby kneeled at Reese's feet and stroked the child's back. "It's OK, honey. You'll be fine."

Robert lifted tormented eyes to Libby's. "But I lost Rollie's binoculars!"

Libby didn't know how she could feel more deeply for anyone than she did for this child in this moment. Except perhaps for the man holding him.

After one of the therapists had driven both Robert and Rollie to the hospital for a once-over, Jenny and Tia caught a ride to the city with Robert's shaken foster brother. That left Reese and Libby alone in the informal lounge attached to the barn.

"Are you *sure* you shouldn't see a doctor, too?" Libby recalled the grueling effort it had cost Reese to rescue the child.

He unbuttoned his wet shirt, shrugged it off his back, and threw it to the floor. "Hand me that shirt of Rollie's. And would you get me a towel to dry my hair?"

"You didn't answer my question." Libby handed him the towel.

"I don't need a doctor. There's nothing they can do for me. Besides, it felt good to be useful." He scrubbed at his head until his damp hair was standing up in spikes. "Maybe I'll change my attitude about physical therapy, though. They want me to do more weight training for my upper body. I could have used that today."

"You were amazing."

He gave her a skew-eyed look. "Right. Wonderful. Sweating like a pig and holding on to the saddle horn for dear life. Just like the heroes in the movies. I'm a gimp, Libby. A cripple. Get real."

You are my hero.

But Libby didn't dare say it aloud.

Reese ate a sandwich from the vending machine in silence, and Libby drank a cup of coffee. She had insisted he put something in his stomach. Reese was pale beneath his tan. The extreme exertion had been hard on him.

Stoic to the end, Reese did it more to please her than for himself. Libby had a hunch it was his tactic for keeping her quiet. But it wasn't going to work. She had things to say and she was bound and determined to say them.

"Candy bar? Twinkie? Little Debbie?" She counted off the offerings in the machine.

"Sugar injected directly into my veins?"

"You're cranky. Why? You saved a child's life! You should be joyous."

He rolled his eyes and sighed. "Give it up, Libby. Someone else would have gotten to Robert if I hadn't."

"I'm not so sure of that. You can't be either. Anyway, you should be *celebrating*. You did something that, six months ago, would have been impossible."

"Whoopee!" Reese circled his finger in the air and looked scornful. "It's hard to celebrate something that would have come easy to me before. . . ."

"First Peter one, verses six and seven."

"Don't get started on that, Libby."

"Don't you want to know what it says?"

"Not particularly, but I have a hunch you're going to tell me anyway." He glared at her. "Are you picking on me because it's hard for me to get away?"

She gave him a serene smile and quoted, "'So be truly glad! There is wonderful joy ahead, even though it is necessary for you to endure many trials for a while. These trials are only to test your faith, to show that it is strong and pure. It is being tested as fire tests and purifies gold—and your faith is far more precious to God than mere gold. So if your faith remains strong after being tried by fiery trials, it will bring you much praise and glory and honor on the day when Jesus Christ is revealed to the whole world.'"

"What does that have to do with anything?" He swilled down the last of his coffee.

"Suffering is nothing compared to what we gain."

"And what have I gained?"

"I don't know for sure about you, Reese, but I know about me. I don't learn very much when things are going smoothly for me. That's when I begin to think I'm pretty smart and competent, that I have a grip on everything."

"What's wrong with that?"

"Easy times don't bring out our toughness or our courage. They lull us into believing we can do everything for ourselves. It's not till we're really pressed that what we're really made of—and what God's making of us—comes out."

"So I should say, 'Hallelujah! I can't walk. That must mean something big is planned for me!' Come on, Libby, you sound just like my sister-in-law. Annie spouts things like 'perplexed but not despairing, persecuted but not forsaken, struck down but not destroyed.' She always puts big emphasis on that 'struck down but not destroyed' part." He grimaced. "As if that's supposed to help."

At least he's listening.

"And don't you dare call me a 'jar made of clay'!" he added, referring to the Scripture.

"We don't get tough if we aren't challenged. It wasn't until I'd torn myself apart over my parents and had given the shreds to God that I found peace. I had to exercise my spiritual muscles."

"Sit-ups for the soul." Reese smiled and shook his head. "You are really too much of a good thing, Libby."

"You *said* you needed more therapy."

"*Physical* therapy."

"Maybe your soul needs an overhaul, too."

"I've told you, Libby. I believed all that stuff once. Look where it got me." He looked at her with something akin to fondness. "I know how hard you're trying, Lib. And I know how sincere you are. It's just that it's not going to work. That bullet took out more than my legs. It also took out my faith."

"Then you have to get them both back!"

The soul first because that's the most important.

"You just keep praying for me like I know you are. Annie is, too. If you can get a thousand or so others doing the same, maybe a miracle will happen." He looked at her steadily. "And it has to be a miracle because there's no other way."

He grew silent, exhausted at his core—spiritually, mentally, and physically.

It was time for Libby to go home and pray for a miracle.

. . . .

"I came to see how Reese was doing today," were Libby's opening words to Annie Reynolds.

Annie rolled her eyes and stepped out of the house. She closed the door gently behind her. "Like a horse with a burr under his saddle. Touchy, jittery, and bad tempered."

"I thought after his saving Robert . . ."

"I know. Rollie called and told us everything. We thought, too, that this would give Reese a real boost in the confidence department."

"But instead . . ."

"Instead he's preoccupied and restless as a frog in a frying pan. Do you have any idea what's gotten into him?"

Libby held up her hands and shrugged her shoulders. "Not a clue. Last time I saw him was after Robert's accident."

"What did you talk about?"

"Somehow we got around to discussing the challenges God allows us to experience. 'Sit-ups for the soul,' Reese called it."

"Aha!"

"What do you mean?"

"That might explain why Reese only appears for meals and to ransack my bookshelves. He's devoured all my books on faith and spirituality." Annie frowned. "Yesterday I heard a terrible crash and discovered that Reese had thrown a book across the room in frustration."

"What book?"

"*Falling Away, Falling from Faith,* something like that. It was a book my pastor gave me after I had a miscarriage. I was questioning God big time back then, and the book really pushed some buttons for me. It made me come face-to-face with the fact that no matter how much I thought I was able, I could *never* get by without God."

Annie shrugged her shoulders beneath her white cotton blouse. "Maybe he's reading things he doesn't want to embrace. That can be an uncomfortable place to be."

"Robert might have drowned without Reese's help," Libby said softly.

"And Reese is dying by pieces inside himself. Pray with us, Libby, that he finds someone to keep him above water."

CHAPTER TWELVE

Quilting made a great resurgence in the 1920s.
The Chicago World's Fair in 1933 had a quilt exhibit, which displayed
quilts made by women across the United States.

"What put the spring in your step?" Jenny greeted Libby upon her arrival at the bakery.

"I'm having so much fun!"

"Sit down and tell me all about it."

"What about work?"

"All caught up. I'm planning menus. When we're done visiting, you can start some asparagus-and-wild-rice casseroles for tonight. Everything else is done."

"Impressive." Libby sank into the chair across from Jenny's desk. "By the way, we're having a horse show this weekend."

"Who, what, when, where, how, and why?"

"Reach Out Ranch, every event a regular horse show would have plus a few extras, Saturday at 10 A.M., our arenas, with lots of volunteers, and just for the fun of it!"

"Can your clients . . . well, you know."

"Do it? Sure, in some form or other. It's like a Special Olympics event. Everybody participates, doing whatever it is they are capable of doing, and we're all winners at the end."

"How about Robert?"

"He'll be in the Western Pleasure class—with help, of course." Libby's smile grew. "Something happened to that little boy in the water at the creek. The experience motivated him. He's eating like a ranch hand and finally beginning to fill out. I didn't realize just how handsome a boy he is without those pale, pinched cheeks and that worried expression in his eyes."

"You really love him, don't you?"

"Yes, I do."

Then Libby's expression clouded. "Bureaucracy is a dreadful thing. If only there were some way to get Robert into my home tomorrow!"

"What else is happening on Saturday?" Jenny inquired.

"That's pretty much it." Then Libby brightened. "But I know a wonderful secret."

"Do tell." Jenny leaned forward and put her elbows on her desk.

"Some of the kids ride barrels. Not fast, of course. The goal is just to get around them. Rollie has them set up in the arena. Yesterday I forgot my billfold in the office and had to go back to the ranch to get it. I heard something in the arena and went to check it out. I thought my eyes were deceiving me!"

"What?"

"Rollie and Reese were in the arena, and Reese was working the barrels himself!"

"For the competition?"

"No. He won't have anything to do with that. But this is better. He's doing it *for himself*. That means he's not feeling as hopeless as he was. He's seen what he can do and knows how much further he can go if he pushes himself. That experience in the water changed him, too."

"Like baptism," Jenny murmured.

"They've become new physical beings," Libby agreed. "Now they need another type of baptism to become new spiritual beings."

She toyed with a pen on Jenny's desk. "It's easy to understand why Reese was so utterly devastated by his injury. Even now he rides like he's one with the horse. It must have been beautiful to see before the accident. He speaks their language. He'll blow up at me in a heartbeat, but he never loses patience with an animal."

"How do you feel about that?"

"It's OK. I keep bouncing back." Libby grinned impishly. "He gives me a zillion chances to be Christlike in my behavior every day.

"Besides, the more Reese rides and the more the horse becomes an extension of the man himself, the more open Reese will be to listen to what I keep chattering about—his faith.

"I keep talking to him about growing through trials. Reese has made himself the author of many of my problems lately. If I tripped up, he'd be right there asking me why I couldn't practice what I preached."

"So he's actually better?"

"Yes. He's less bitter and turned inward. That is a miracle in itself!" Libby snapped her fingers. "I almost forgot. Would you and Tia like to come to our dance on Saturday night?"

"Dance? Who's dancing?"

"Everyone who takes part in the horse show activities and any guest who wants to try it. It's going to be fun!"

Jenny looked at Libby as though she were paddling with only one oar in the water. "Have you forgotten the physical state of the riders at the ranch?"

"Not for a minute. We'll be square dancing—in wheelchairs and on horseback."

"You can *do* that?"

"Why not? We've been practicing. The sidewalkers and therapists are all for it, and they are the ones who'll get the brunt of the work."

"This I have *got* to see. Can I bring Mike and Luke?"

"Of course. Luke will have a great time. We're also having a little carnival—games, food, prizes."

Jenny studied Libby for a long time before speaking. "He really did it, didn't he?"

"Who?"

"God. He brought you through the worst time in your life and you arrived on the other side even better than you were before."

"Joy in suffering," Libby said. "I wouldn't want to repeat those dreadful days with my parents ever again, but I don't want to give back what I learned from them either."

"I felt much the same about my growth after Lee's death. Been there, done that, bought the T-shirt."

The two friends sat in companionable silence, each giving thanks for the blessings God had given them.

. . . .

"Does your head hurt as much as mine does?" Libby found Reese in the lounge drinking a soft drink and staring out the window.

"Those kids can make more noise than all the marching bands at the Rose Parade," he said without turning around. "But they are having fun."

"It was a great idea to turn this into a fund-raiser. We should get another scholarship out of this."

Libby put coins in the machine and chose an iced tea. Her back was toward Reese.

"I've watched you with Robert," Reese said unexpectedly.

She turned around and took a sip before speaking. "He's a honey."

"He's more than that to you."

"You can see it then?"

He chuckled. "I've seen girls in love a few times, and you are crazy in love with that child."

"I'm looking into becoming his foster parent—or adopting

him." Libby waited for Reese to tell her she was crazy—a single woman with no parenting experience and a host of responsibilities adopting a child with handicaps.

But he didn't. Instead he said, "That's nice."

"You aren't going to tell me I'm crazy?"

"No. You'll be a wonderful mother. He's a lucky little boy."

"If it works out. There's nothing definite yet. I'm not saying anything to Robert until I have good news for him."

"That's smart. He'd be devastated if you built up his hopes and it didn't work out."

"That's what I'm afraid of." Libby sighed. "There are certainly lots of opportunities to develop patience and endurance, aren't there?"

She waited for his response and was again surprised by what he said. "I always thought I'd be a good father."

"I'm sure you would. Maybe you will someday."

Reese turned his chair to face her. His eyes were black with pain and frustration. "Look at me, Libby. Do I look like promising husband or father material to you? I don't think so."

"Because you are in a wheelchair it doesn't mean you can't father children. . . ." Libby's voice trailed off. This was very personal territory.

"So says my doctor." His voice was rough, scornful.

"Well, then?"

He looked at her pityingly. "I'm not going to marry, Lib. I'd never saddle someone with my problems. I'm a full-time job. Ask Annie and Bill. Why would I burden someone else with this?"

"You're independent. Annie says she hardly ever sees you anymore."

"I stay away out of self-preservation. Annie thinks I'm her mission from God."

I've thought the same thing.

"Some days it's a nuthouse at home—and the inmates are running the asylum."

Libby smiled. "Would you like to have your own place?"

"Yes."

"And is it possible?"

"They tell me it is."

"Then it is. And if you live independently, why couldn't you date or marry or have a child? If you don't want one of your own, there are plenty out there like Robert."

"You don't get it, do you, Libby?"

"Apparently not. Explain it to me."

"I'm only half a man now. They've asked me to come back to work at the police station—behind a crummy desk. I've relearned to ride, but only with help. I wake up at night and think I'm going to get up to get a glass of water. Then I remember I can't unless I haul myself into that chair. *Half a man*, Libby. No woman wants that."

I might. Aloud she said, "It's possible that you'll change your mind. . . ."

"Not about this I won't."

"Never?"

"Ever."

Signed, sealed, and delivered. That was Reese's message. And Libby hadn't known how much she'd cared until she realized that she could never have him.

"What are you moping about?" Tia demanded. "I'm going to have to find a sling to hold up your face."

"I dunno."

"Tell Auntie Tia your problems." Tia plopped down on the couch in her office and patted the cushion next to hers.

Libby sighed and relented. Tia would hound her until she spilled it anyway. "Disappointment, I guess."

"About what?"

"Everything I want is taken."

"What does that mean?"

"I can't get any word on the status of Robert's situation. They promise to call and never do. I have a hunch that someone somewhere doesn't think a single mother is right for a child with handicaps."

"So get married."

Libby glowered at Tia. "To who?"

"Actually, I was thinking of Reese Reynolds."

"Wha . . . How did you . . ."

"Know you were in love with him? Darling, it's written all over your face and oozing out of every pore. I've known you practically since birth. You don't have to tell me things about yourself for me to know them!"

"It's not that apparent, is it?" Libby was horrified.

"Only to me. And probably to Jenny. But we haven't discussed it. I'm sure we've both had confidence that you'd tell us—after you discovered it yourself."

"I'm bright as a stump, aren't I?"

"Only in the ways of love, darling. In that area you are an innocent." Tia smiled complacently. "But I knew you'd figure it out sooner or later."

"Well, I wish I hadn't. Reese has already told me that he will never marry."

"Why not? He's a hunk and a half! The man is to die for!"

"He doesn't see it that way. He doesn't want to burden someone with a 'cripple.' He's willing to give up a chance at happiness to save someone from that awful fate."

"A martyr. How dramatic. Don't worry. He'll get over that."

"I don't think so."

"Not without help, perhaps."

"Tia, I am *not* going to allow you to play matchmaker to Reese and me. No way, no how!"

"But it would be so much fun!"

"No!"

Tia lifted one perfectly groomed eyebrow. "We'll see."

"Besides, he's not a Christian."

"But I thought . . . Bill and Annie . . . ."

"He was once—before the accident. Now he's turned away from that completely."

"And now you are concerned about being yoked with an unbeliever as well?"

"Wouldn't you be?"

"Don't give up on the man yet, Libby! His background is rooted in faith. He's just wandered away for a while. Pray he'll come back—for his sake, not yours."

"I've been praying—until I'm hoarse and exhausted."

"What's that thing your mother used to say? 'God is never late but he's rarely early either.'"

"It's not that simple, Tia."

"Simple? You think what I'm talking about is *simple?* It's just God making miracles, that's all! Moving heaven and earth to convince Reese that there is someone who loves him just like he is, that he's been chosen to be one of God's children and given eternal life if only he'll accept it? That's not simple, but it is *possible.*"

"God willing, you mean?"

"Amen to that."

When God finally did go to work, Libby was to muse later, he really worked. And then things started popping like the Fourth of July—but not, of course, in any way Libby might have imagined.

. . . .

A single phone call turned Libby's life upside down.

When she hung up, she sat down on the couch and stared at the wall, stunned. When she was able, she picked up her keys, went to the garage for her car, and drove faster than she ever had before to Fraiser Towers.

Forgoing the elevator, she took the stairs two at a time to her parents' room.

Mr. and Mrs. Morrison were engaged in the thousand-piece puzzle Libby had brought them last time she'd visited. Oddly, her mother still had the ability to pick out most of the straight-sided pieces for the outer rim of the puzzle. While she fingered each piece, exploring every side, Mr. Morrison worked on putting the edges together and filling in the middle.

"Hi, Libby." He looked up from his project. There was color in his cheeks and he looked very businesslike in his half glasses. Her mother waved absently and kept on with the puzzle.

"What are you up to today?"

Libby sat down on a straight-backed chair across from him and said, "I'm going to be a mother."

Mr. Morrison's glasses slid to the very tip of his nose as he jerked backward. "Libby . . ."

"It's OK, Dad." She blushed. "That didn't come out quite like I meant it to. I got a call from the agency about Robert. I'm adopting him!"

"You are? I mean, *you are!* Well, hallelujah! That *is* good news! It's about time."

She sagged in her seat. "And now that I'm getting what I've wished for, I'm scared stiff. What if I can't do it? What if Robert is too difficult for me to handle? What if he doesn't *want* to be adopted by me?"

"You haven't discussed it with him?"

"I was afraid. I thought that if it didn't work out, the disappointment might discourage him too much. He's a child who has had far too many of his hopes dashed already. I didn't want to be guilty of putting him through that, but now . . ."

"Now you wish you'd asked him."

"I forgot to protect my own heart, Dad. I love this little guy so much! What if . . ."

"Have you prayed about it?"

"Daily. *Hourly.*"

"And you are still sure that God is telling you to do this?"

"Yes, but . . ."

"There shouldn't be any 'yes, buts' concerning the Lord. Go with it Libby. If it is right, then it will happen."

"Do you think I'm crazy?"

"No more so than usual, darling."

"Oh, Daddy!" She flung her arms around his neck and hugged him.

As she did so, she got a glimpse of the clock on the bureau. "I've got to go! I have to tell Robert!"

She kissed her parents and started for the door. As she turned the corner into the hall, she heard her dad say to her mother, "Honey, you're going to be a grandmother!"

A long talk with Robert's foster mother at the ranch while Robert was riding soothed Libby's psyche. The woman, a portly, cozy lady with a wide smile, was delighted.

"He is just the sweetest boy! I'm so glad he'll have a permanent home!"

"You don't mind?"

"I'd keep him if I could, Libby, but I can't. I see my job as taking care of children until they find a permanent home. If I had kept every child who came to me and stole my heart, I'd have to live in a hotel by now in order to have enough rooms. No, this is my dream for Robert—a real family. And his dream, too."

"What if he doesn't want to leave your home?"

"For one of his own? Don't be silly." She tapped Libby on the arm. "Here he comes now."

"Mairezedotes and I had a great time today. Did you see us?"

"You were wonderful." His foster mother ruffled his hair. "I'm going to speak with your therapist. You stay here with Libby. She has something to tell you."

Robert looked up expectantly. He was as brown as a little nut from the sun. He looked sturdy as a result of his improved appetite, exercise, and self-esteem. Libby wanted to gather him into her arms and squeeze him forever.

Instead, she dropped to her knees in front of him and took his hands. "Robert, I have something I'd like to ask you."

His eyes widened and he took in her bended posture and the intense look on her face. "Are you going to ask me to *marry* you?" He pulled one hand away to cover his mouth. "I'm not old enough to get married!"

"What made you think . . ."

"I saw it on television last night. This guy got down on his knee, and . . ."

Libby burst out laughing. "No! I'm going to ask you something even better! Robert, you are free to be adopted. Would you consider . . . would you like . . ."

"Could you be my mother?" The words came out with such longing that they nearly shattered Libby's heart.

"Could you be my son?"

"Yippee!" He flung himself forward to reach her neck and nearly toppled them—chair and all—onto the ground. "Can we go home now?"

Home. Where the heart was. What she'd been missing until this moment.

"Is everything all right?" Reese's concerned voice interrupted her thoughts. He stared at the youngster clinging to Libby's neck with a death grip.

"You bet!" Robert assured him. Then, with wisdom and perception beyond his years, he said, "I'm going to tell my foster mother something. OK, Mo . . . Libby?"

She nodded and he spun off, his cowlick sticking straight up in the air like a flag of victory.

"What's going on?" Reese looked even more robust than Robert. Libby knew from Rollie that Reese had gone back to physical therapy with renewed vigor and an improved attitude and that he was making astounding progress. And his internal progress had been as impressive as his external. He was calmer, more at peace with himself and his injury.

"Robert has just agreed to be my son."

He leaned back in his chair as if he'd been slapped. "What?"

"I'm going to adopt him. I'm going to be a mother!"

"Congratulations." He said it but he didn't sound like he meant it.

Libby stared at him. "Aren't you happy for us?"

He blinked and looked away. "Yeah. Sure."

"What's wrong, Reese? You've known for a long time how I've felt about this child. . . ."

"It's not that."

He looked at the ground, and Libby was sure that, had he been able, he would have scuffed his toe in the dirt.

"What, then?"

The words jerked roughly out of him. "Every time I think I'm catching up to life, something happens to remind me how far behind I am."

"What do you mean?" Libby put her hand on his wrist and was grateful that he did not pull it away.

"I'm constantly amazed by you, Lib. You are the bravest person I've ever met."

"Me? Hardly. Look at Robert, look at the clients out here and their families, look at *you*."

"You've picked yourself up and dusted yourself off too, Lib. You kept on living when you didn't feel like it. You've made yourself a fulfilling life out of thin air and dreams. Now you've made yourself a family. I'll never be that brave."

"I don't understand."

"I can't get attached to anyone. I can't be there for them fully. You, on the other hand, keep taking leaps of faith and landing on your feet—just like you're doing now with Robert."

"You can too, Reese. Look how far you've come!"

"But I won't drag anyone else into this. That means I have to accept the fact that a family just isn't in the cards."

"It's a *choice*, Reese. That isn't etched in the heavens or anything!"

"And it's a choice I'm determined to live with. Congratulations, Libby. I really am happy for both you and Robert."

She stared helplessly after him as he moved away.

....

Libby hadn't seen or spoken to Reese for nearly two weeks. She thought of him often, but she'd had no time to pursue their conversation further. Carpenters were making her house handicapped accessible. She'd shopped for clothes and toys for Robert and cooked meals and frozen them so that she wouldn't have to waste time cooking when she brought her new boy home.

Together they had made the decision that Robert would stay where he was until all was ready for him. Still, they'd spent many hours together deep in mother-son conversation that Libby had already grown to love.

She was at the ranch delivering a quilt when she saw Reese outside the arena. Mustering her confidence, she walked toward him.

"Hi."

"Hi, yourself."

"What's going on?" At least they had this much conversation perfected, Libby thought ironically.

"They are having trouble with a rider. She hasn't developed any emotional control and has a tendency to screech every time the horse moves unexpectedly."

"That doesn't help anything."

"I know that. And you know that. But she doesn't. Not yet, anyway. It hasn't occurred to her yet that emotional outbursts can startle the horse and scare the wits out of the rider." He looked past the scene in the arena. "There's a lot to learn on the back of a horse."

"She'll learn quickly—manners, at least. She won't risk losing the chance to ride."

"A missed opportunity," Reese murmured. Libby sensed that he was talking about something other than horse etiquette.

"What have *you* learned from the horses, Reese?"

"Outside of the obvious?" He tapped his fingers on the wheel of the chair. "Controlling a powerful animal gives you the idea that perhaps you do have the ability to choose for yourself."

"Choose what?"

"Where you live, what you do, how you feel."

"Are you making those choices?"

"Getting there."

"And how about choosing God?"

He looked at her, amused. "You don't give up, do you?"

She sat down on the grass in front of him. "So how about it?"

"I'm getting there. I do live with Annie and Bill, you know. She's after me every day to recommit to my faith."

"And?"

But before Reese could answer, Rollie's pickup truck rattled into the yard and straight to where they were sitting.

. . . .

When Robert was in school and Libby had time off from work, she spent her free time at the ranch. The facility was booked almost to capacity, and she and Rollie were planning a new fund-raiser to build another barn. Her days were fuller and happier than they had been in a long time, and Libby gave thanks every morning for that fact.

She looked up from the papers before her when Rollie entered the office. "Has Reese been here lately? I haven't seen him for at least two weeks."

"No. He called one day and said that he wouldn't be able to help out for a while. I didn't expect him to be gone this long.

He's been missed. I've thought of calling him, but I figured it would be better if he called me first."

"Do you think something is wrong?" Libby felt a pang of alarm.

"He wouldn't say if there were. You know how Reese is—the strong, silent type."

"Would it help if I called him?" Libby asked.

Rollie took the matter under consideration before shaking his head. "I don't think so. I got the impression that he wanted to be separate from this place for a while."

"Why?"

"He said he needed time to think. I just wonder what is so important that it needs weeks to consider."

"He didn't sound depressed, did he?"

"Not really. More like determined." Rollie looked over the papers on Libby's desk. "By the way, have you got the bids on the new barn?"

Diverted, Libby began discussing their new project. Thoughts of Reese slipped into the background of her mind until she was on her way home.

She glanced at her watch. Ten minutes before two o'clock. The bus wouldn't be bringing Robert home for two hours yet. Without making a conscious decision, she turned toward Bill and Annie's.

It occurred to her as she neared their place that she was in serious danger of overstepping her boundaries with the Reynolds family. Reese had made it very clear to her that the only part she could play in his life was that of friend.

And friends respect each other's privacy.

Libby pressed on the brakes at the corner, gave herself a mental reprimand, and began to turn around and go back to where she belonged—out of Reese's personal life.

She didn't see Reese's van until she'd almost backed into it.

"Rats," she muttered. *Caught.* She wished for the umpteenth time that she could remember to put her brain in gear before the rest of her. Now Reese was waving her toward the yard, and she had no choice but to obey since his vehicle was practically riding on her bumper.

Vowing to say hello and then leave quickly, Libby leaned out her window to speak but Reese beat her to the punch.

"Come on inside. Annie's not here yet but she will be soon."

"That's OK. Another time."

"Now is fine." He turned off the motor and moved into the ritual of lowering himself from the van. Libby, not wanting to be inexcusably rude, had no choice but to join him.

"I didn't plan to stay. . . ."

"Then why did you come?" He wheeled toward the house and up the ramp to the kitchen.

Because I'm a meddler.

Resigned, she followed him into the kitchen.

"Listen, Reese," she began as he took a carton of orange juice from the refrigerator and poured two glasses, "I really shouldn't be here. I asked Rollie where you'd been, and he told me you needed time off to think. I have no right to intrude on your solitude." She hung her head. "It's just that we all miss you."

When she looked up, he was watching her with amusement. It occurred to Libby that the time at the ranch had erased several years from his features. In fact, he was incredibly handsome.

"Thank you. That's nice to know."

He certainly wasn't giving her any help or a way to gracefully bow out. Libby felt a bit like a bug under a microscope.

"How's Robert?"

She lit up. This was safe ground for her. "He is absolutely wonderful. He appreciates every little thing I do for him and he's so cheerful! I can't imagine how I got along without him."

"You aren't having any trouble with his chair?"

"In the house, you mean? No. There were two bedrooms on the first floor. One was used as Dad's den, the other as my sewing room. I converted the den back into a bedroom and did a few changes on the bath to make it handier. I moved a little furniture to make room, added ramps to the outside of the house, and presto! Space for Robert, wheelchair and all."

"*No* trouble?" Reese sounded surprised.

"Nothing serious. We've become very creative when we need to be, but the house is working out fine." She smiled. "Robert tells me we have room for a brother or sister who is also wheelchair bound."

"What do you think about that?"

He was certainly grilling her today. "I've said I'd consider it but that he's already brought me so much joy that I wasn't sure how much more I could stand."

"Really." Reese was silent until Libby felt compelled to speak.

"What have you been up to?"

"A lot of physical therapy and weight training. A little wheelchair basketball. And I got a new job."

She almost didn't catch that, thrown in as it was as a casual, offhand remark.

"A job? How wonderful! Where . . . ?"

"I took the one they offered me at the station. I am now officially a pencil-and-paper pusher but with potential for advancement."

"What kind of advancement?"

"An investigator. They think my experience might benefit them in some way. Time will tell."

"How wonderful for you!"

"Is it?"

"Of course. You can have a more normal life—going to work, grousing about your paycheck and lousy benefits—you know, all the kinds of things people who work like to do."

He laughed. "I hadn't thought about it that way."

"What inspired you to do it?" Libby asked.

"Something Annie said to me in a fit of irritation. I'd been staring at the window so long she threatened to start dusting me when she did the rest of the furniture."

"I can just hear her."

"She was really upset. I didn't realize how much she'd worried about me. Apparently I'd pushed her to the edge. I suppose I was too busy worrying about myself to notice."

He winced at the memory. "She started flapping her dust rag at me and calling me a coward, claiming that since the accident I'd been afraid to live my life, to try the things I'd always done."

"That doesn't sound like Annie!"

"If she's angry enough it does. She also told me that fear wasn't from God and as long as I chose to wallow in it, I'd never grow."

"Ouch."

"But I saw she meant it—and how much I meant to her. So I decided to listen."

"And what did you hear?"

"About her faith, her beliefs, her rock-solid commitment to help me see the light."

"And?" Libby was a rapt audience.

"And I decided that if I couldn't lick her I'd have to join her."

"You mean . . ."

"I thought I might as well give God another chance, since apparently he is even more determined than Annie not to give up on me."

"And how's he doing?" Libby whispered.

"So far, so good. I may have misjudged him."

"Are you saying . . . ?"

Reese rolled his eyes. "Yes, I *am* saying . . . we worked up a new partnership agreement."

Libby launched herself out of the chair and into Reese's arms. She hugged his neck until he yelped.

"Oh, sorry . . . I didn't mean to hurt you."

"No damage done. I just didn't expect quite that enthusiastic of a response."

"There is rejoicing in heaven when someone returns to God."

"So I'm beginning to understand." Reese looked down at his

jean-clad legs. "I'm also beginning to agree with Annie. Fear isn't something God hands out. Just the opposite, in fact."

"I was very fearful before I took Robert," Libby admitted. "I know now that it was a trap, a means by which to convince me that I couldn't handle a handicapped boy alone. But once I acknowledged the fear and moved ahead anyway, it seemed to fall away."

"Are you sure that's how it works?" Reese seemed unduly interested in her answer.

"It worked that way for me."

"And if it worked for you, do you think it might work for me?"

She looked straight into his eyes. "Yes. I do. What are you so afraid of, anyway?"

He swallowed thickly. "Of the most frightening, dangerous thing I've ever done."

"You've faced plenty of danger as a policeman."

"But this is worse."

Libby began to feel sick in the pit of her stomach. Was he trying to tell her that he'd had bad news from his doctor? That he had to have surgery?

"I'm terrified of asking you to marry me."

She stared at him blankly as her mind switched gears. "Of *what?*"

"Proposing. Having the nerve to think you might consider marrying me." He looked at her with eyes so vulnerable she nearly wept. "Of being turned down."

"Why would I turn you down?" she whispered, her mind still in shock.

"Because I'm in a wheelchair. Because I'd be a whole new set of problems for you. Because you don't love me . . ." He was visibly steeling himself for rejection.

"You aren't a *problem!* I love guys in wheelchairs! Haven't you realized that yet?"

He smiled a little. "Even me?"

"You most of all." She grabbed his hands and felt their strength and the calluses he'd earned riding the horses. "If I were afraid of wheelchairs and the people in them, would I have adopted Robert? Would I have fallen in love with you?"

Reese looked stunned. "Would you repeat that falling in love part?"

"Yes, you big out-to-lunch cowboy! Can't you see it? Tia says it's written all over me. I love you. I think I've loved you almost since the night I met you!"

He leaned forward. "Why didn't you tell me this earlier?"

"What good would it have done? You were too busy at your pity party to believe me."

"I was that bad?"

"Not so bad. But I knew how good you could become."

"So then, is that a yes?" His devastatingly handsome face relaxed. The twinkle returned to his eye.

"Yes!" She squealed so loudly that Annie's parakeets began to chatter in their cage. Then she paused to collect herself. "Would you ask me again now that my brain is working?"

This time he laughed outright. "You are too much of a good thing, Libby Morrison, but here goes. Robert needs a family. I need a wife. The only wife I want is you. You hold my heart in your hands." His voice softened. "Will you marry me?"

"Yes! A thousand times yes!" She leaned to kiss him and then suddenly pulled away. "What took you so long to ask?"

He took her face in his hands and sighed with vast patience. "You didn't quit talking long enough for me to do it."

"Oh." With that, Libby melted into his arms, and she didn't talk for a long, long time.

Not only was it the first wedding ever held at Reach Out Ranch, but it was the first one in which the bridal party sat and the guests stood.

Even the pastor, seated on a stool, was eye level with the bride and the groom in his wheelchair. Mike, Robert, and Bill sat to Reese's right; Jenny, Tia, and Annie, to Libby's left. The guests, many of whom were employees, volunteers, or clients at the ranch milled around, as did several horses that were eating the hay Rollie had dumped near the fence.

Only Reese's black-and-white paint was more interested in the ceremony than the food. He'd had his head stuck between the two top rungs of the fence observing everything with an alert eye.

The yard, barns, and horses had been groomed to a high luster. Reese, Bill, and Mike looked at home in Western suits. Even Robert, in his first suit ever, seemed at home, although his chest was swelled so large with pride and happiness that his buttons threatened to pop.

Tia, ever the fashion maven, had found the bridesmaids' dresses—simple, elegant, and amazingly well suited to cowboy boots. Libby had opted for dazzling white, a bright foil for her tan and the radiant glow in her cheeks. Her parents, also in wheelchairs, the theme of this celebration, looked proud and happy. Tears of joy streamed from Mrs. Morrison's eyes, and Libby was confident her mother understood the occasion.

Not many feet away was the wedding buffet on picnic tables lined with white. The cake, a multilayered affair designed by Jenny, had a bride and groom on top, each, of course, leading a horse.

"And this is a message to all of us present," the pastor said. "'Dear friends, let us continue to love one another, for love comes from God. Anyone who loves is born of God and knows God.'"

And there was much love here today, Libby thought as she turned to her new husband. And God was here. She knew it with full confidence and with every fiber of her being. And Reese knew it, too. That was the very best wedding gift of all.

Judy Baer lives in Minnesota and raises quarter horses and buffalo in North Dakota. She is the mother of two grown children, Adrienne and Jennifer.

Judy began writing in 1982 and to date has published more than sixty books. During her career she has been the recipient of numerous awards, including Woman of the Year in 1995 for the North Dakota Professional Communicators' National Federation of Press Women, and the Concordia College Alumni Achievement Award in 1997.

Libby's Story is Judy's second full-length Tyndale House novel. *Jenny's Story* was the first. Previously she was the lead author for the Tyndale anthology of romance novellas entitled *Reunited*.